D1810576

Twenty Stories From South Asia

OUR RECENT RELEASES

Short Fiction

Asomiya: Handpicked Fictions
  Selected by NEWF
Inspector Matadeen on the Moon
  By Harishankar Parsai
  Trans C M Naim
Seven Sixes are Forty Three
  By Kiran Nagarkar
  Trans ShubhaSlee
Hindi: Handpicked Fictions
Trans & Ed Sara Rai
Waterness
  By Na Muthuswamy
  Trans by Lakshmi Holmström
Downfall by Degrees
  By Abdullah Hussein
  Trans by Mohammad Umar Memon
The Resthouse
  By Ahmad Nadeem Qasimi
  Trans by Faruq Hassan
Katha Prize Stories 12
  Ed Geeta Dharmarajan
Best of the Nineties:Katha Prize Stories 11
  Ed Geeta Dharmarajan

Non-Ficton

Links in the Chain
  By Mahadevi Varma
  Trans by Neera Kuckreja Sohoni
Travel Writing and the Empire
  Ed Sachidananda Mohanty

ALT (Approaches to Literatures in Translation)

Ismat: Her Life, Her Times
  Eds Sukrita Paul Kumar &
  Sadique
Translating Partition
  Eds Ravikant & Tarun K Saint
Translating Caste
  Ed Tapan Basu
Translating Desire
  Ed Brinda Bose
Vijay Tendulkar

Trailblazers

Ambai: Two Novellas and a Story
  Trans by C T Indra,
  Prema Seetharam & Uma Narayanan
Paul Zacharia: Two Novellas
  Trans by Gita Krishnankutty
Ashokamitran: Water
  Trans by Lakshmi Holmström
Bhupen Khakhar: Selected Works
  Trans by Bina Srinivasan,
  Ganesh Devy & Naushil Mehta

Katha Classics

Pudumaippittan
  Ed Lakshmi Holmström
Basheer Ed Vanajam Ravindran
Mauni Ed Lakshmi Holmström
Raja Rao Ed Makarand Paranjape
A Madhaviah: Padmavati
  Trans by Meenakshi Tyagarajan

Katha Novels

Singarevva and the Palace
  By Chandrasekhar Kambar
  Trans by Laxmi Chandrashekar
Listen Girl!
  By Krishna Sobti
  Trans by Shivanath

YuvaKatha

The Mountain of the Moon
  By Bibhutibhushan Bandopadhyay
  Trans by Santanu Sinha Chaudhuri
Lukose's Church
Night of the Third Crescent

<small>FORTHCOMING</small>

Short Shorts Long Shots
  By Uday Prakash
  Trans Robert A Hueckstedt &
  Amit Tripuraneni
JJ: Some Jottings
  By SuRaa
  Trans A R Venkatachalapathy
Upendranath Ashk: A Critical Biography
  By Daisy Rockwell

Twenty Stories from South Asia

Great short fiction in
award-winning translations, from the
First Katha South Asian Translation Contest 1999-2000,
held in association with the British High Commission,
British Council Division

ф

KATHA

First published by Katha in 2003

Copyright © Katha, 2003

Copyright © for original stories
held by the authors.

Copyright © for the English translations
rests with KATHA.

KATHA
A3 Sarvodaya Enclave
Sri Aurobindo Marg,
New Delhi 110 017
Phone: 2652 4350, 2652 4511
Fax: 2651 4373

E-mail: kathavilasam@katha.org
Internet address: www.katha.org

KATHA is a registered nonprofit society
devoted to enhancing the pleasures of reading.
KATHA VILASAM is its story research and resource centre.

Cover Design: Geeta Dharmarajan
Cover Photograph: Mahesh Bhat

This volume has been edited by Indira Chandrasekhar

In-house Editors: Gita Rajan, Shoma Choudhury
Assistant Editor: Smita Mishra Chaturvedi
Production Coordinator: Sanjeev Palliwal

Distributed by Katha Mela, a distributor of quality books.
A-3 Sarvodaya Enclave, Sri Aurobindo Marg, New Delhi-110 017

Typeset in 12 on 15pt Lapidary333 BT by R Ajith Kumar
Printed at Usha Offset, New Delhi

Katha has planted two trees to replace the tree that was used to make the paper on which this book
is printed.

ISBN 81-87649-71-2

1 3 5 7 9 10 8 6 4 2

CONTENTS

Introduction

For the past fifteen years, Katha has been trying to build bridges between language, culture, caste, class and nation by publishing the best of regional writings in translation. The Katha Translation Contests are a special project under Katha Vilasam, Katha's Story Research and Resource Centre and are crucial to the achievement of Katha's goals of excellence in translation and publishing and creation of an ever increasing pool of sensitive translators.

Ten years ago, in an effort to tap the wealth of fiction in a multilingual country, and take it to a wider readership, Katha, with support from the British Council, British High Commission, conducted the first All India Translation Contest in 1993. The response was encouraging – Katha received more than a thousand entries. The success of this first collaboration led to a second All India Translation Contest in 1996-97. The fact that the participants wanted to translate from two, three, even four languages revealed the rich multilingual skills that were waiting to be tapped. The winning translations published in the series, *Visions Revisions 1* and *Visions Revisions 2*, reprinted as *Silak's Daughter* and *The Will*, were very well received by readers and reviewers.

Encouraged by the tremendous enthusiasm shown by potential translators, Katha decided to expand the scope of the contest to include languages from the SAARC countries – Bangladesh, Bhutan, India, Maldives, Nepal, Pakistan and Sri Lanka. The British Council once again came forward with assistance and enabled Katha to conduct a South Asian Translation Contest.

The process began with a massive publicity campaign in India and the other SAARC countries. Next, twenty short stories by eminent writers from Bangladesh, India, Nepal, Pakistan and Sri Lanka were selected by a panel of writers and scholars. The languages chosen were shared by several countries yet the fictions were unique to their respective cultures. This, we hoped, would offer a real challenge to our translators and to our delight, they rose to it. Once again contestants wanted to translate from more than one language, but were given the option of selecting only three. They were charged a nominal registration fee of fifty rupees per language and were given two months to submit their translations.

The adjudication process for the translations received was quite exhaustive. All the translations underwent screening at Katha where translations that were incomplete, handwritten or not accompanied by registration forms were weeded out. The translations were then shortlisted by external examiners based on language skills, readability, spelling and grammatical accuracy, degree of regional flavour and general overall expressions. After that, the Katha editors screened the translations to select entries that read better and displayed greater command over language. The next stage involved close comparison of the translations with the originals by the resource people in each language to check for fidelity, readability and syntax and also whether the translations carried the essence and flexibility of the originals. Based on the above, three translations in each language were selected for the final round of adjudication.

After careful scrutiny, the judges came up with a list of winners, one in each language, from as diverse backgrounds as engineering, the civil service, agriculture, teaching and creative writing. What all of them shared was a fluency in the target language, and a strong bond with the ethos, the culture and of course the linguistic niceties of the source language. They had to be sensitive readers to be able to go beyond the word and convey the deep story to the readers in English, sometimes woefully inadequate a medium. Their attempts have been recognized and commended by the judges, and now you, the readers must savour the success of their efforts.

20 Stories From South Asia is the outcome of the first Katha South Asian Translation Contest, a major bridge-building initiative towards culture linking. This collection brings to you twenty fascinating stories, in award-winning translations, by master storytellers in different languages. Happy reading.

Desert Nymph
by Arupa Patangia Kalita
translated by Bonita Baruah

When the Lions Club proposal first came, Dr Emily Bedi didn't give it much thought. But having tea with Nidhi, Aneesh, Jessie and Debbie at the medical college canteen, she was forced to think about it again.

Aneesh was literally jumping about with excitement. The Lions Club was organizing a medical camp in drought affected Kishangarh. For Aneesh, an MS student of ophthalmology with a passion for photography, the desert meant innumerable new photo opportunities – endless stretches of wind caressed sand, camels, cactus, the colourfully costumed women. He could not wait to go. In fact Aneesh, who had received several awards and always carried a camera in his bag, was going only in the hope of getting some good photographs.

The Club had made arrangements for eleven doctors. Nidhi suffered from dust allergy, so there was no question of her going. The canteen boy was cleaning the table on the other side. Sneezing loudly a couple of times, Nidhi exclaimed, "Me and the desert! No way."

Debbie wouldn't be allowed by her family. Jessie was a bookworm, she would not miss classes for even a week before exams.

A thrilled Aneesh paid for the tea, then drew up his chair close to

Emily. "Emily, please." Everyone burst out laughing at Aneesh's desperate tone. All their friends knew that Aneesh worshipped the beautiful Emily. Muttering "Have to think about it," Emily got up to leave.

All heads in the canteen involuntarily turned to look at her. But Emily was used to being stared at ever since she was thirteen. She walked out slowly, the stares following her slender five feet, nine inch frame until it disappeared from view.

Emily, who had two months left to become a full fledged gynaecologist, had inherited her rose pink complexion from her mother, a Kashmiri brahmin, and her height and bone structure from her Punjabi father, an army officer. This perfect combination of toughness and softness made her a head-turning beauty. Her stunning looks had also made Emily Bedi a familiar name in the modelling world. Modelling though was just a hobby, not a profession. Emily's mother was not at all in favour of it. If Emily modelled once in a while, it was because her indulgent father allowed her. While she herself did not take it too seriously, she didn't dislike it either. And even though she was not blinded by the glamour, she quite enjoyed reading about her modelling sessions, and the complimentary phrases the journalists used to describe her. The fan mail was also easy to get addicted to.

Emily loved the exquisite designer dresses – every time she put one on, she felt transformed into a new person. She had really liked the one made by a Bombay firm last time. In that silver embroidered black silk dress, she had felt like a fairy queen cloaked in a star studded night sky. The photographs made it to the covers of several magazines.

Her television assignment for a famous sari mill had created quite a sensation. The theme of the advertisement had been – "Our colours, nature's colours." A pink sari sliding off her arms to fall on a ripe, sliced pomegranate. A shower of sunflower petals fluttering down onto a sunflower coloured pallu hiding Emily's perfectly chiselled face. A parrot green sari flowing gently away towards a flock of parrots in the sky, exposing her slim waist. A peacock hued sari blending with the spread out fan of a peacock, revealing her breasts. After that advertisement, she was flooded with offers. Several soap companies offered her big money. There was only one problem – they all wanted her to expose some part of her body. Some wanted her soaked to the skin, others wanted her in a bubble bath or half-draped in a towel. This upset her mother so much that she refused to touch food one whole day. Her father, respecting her independence, left it to her saying, "You are a big girl, capable of taking your own decisions." Yielding to her parents' feelings, Emily refused the offers.

The offers Emily rejected were accepted by Shobha Deshpande. Shobha was Emily's friend since school. She had made a career of modelling after graduating, and was willing to do anything to make it big. One of six children in a middle class family, she moved out of her parents' two bedroom flat as soon as she made some money. Shobha never tried to hide her envy towards Emily – her huge house, car and the privileges she enjoyed as an only child. On her part, Emily accepted Shobha's disgruntlement with life.

Coming home from college that day, Emily sat in the balcony in a melancholic mood. A patient had died in her arms that day. The woman would have died anyway. After suffering for a whole year from a hundred and one ailments, the woman had come to the medical college eight months pregnant. Emily had looked at the husband's face and had wanted to yell at him, but stopped herself. What was the point? She remembered the woman's helpless expression as she looked at her husband while being taken to the operating table. His face had been devoid of expression. A tear escaped Emily's eye. She didn't realize that her mother had come out and was standing behind her. She silently handed Emily a cup of coffee. She knew something had happened to disturb her, she also knew that the tenderhearted Emily would burst into tears if she said anything.

Suddenly the bell rang, and moments later Shobha walked into the house. Emily's mother didn't really approve of Shobha — her reckless lifestyle, her revealing ads. But for once, she was glad to see Shobha walk in noisily — she didn't want to see her daughter mope around the whole evening. She left the room on the pretext of getting the girls something to eat.

Shobha was dressed in a body hugging yellow top and skin tight jeans, earrings dangling down to her shoulders, dark, coffee coloured lipstick on her lips. Apart from her five feet eight lissome frame and dusky skin, the key to Shobha's success was her willingness to expose. She was in a very good mood that evening. She had just bought a second hand Fiat with the fifty thousand she had been paid for a revealing centrespread in a business magazine. She gave Emily the news — "Emy! I've bought a car. I want to treat you today. Let's go." She burst into expletives suddenly. "Bloody relatives! Those are just photographs of my body, I'm not selling my body. They're acting as if they'll eat me alive. Trying to be my moral guardians." She started pacing up and down the balcony. "What can they give me? Give me one lakh and I'll drop even the little I wear. If I had a body like yours, I would have a bungalow by now, and a brand new car."

Emily didn't like it at all when Shobha talked like this. "Why do you think of modelling as prostitution, Shobha? It's a beautiful thing."

Shobha laughed mockingly. "It's easy for you to say so, you live in a doll's house. Your father's friend makes a film for you, and you become a hit. If you were the daughter of a drunkard and a gambler, would you have got this opportunity? For girls like me who don't have rich fathers, it's a constant struggle, a battle. And I'm willing to take off my clothes again and again if I have to." Usually, Emily didn't respond to such talk. And Shobha would calm down eventually. "Gave a thousand rupees to Ma today. I thought I'd take her to the temple in the car. But Mama came and spoiled everything."

"Why?" Emily asked after a long pause.

"He saw my photo and raised a stink."

"What did your mother say?"

"Is Ma capable of saying anything? If she was, she wouldn't let herself be kicked around for a handful of rice and one sari. Ma's not human, she's a machine. If she was human, she would have come away with me a long time back."

In Emily's sanitized life, it was through Shobha that she had first come into contact with poverty. She saw for the first time eight people living crammed together in two small rooms. And Emily had developed a great fondness for Shobha. She said softly now, "You are doing the right thing."

This somehow calmed Shobha down. She sat on a chair, propped her cheeks up with her hands and said, "I'm earning a few rupees by showing off my body, what's wrong with that? If only I'd been born in the West! Bloody Indian morality!"

Emily's mother came in with the tea and left. Shobha started again, "Nani was shocked to see me spend fifteen thousand rupees on clothes, and scolded me. It's my money, why does it bother others? Indians don't know how to dress up. If Nani has four new saris, she exaggerates and says she has thirteen. Poverty has turned them all into beasts."

Like anyone else, Emily too liked clothes, what was so unusual about it? Earlier Shobha could not afford them, now she could. Why did Nani have to get worked up over it? Shobha showed her yellow earrings to Emily, "Like them? They come in a dozen different colours, a thousand a pair. Couldn't buy all of them. Do you want to?" Shobha often got Emily to buy the things she liked. Emily bought them, but Shobha wore them. Shobha put the earrings on Emily and said excitedly, "You look so beautiful!"

Emily made a quick mental calculation – twelve thousand rupees. All she had to do was request her parents, grandfather, or uncle. Shobha was looking at her with hopeful eyes, and Emily could not say no when anyone looked at her like that. Her grandfather had been calling up, to know what she wanted for her birthday. She had been undecided, but now Shobha had helped her.

"I'll ask Nana on my birthday. Where did you see them?"

"But there's only one set. In the Worli complex."

"You get good things in Worli, but the stocks are always limited."

"The owner says there's no point in keeping expensive things – there are no buyers. Everybody wants cheap stuff. How would poverty stricken Indians know the value of good things?"

Whenever the word poverty cropped up, Emily always accepted what Shobha had to say. Shobha knew what poverty was, she understood it better.

"Come, let's go for a ride in my car," Shobha proposed. "It's my treat today." Emily agreed. Her mother was happy too – going out would be good for her. Emily was about to take off Shobha's earrings, but she would not hear of it. "You wear them," she insisted. "What'll you wear them with?" The two went into Emily's room. The cupboard that ran along the length of one huge wall was filled with clothes. After rummaging through the clothes on their hangers, they took out a yellow churidar kurta. Applying some eyeshadow on Emily's lids, Shobha looked at her. "You really are very beautiful, Emily." She looked at Emily's shoes. "Why don't you buy one of those with ankle straps? They'll look good on you."

Shobha didn't suggest this with a selfish interest – her feet were larger than Emily's.

"How much are they for?"

"About two, two and a half thousand."

"Don't they look like the ones Alexander the Great wears in our history books?"

"Yeah, these shoes did originate in Greece."

Shobha's car, though old, was in good condition. She had learnt to drive from Emily. Shobha's face was shining today – she had long dreamt of buying a car for herself. Seeing her like this made Emily happy as well, for she was someone who naturally liked others to be happy.

They walked into a restaurant and ordered chicken biryani, "I love Indian food," Shobha announced, "and I hate fast food."

"Weren't you cursing Indian morality and Indian poverty seconds ago?"

"Arré ... Are morality and food the same thing?" Shobha didn't like it when Emily became serious. "Why shouldn't I like the West?" she asked, putting her spoon to the biryani. "Life is so free there, no ugly poverty." Emily wanted to remind her about the economic crisis in America and England, the condition of the Blacks. But while eating the biryani that Shobha was so joyously treating her to, Emily couldn't bring up serious topics she knew Shobha so disliked.

Shobha polished off the plate of biryani and asked for coffee. "You know Emy, I read in a magazine the other day, that an actress in Hollywood wore a dress made of moss."

"A dress made of moss?" Emily laughed out loudly.

"This super rich beauty had touched the soft as velvet moss somewhere, and fancied herself in a dress made of it. Most fashion houses admitted their inability to oblige her. Finally, one volunteered for ten lakh rupees."

Emily tried to imagine a blue eyed, golden haired seraphim in a green dress made of moss. She stared at Shobha in amazement. "What cloth did they use underneath it? Moss is a kind of plant, it dries up when it doesn't get any water."

"The lifespan of the ten lakh rupees costume was just twelve hours," Shobha said as she finished her coffee.

"Moreover, every half hour the dress had to be sprayed with water." Both Emily and Shobha burst out laughing. "The actress threw a party in honour of the moss dress, and posed before the flashbulbs, proud of her unique idea. And between the photo sessions, someone had to keep spraying her dress. At the end of the twelve hours, it was the end of the ten lakhs as well." Again the two started laughing.

Emily had read about an actress who faced the wrath of animal lovers for having a nightgown stitched from eighteen tiger skins. She'd heard of necklaces made from pearls the size of pigeon's eggs. She'd also seen a photo of a gold embroidered dress worth twelve lakh rupees worn by a model. But a moss dress that lasted for twelve hours! It was too much.

Shobha bought two packets of chips. "Come on Emy, let's sit in the park for a while." The chips were about to finish, so she picked up two more packets, and they sat down on the smooth lawn of the nearby park. Shobha lay down on the grass, munching lazily. "The rate at which you're eating, it won't be long before you become like your nani," Emily remarked. Shobha just smiled mysteriously. Finishing off the last of the chips, she sat up. "I still have to give you a piece of news. There's a fashion show on the fifteenth of next month, sponsored by a famous mill." Shobha grabbed Emily's hand excitedly, "They'll choose one model for Paris. This is your chance, Emy. Radha Verma is so sure she will be chosen," Shobha grimaced. "That snob! She's made it big only because of your medical career."

"Who'll design the costumes?"

"You have to do it yourself. Nowadays, a successful model needs a good body as well as brains. Monsieur Forraze is coming himself. If you catch his eye, the entire world will be at your feet. Wow!" Shobha smacked her lips greedily, as if savouring a pickle.

"Are you taking part?"

"Of course! I should think myself lucky to be able to stand before Monsieur Forraze. I'm just wondering what to wear. What's the latest trend in Paris? I must find out, but I don't know anyone in Paris. Shobha Deshpande's Paris link surfaces again." There was that dissatisfied look on her face again.

Shobha was now lying on the grass, her face resting in her hands. In her clinging dress, she looked like a figurine. Several young lads had started hovering around. The boys, the men who passed by, every vendor in the vicinity ogled at Shobha, who was stretched out as if she was posing in front of the camera. Suddenly Emily noticed that Shobha's breasts were looking fuller. She looked closely, as if examining a patient, then burst out – "What have you done Shobha? Is it silicon? Hormone creams? Or hormone injections?"

Shobha's laughter was cynical. "Doctor Sahiba, silicon is a very costly affair. All Shobha Deshpande's budget can afford are hormone injections."

"You think it's a joke, Shobha? Do you know about its side effects!"

"Sores on the face, messed up periods, even breast cancer."

"Then? Do you want to die?"

"I want to go on living Emily, but not like Nani or Ma. Do you call that living? I'm getting ready to face Monsieur Forraze."

Shobha broke into small sobs. "I despise poverty. If I'm not successful as a model I'll have to go back to that two room hell. My hair's getting split ends from all that blow drying. I'm terrified of putting on weight ..." She swallowed hard mid sentence. "I'm really punishing myself, Emily!"

Emily felt a familiar concern for her childhood friend.

"I want to be like Madonna, Emily. She's my ideal. She's just five feet five, but she has been able to become famous because of her gutsy, Couldn't Give a Damn attitude!"

Emily wiped a tear off Shobha's false eyelashes, and changed the topic.

"My aunt had been to Paris recently."

The word Paris had an electrifying effect on Shobha. She cheered up. "Amarjeet Auntie, who's married to a pilot?"

"Auntie took her most expensive churidars – all her silks and minawork. But she was too embarrassed to step out on the streets of Paris in them."

"Why?"

"The latest fads in Paris are tea, cotton and bidi. Auntie says if she had worn one of those cheap cotton housecoats off the footpath, which the women in her colony wear, she would have been more in fashion."

Shobha was listening intently to Emily. "Does that mean I should dress like a jhonpadiwali for Monsieur Forraze?" She pondered over it. "Tea and bidi ... that means something oriental. Hand embroidered costumes are the craze here too. Have you seen the dresses the banjarans wear? Such exquisite embroidery and mirrorwork. Radha Verma has picked up a beautiful ghagra choli."

"Where did she get it from?"

"She's not telling anybody, she's afraid someone might steal her idea. She's going around saying she'll be the one to be selected. Radha was looking truly ravishing in her last photos."

"She does have a perfect body."

"And she knows how to show it off. She's taking modelling very seriously. Last winter she roughed it out for twenty days in an adivasi village in Bengal."

"What was she doing there?"

"Collecting jewellery. Did you see her latest centrespread?"

"No."

"It was brilliant. She was nude, but a colourful tribal necklace covered her top half. A big metal bell hanging from a girdle covered her lower half. The kind of girdle tribal women wear on their wedding night."

"Why do they wear it?"

"To protect themselves from their husbands' atrocities."

"You keep abreast of a lot of news, Shobha."

"I just read about these things. Radha Verma goes a step beyond. That's why her rate's gone up so much. She went to the fashion show in New Jersey last time. You know that. Before going to America, she grew her hair and sunbathed every day to acquire a tan. With her long open hair, her broad bordered Banarasis, south silks and woven saris from Bengal, she was an instant hit."

Dusk had set in slowly while the girls were talking. Emily and Shobha got up. Shobha kept spitting at intervals. Starting the car, Shobha said without looking at Emily, "A magazine has chosen me for its centrespread."

There was anger in Emily's voice, "How much are you taking off this time?"

"Just till here," Shobha pointed expressionlessly to her hormone enhanced breasts, as if they were some ornament around her neck, not part of her body. "I'll wear Nani's rudrakshas round my neck, and on my ears."

Shobha stepped on the accelerator. She asked softly, "Are you angry with me Emy? Radha bares her whole body. I've just ..."

"Please Shobha, let's just forget it."

"I'll make fifty thousand from this contract. I'm going to save it all. There's no one to look after me if I fall ill."

"Why, are your parents dead?"

"Ma's warm water and Nani's tulsi leaf won't cure me, I need money." Again there were real tears on Shobha's false lashes.

Emily steered away from the topic. "You know Shobha, the Lions

Club is holding a medical relief camp in Kishangarh, a fifteen day programme. They've called us. Dr Kapoor, our department head, is going. She has asked me to go along too."

"Why has the Club chosen that place?"

"You don't read anything besides fashion magazines, do you? Haven't you heard? Kishangarh has been in the headlines, there have been so many debates in Parliament. A lot of people have died because of the drought there. Many foreign countries have sent relief to that place. And you have no idea!"

Shobha suddenly brought the car to a halt. Her eyes and face had reddened. She sat on the roadside and threw up. The chicken biryani, the potato chips, all came out the way they had gone in. Taking over the wheels, Emily chided Shobha. "You've chosen the deadliest method to keep slim – gorging on food and then throwing it up. What beauty care! When Radha and the rest count calories at parties, you continue to gorge. Do you then go and vomit it out in the toilet? You want to create a myth – no matter how much Shobha eats, she's always 36-24-36."

Shobha kept quiet. Emily felt bad. "Are you feeling unwell?"

"Just a little dizzy."

"You have low blood pressure. Why are you obsessed with just one aspect of beauty, Shobha? Bantu women stretching their necks, Chinese women squeezing their feet to keep them tiny, the slim figure dictated by current fashion – they are all the same thing. Radha had to be admitted in the Intensive Care Unit once. Don't you remember Doreen – she went into a coma. Will you be dictated by what others want? Beauty lies in good health."

"You're right Emy. But no one's going to give me any assignments if I have normal pressure and a normal haemoglobin count. My vital statistics are more important."

"Since when has this been going on?"

"Since my first assignment, four years now."

"Since when have you been unable to eat?"

"For about a month. If I eat just a bit too much, I throw up."

"What do I do with you, Shobha? You're heading the same way as Shyamoli Desai."

"Shyamoli who?"

"That tall, slim friend – you used to praise her a lot – Shyamoli used to be a hostess at Air India's VIP lounge. She left the job and made quite a name in modelling."

"How did Shyamoli die? Because she couldn't eat, just like me?" Emily was becoming emotional.

"Do you think life is a modelling assignment that you can accept and reject when you want to?"

"I'm feeling fine now. Let me drive. You're not used to driving an old car." Emily was indeed finding it difficult. Against her will, she let Shobha drive. The two friends sat quietly for a while. Even under Shobha's heavy make-up, her paleness was evident to Emily. She couldn't help remarking, "You're anaemic, Shobha! If you torture your body like this, how long will you survive?"

Shobha had that lip curling, Couldn't Give a Damn smile again, "Shyamoli Desai lived only for thirty five years, but during those short years she lived like a queen! Paris ... London ... My nani is eighty years old, my mother fifty. I want to live like Shyamoli, not like them, like animals."

"Why are you modelling full time? I can give you a job."

"How much will you pay me, Doctor Sahiba? At the most, three thousand rupees. The rent for my flat is two thousand. If I open the east window I can see the sea, and such a beautiful breeze. After my father's dingy flat, I feel a sense of freedom here. I'd rather live with my happiness, my privacy, for a short time. When the dining set comes, I'll invite you to dinner. You'll come, won't you Emy?"

Again that familiar tug at her heart.

Suddenly Emily blurted out, "Why don't you get married?"

Shobha burst out laughing, "You think marriage can rescue your poor friend from this rut?" She turned serious, "If I get a smart handsome boy like Aneesh, a rich doctor's son, I would get married today. Tell me, would your friend marry the daughter of an alcoholic, and rescue her from that two room dungeon? Judging by the specimens who have asked for my hand, it'd be back again to that hell."

Emily did not want to be with Shobha any longer, "Drop me off here, Shobha, I want to visit Amarjeet Auntie."

Emily headed towards her aunt's. Both she and her uncle had gone out. Emily asked Janakibai for a glass of water and went to the balcony. From there, she could see Aneesh's house. She kept looking at the grey house. What was Aneesh doing? Janakibai brought her tea and sweets. She drank the tea and set aside the sweets. "Where have Uncle-Auntie gone? When will they be back?" "To the movies." Janakibai spoke very little. Emily listened to music for a while and pondered over whether she should go home or wait. Looking at the house to the south, she decided to call up Aneesh. "Aneesh, I'm here looking at your window. Can I see you?" Five minutes later Emily saw Aneesh's bike heading towards the apartment. Watching him park the bike below, Emily felt a little awkward, and blushed. Had she really come here to meet her aunt? Why had she left Shobha midway? Why had she been so upset to hear Aneesh's name on Shobha's lips? She rang up her mother and told her she would be staying the night at her aunt's.

Aneesh was wearing a loose white T-shirt over a pair of old jeans, a pair of Kolhapuris on his feet, his thick hair tousled. Emily looked at Aneesh's feet — always hidden by socks and shoes, they were very fair, the heels reddish. Whenever she stood before Aneesh, she felt as if she was in front of a camera. Emily stood before the yellow flowering bougainvillea, as if she was being photographed. Aneesh was looking at her with one eye closed. "Yellow flowers in the background and you in a yellow dress! In my hurry to meet you, I forgot my camera." Emily broke into laughter. There were two and a half hours left for her aunt and uncle to return. Emily decided it would be a better idea to spend the time with Aneesh, than looking at Janakibai's sour face. Sipping tea with Aneesh in a restaurant, driving around on his bike, Emily promised him that she would go with the relief team to Kishangarh.

Dropping her off, Aneesh told her how thrilled he was. "The wind blown sand, you and my camera. Ah!" Emily laughed once again – "Aneesh, you view everything as if you were looking through the lens of a camera." Aneesh took off his glasses, "Really?"

After the two day long, tiring journey, when the medical van entered the desert, everybody, Aneesh's camera included, had fallen silent. Emily felt as if the van was heading towards a huge blaze. The heat was scorching. Where Emily lived, it was quite hot. During summer the temperature often rose to above forty degrees. But the coolers, fans and air conditioners kept her protected. The wind blew in specks of sand into the van when she tried to roll down the window a little. Where her hand touched metal, it felt as if she had touched a saucepan on fire. Emily looked outside – the sand stretched out before them like a crumpled chiffon sari, on the horizon the sun, a brightly shimmering piece of glass, cactus bushes beginning to darken under the fading light, a couple of camels.

As soon as they reached the government bungalow in Kishangarh, Emily lay down on the bed and fell into deep sleep. In the middle of the night she woke up. The fiery heat of the day had gone, it was cool now. She opened the window and looked outside. A few scattered shops, some dwellings and some street lights. Beyond, infinite darkness. The darkness was more intense in patches where the thorny bushes one had become so tired of seeing grew. In the dark they resembled crouched camels. The dark, quiet night caused a chill to run down Emily. Her throat was parched, she wanted a drink. But there was just enough water in the bottle to wet her throat. If only she could have a bath. She saw her pink, marble-floored bathroom – her body felt the touch of a cold spray from the shower. A government car had come in the evening with water for the medical team. It was supposed to last three days, but she needed that much water for just one bath. Emily had read about the drought, but being used to the twenty four hour running water at home, she had not imagined such terrible scarcity. What little water they had here had been made possible because of Dr Kapoor's contacts. Emily wet a towel and wiped her face. She stood in front of the window again. It was a clear, star studded night. She had never seen the sky loom so large before. She was used to seeing only snatches of it. Watching the stars she thought of lines from a book she had once read.

It was about a famine. Sitting amidst his dying crops, the farmer looked at the starlit sky above, so beautiful yet so cold and heartless, and could only curse it. Somewhere in this darkness as well, was there a farmer cursing the beautiful stars that shone like diamonds? A sound – like someone wailing – wafted in. Emily listened for a while and recognized it to be a local violin like instrument. Its sound had been rendered unrecognizable by film music producers who used it along with drums and guitars. It was hard to believe that its strings could produce such heartrending tunes. Emily strained her ears to catch the sound amidst the swish-swishing wind.

The tune brought to her mind the picture of a desert belle – a beautiful banjaran in her flowing colourful costume swaying gracefully across the desert, anklets on her feet, bangles on her arms, a painted earthen pot on her head. She had seen a movie once – she didn't remember much of it, but the vision of the "desert belle" had stayed. The camera had focused on her first from the front, then from the back, then sideways. Emily wanted to dress up like that and walk through the soft desert sand. She imagined Aneesh looking at her through his camera – he was a different person when he was behind it. "Emy, what a snap! Your profile looks superb from up close. You're truly beautiful, Emy." If only Monsieur Forraze could see her in that banjaran's dress, captured by Aneesh's camera ... She remembered Shobha's words – "The world will be your oyster." Right after this was the fashion show. A desert belle's dress would be perfect. Who were the women who made these lovely mirrorwork dresses? She would try to take back a dress for herself, and one for Shobha too.

Emily woke up the next morning and was embarrassed to see that the tent had already been drawn outside and Dr Kapoor was in her white coat, ready to start work. Aneesh was busy clicking a camel draped in a colourful cloth. He had already been scolded once by their team leader, Dr Mehta – "Aneesh, you and your camera!" The tent was half full. Aneesh quickly put his camera away. "At this rate, you'll finish your camera film," Emily told him quietly. Aneesh forgot everything when the word camera was mentioned. "I've brought five reels – one for the desert, and the rest for you."

"Let me get a costume first."

"Wind patterns on the sand, and you in a desert woman's dress. I want to take some photos of you on a camel!"

Emily and the others gradually got involved in work. Examining the patients who had come – some walking all the way, some virtually crawling, some on camelback or on camel-drawn carts fitted with car wheels – Emily was awestruck. How could people be reduced to such a sorry state, she wondered, dazed.

Throughout the day, only menfolk came, there was not a single woman. The mukhiya, the village headman, with his bright colourful pugdi and white curled moustache which dropped down on his lips, told Dr Kapoor that their womenfolk would not come here, the Doctor Sahibas would have to go to their village. Aneesh, Dr Mehta and Dr Sethna tried arguing with him, but it was of no use. Finally, Dr Kapoor and Emily decided they would go to the village. They would take the van. The senior doctors offered them words of advice. It would mostly be gynaecological problems. They were also warned to take along drinking water.

Emily was beginning to realize just how valuable water was. She hadn't bathed for the last three days. The water available was just about enough for drinking and cooking. The tanks and the taps in their government bungalow were all dry, the water level was too low for the pump to draw water. Emily put on a cotton sari and combed her hair. About to wash her face, she changed her mind and put the water away.

The medical van made its way through the desert. Accompanying them was the mukhiya. The heat was tolerable in the morning. Also, Emily had started getting used to it. She was beginning to think that Dr Kapoor was made of steel, nothing could frazzle this fifty year old woman. Now, before them stretched the real desert – only sand as far as the eyes could see, stark bare trees, not a trace of life even in the small thorny bushes. Dr Kapoor was talking to the mukhiya. He owned two shops in Kishangarh. He bought cloth from the city, on which the womenfolk embroidered intricate designs. The mukhiya paid them for their labour. He then sold these in the city. Dr Kapoor had endless questions. Emily had never seen Dr Kapoor from up so close. A woman who had no ties to bind her down, there was no place perhaps that she had not visited. Besides work and travelling, her other passion was collecting cactus. There was every imaginable variety at her house.

Suddenly Dr Kapoor ordered the driver to stop and got down. Next to a bare tree, there were a few green stick-like cactus plants.

Dr Kapoor tore off one of these, "I've been searching for this variety for a long time." Emily could not see any beauty in those thin green sticks. They looked as if somebody had stuck them in the sand. Dr Kapoor began talking excitedly, "Do you know, Emily, there are several gallons of water inside this plant. When the aridity rises even a little bit, they start drawing in whatever moisture they can from the air and the soil." Emily was beginning to get interested in what Dr Kapoor was saying, "But how do these plants retain the moisture?"

"That's one of nature's wonders. Look closely, there's a shining, white, waxlike substance on their surface." Emily looked. Yes, indeed.

"It's a kind of protective armour. These plants grow so slowly that it takes about a hundred years for one of them to reach their full height."

Emily looked around. It was dry and bare, except for a few carcasses of some animals. These had died because of the drought, the mukhiya said. There was about an inch of water left in his well. If it didn't rain soon, his camels too would die. Dr Kapoor tried to offer some hope, "Don't worry, it's bound to rain soon." She looked at Emily, "You cannot imagine the magic a little bit of rain can weave in the desert." Dr Kapoor started telling them about the Kalahari Desert. "Dr Peter took me there. I was then a visiting lecturer in Africa. The magic played by the rain was awesome. The night before, there was only sand, no trace of any life. Then it rained a little. In the morning the desert was alive with countless tiny white flowers. So many of them ... These plants lie under the sand, a little water and they come out. I witnessed this hide and seek game of life several times in Kalahari."

Their van was crossing a bridge. Under the bridge ran a long winding ditch. There were stones and sand on its bed. This "river" was their lifeline, the mukhiya said. If the people were still alive it was because of the little water they got from it. When even that got over, they would all have to leave. This ditch they called a river ran a mile from where they had camped. It was another five miles from here to the village. Soon after crossing the bridge, Emily noticed six women carrying earthen pots on their heads making their way across the sand, through the leafless trees and thorny bushes.

Emily became excited, she was finally going to get a glimpse of her desert belle! But before she could make out anything, the women had disappeared. Looking towards them, the mukhiya spoke as if to himself, "The women have to spend so much time in search of water, my business is getting ruined."

The van halted near a dilapidated hut, where several women sat huddled together. From a distance they looked like a heap of dirty rags. Dr Kapoor and Emily took out the equipment and medicines from the van, and got ready.

The mukhiya brought four women to them. Emily got the shock of her life. These bedraggled, ghost-like creatures looked nothing like her desert beauty. She had once visited a silver mela held for tourists at the Jodhpur Palace, with her father. They had tried to recreate the royal ambience in the palace which had been converted into a grand and modern hotel. A banjaran woman was dancing in the Rangmahal. Writhing like a snake, she kept the foreign tourists, and Emily, enthralled by her fluid movements. There was nothing in common between that beautiful banjaran dancer and these women in their torn and tattered clothes. Their hands and feet were laced with cuts and bruises. Their skin was all shrivelled up like burnt potato jackets. Their teeth were as black as any animal's. Their tangled, matted hair looked like they had never been touched by water or oil.

Emily was stupefied. Meanwhile, Dr Kapoor made one of the women lie down on the bed inside the van. A horribly foul smell emanated from the woman's body. Emily's stomach started to turn. "Come nearer." Dr Kapoor ordered her sternly. She was putting on her gloves for an internal examination. The woman was terribly anaemic and had had two miscarriages. At first she just watched Dr Kapoor's gloved hands dumbly. But when Dr Kapoor placed her hands on her ghagra, the woman jumped up, violently flailing her arms and legs. The experienced Dr Kapoor somehow brought the near hysterical woman to her senses, speaking in a stern, yet kind voice. The woman's genitals were infested with blood and pus-filled boils and wounds. While Dr Kapoor and Emily were consulting each other, the woman, who had remained mute, refusing to reply to any query, jumped up and disappeared. Emily got down from the van and saw the woman, carrying an earthen vessel on her head, limping away slowly along with two others.

All the women gathered there came to be examined one by one. It was the same story with each one of them – they were all extremely anaemic, had innumerable childbirth-related ailments, and bodies ravaged by hunger, hardship and poverty. Their private parts were rotting with infections. Writing down their names and ages, Emily received another shock – twenty four, twenty, thirty. These women had been wasted in their youth. Emily's heart broke.

On their way back to the camp, both Dr Kapoor and Emily were very quiet. The van was crossing the same bridge. Under the bridge sat a group of seven women. Emily stopped the van and got down. She was joined by Dr Kapoor. One by one, the women were taking out water with a small vessel from a hole dug in the sand and stones and filling their pots. The women looked up at them. Their faces were hidden, but Emily recognized one of them. It was the first woman they had examined that morning. Emily grasped Dr Kapoor's hands. She made it back to the van only with Dr Kapoor's support. Emily was aghast – that woman had walked five miles with her boil infested body for a small pot of water!

The sun, a red hot dish on fire, was merging into the horizon. The white film on the cactus was gleaming in the sunlight. Soon, the plants would blend with the black night. Emily fell asleep and started dreaming. Her hands were smeared with blood and pus from the insides of the women. She kneeled near the ditch under the bridge, to wash her hands. She kept trying to fill water in a small vessel, but it wouldn't fill up.

As soon as they reached the camp, Emily got off the van and threw up near the stairs.

Next morning, Emily found Dr Kapoor discussing the women's problems with the senior doctors. Gulping down her tea she joined Dr Kapoor in the van. The women's wounds, she learned, had been caused by the unhygienic conditions and aggravated by the water scarcity.

A young girl was the first to be brought in. She had come with her mother, whom Emily recognized as the same woman who had run away. When Dr Kapoor sternly asked her why she had done so, she replied from behind her veil that there was not a drop of water in her house that day.

Emily made the thirteen year old lie down on the bed. Her body still displayed some signs of youthful softness. The girl had an eye infection. A lack of vitamins combined with hours of peering over stitching was causing night blindness. When Emily tried to examine her genitals, she objected more fiercely than her mother. Emulating Dr Kapoor, Emily calmed her down. The skin on her vagina had peeled off. Emily found something stuck there. She took it out with a pair of forceps, it was a blood-soaked piece of earth!

The next day, as they were about to set out, Dr Kapoor noticed a large bundle in Emily's hands. "Emily! What are you taking?"

The bundle contained pieces of cloth – torn from the cotton churidars, saris and housecoats that Emily had brought with her. Dr Kapoor laughed, "Silly girl! These women will never use them for the purpose you intend."

"Why?"

"Water."

Emily was almost in tears. "Sanitary napkins are an unimaginable luxury for them – something beyond their imagination," said Dr Kapoor. "When people don't have water to drink, washing clothes is out of the question. When they don't have clothes to wear, they can't throw them away."

Tears rolled down Emily's face. "What can we do, Madam?" Dr Kapoor placed a hand on her shoulder, and both remained silent for a long time.

The van had reached the broken down hut where the women were gathered. Emily stared speechlessly as if she were witnessing the most unbelievable sight on earth. Sitting in a circle, the women were singing. A young girl was dancing in the middle. It was the same dance performed by the banjaran at the Jodhpur Palace. The girl's ghaghra choli was whirling in the air. Emily clasped Dr Kapoor's hand – "Madam! They are dancing and singing."

Dr Kapoor was laughing. "Of course, they are alive, and they are living."

The team arrived a bit late that day. Sorting the new stock of medicines had taken a long time. Emily and Dr Kapoor now found it easier to relate to the women. The two citybreds who cleaned the pus off their wounds with their bare hands had become goddesses in the eyes of the womenfolk. Dr Kapoor was the Maji who scolded and Emily the Farishta Didi. Seeing them, the women chorused forward, "Farishta Didi! Scolding Maji!" Dr Kapoor's antibiotics and disinfectants had worked wonders. The wounds were well on the way to healing. Saving as much as they could from the bandage roll and cotton they had, Dr Kapoor gave them the bundle of rags Emily had brought. In a second, there was chaos. The women were mesmerized by the multi coloured clothes. The next day Emily was astounded by how they had used the rags. The young, dancing girl had stitched a red flower from Emily's old housecoat on to her blouse. Another had lined her ghagra with a sari border. They had transformed their old clothes into new ones. When Emily pointed this out to Dr Kapoor, she remarked, "It's their profession."

The fifteen day camp was nearing its end. They stopped seeing patients a day before the campfire. That day, a sulking Aneesh said to Emily, "Emy, I'm hurt. Where's my village belle? Where are the photos amid the patterned sand? You leave early, and when you're in the camp, you're busy with Dr Kapoor. You're boring me, Emy." Emily smiled weakly. Dr Kapoor, passing by with cactus in hand, said, "Aneesh! Take Emily out for a while. She has been very disturbed." Aneesh was looking at her, and not through his camera lens. "Please, Emy." When she looked into his little-boy eyes, she could not refuse him. Emily went out with Aneesh.

"Emy, you'll have to walk."

"Did you know, Aneesh, the women here walk ten to fifteen miles every day for just a mug of water, and even then ..."

She stopped midway.

"The people here lead a very hard life. There has been no water here for a year now, and no farming." A herd of camels passed by, carrying bundles and people – old men, women, children. Walking alongside were some men. "These people are leaving the village," Aneesh explained.

"Where are they off to?"

"Where they can eke out a handful of rice."

"Why?"

"The water has completely disappeared."

Emily was staring at the people.

"Emy! You've changed after coming to Kishangarh."

"Possibly, Aneesh."

Aneesh forced Emily to go into a dress shop. It was the mukhiya's shop. Foreign tourists and fashion houses came here to buy the clothes embroidered by the women. Aneesh bought Emily a dress. The shop was almost bare, there were hardly any dresses.

All this while, Emily didn't smile even once. When they were back at the camp, Aneesh asked lovingly, "Won't you wear this dress? Please? I've kept a camel waiting, the sun is about to set, soon it'll be all over ..."

Emily went in to don the orange coloured dress. There were small round mirrors and green embroidery all over the ghaghra, a reddish yellow flower on the blouse. Once dressed, Emily looked at herself in the mirror and gave a start. Each thread of the dress was stained with blood and pus, with the sweat of these women who walked fifteen miles every day in search of water, with their tears.

Emily tore off the dress. She came out wearing the same dress she had on earlier. Aneesh, who was waiting eagerly, asked why she hadn't put on the dress. Emily spoke haltingly, "I can't."

"Why Emy? You had said ..."

"Please Aneesh, don't ask me anything."

Emily went indoors. A speechless Aneesh put his camera away. Early next morning, as they were about to close camp and return, they noticed that a group of women had gathered outside. They were all sitting very quietly. Emily was amazed to see them – they must have set out in the middle of the night to have reached this place, twenty miles away, so early in the morning. Handing a bundle to Dr Kapoor and Emily, they broke into tears. Emily started to sob, and Dr Kapoor's eyes glistened.

From the van Emily looked back at the women. A cluster of green cactus was growing nearby. To Emily, these women seemed like the cactus. The plants thrived on the little moisture present in the dry desert air. The women, too, drew sustenance from wherever they could, finding a reason to live. Like the plants, they seemed to possess an invisible shield which protected them from life's extreme hardships. It was an unbearable, hopeless existence. Yet exist they did.

Emily opened the bundle. There were two embroidered sets of ghagra cholis and chunnis. Emily had almost forgotten – on her arrival here she had given the mukhiya money for two dresses. He had mentioned that the women were making her dresses, but Emily hadn't paid attention. Emily stopped halfway as she was taking out the dresses from the bundle. They were covered with embroidery, like a beautiful painting. Emily thought of the painstaking labour that had gone into its making, the callused hands that had woven such magic. She thought of the young girl with failing eyesight weaving the beautiful flowers on the fabric.

She handed one of the dresses to Dr Kapoor, who looked at it for a while, then returned it to her. "What will I do with this? You keep it." Emily was mesmerized by the dress. A long green snake covered with tiny pieces of mirror ran along the entire ghagra, the border had chamkis. She held the dresses in her lap for a long time.

Shobha came as soon as she heard Emily was back. One look at Emily, and she burst out excitedly, "Emy! You're looking so nice. I've heard Monsieur Forraze likes tans."

Emily gave a wan smile, and took Shobha indoors. Seeing the dresses, Shobha asked excitedly, "Did you bring these?" Shobha ran her hands over them greedily. " With this exotic dress and your suntan, you're sure to be selected, Emily!" Shobha hugged her from behind. "Will you forget me after that?"

Emily removed Shobha's hands. "I will not participate. I'm giving up modelling."

Shobha was astounded. "What are you saying? Do you know, in Paris …"

Anger was writ all over Emily's face, "Stop it, Shobha."

"What's happened to you, Emy? Kishangarh has changed you."

Emily sat without uttering a word. Then she broke out in a cry – "I have no right. No right to flaunt clothes in a country like ours."

Shobha was dumbstruck. Haltingly, in a small voice, she asked Emily, "Will you let me wear one for the fashion show?"

Emily almost snatched the dresses away from Shobha. "No." She touched the green dress lovingly. The dresses in the mukhiya's shop had only one or two flowers, hers was entirely covered with tiny white flowers. Emily thought of that young girl and the red bruise on her hands. Hadn't it hurt when the needle or thread touched it? She couldn't even give her a hand lotion. The bruise, she had said, was from continuously drawing water from the government well. Emily's heart ached thinking of the fate of that pair of hands, hands that could weave such beauty.

The mirrors on the dresses caught the sun's rays and glistened like the desert sand. Who had taught those illiterate women how to bring nature alive on a piece of cloth? She remembered Dr Kapoor's words. "They are alive, they are living." Emily remembered the day they had sat together singing. She hummed and tried to remember the tune. How long before that young dancing girl became like her mother, prematurely old? How different would be her fate? If it wasn't for the drought, she would probably be carrying a baby in her lap. For how many years had these women been living like this? It sometimes took up to a hundred years for the stick-like cactus plants to reach their full height, Dr Kapoor had said. How long would it take for these desert women to start living?

Once more Emily touched the white cactus flowers. These plants, life itself, lay buried under the sand. A few drops of rain, and the whole desert would come alive. The young girl's voice rang in her ears, "Farishta Didi, when will it rain?"

"Desert Nymph" was originally published in Asomiya as "Morubhumit Menaka."

The Festival
by Akhtaruzzaman Elias
translated by Amar Kumar Majumdar

Anwar Ali should have been in an excellent mood. Only a short while ago, he was at a rich friend's big house in Dhanmandi, to attend his marriage ceremony. It was a modern, well finished house in inner Dhanmandi. He was able to feast his eyes on the charming grace and beauty of a host of fashionable and attractive women. He even got acquainted with a few of them. The elegance and festive mood of the congregation had provided him with sensual pleasure that should have lasted for at least a week.

But Allah willed otherwise. As soon as Anwar Ali entered the narrow lane of his locality he was disgusted and became depressed. The objects of his disgust were these. The dirty, yellow and muddy water in the open drain looked on with a turbid, indifferent stare under the dim light of the lamp post. On the edge of the drain, colliform heaps of human excreta and dog stools lay side by side, as if sleeping together in a curled up fashion. And the people. The people also caused irritation in Anwar's mind. With half an hour still left for the end of the night show in the cinema hall, the local youths were already preparing for their daily ritual of eveteasing. To the left, on the main road, gambling was on in full swing. In the Ahmadia Hotel and Restaurant, a disc record of a twenty year old song, *Chode babul ka ghar,* was being played continuously. It was only fifteen minutes past eleven, the cacophony would go on for another two hours.

His own shabby environs and the festive house in Dhanmandi, were lodged firmly and uncomfortably together in his mind. In that posh area, all the roads are wide and smooth. All through the day and night, they relax and bask under milky white bright light. Lying down, they look up at the mysterious, eternal space above. One after another carfuls of local and foreign ladies come out of the royal mansions and head for some other palatial building. Jewel studded huge mansions stand at respectable distances, in a negligent manner. One can be sure that a quarter to half a dozen beauties converse among themselves in strange languages in those mansions, as inaccessible and forbidden as planets and stars. One moment one among them plays Raag Malkosh and the next moment she sleepily turns the pages of a book with lazy fingers. When Muntashir, Ishtiaq or Ahrar comes, she talks about socialism in a soft silky voice against the background of a softly singing long playing record of Kanika Bandyopadhyay, a leading exponent of Tagore songs. She also finds the time to suffer sweetly from loneliness. At such times, there is no way to listen to the jazz king Duke Ellington for a full two hours, with the fan running full speed in an air conditioned room.

And just look at the condition here! At this late hour, eight to nine dogs can be seen running about madly from one end of the lane to the other. Not that there are no dogs on the other side. One of a venerable breed was there at the venue of the marriage ceremony. What grave expression, what physique! How proudly he stood there, wagging his tail just a little. Like a landlord in a Bengali film sequence enjoying the sunset, sitting on his first floor balcony in a deck chair. The mere sight of such a dog gives rise to a feeling of awe in the onlooker's mind.

And look at the sons of bitches here! All of them bloody street dogs, with not a strand of hair on their scarred bodies – they can only wail pathetically. Bastards, they have become ugly and fat, eating all the rubbish, and stare vacantly while creating nuisance in trickles whenever they come near a lamp post.

Entering his room, he felt as if it was an offshoot of the main lane. The same damp, stale odour. A white tooth and a yellowish one peeped shamelessly through the gap between the thick lips of Saleha Begum who had been asleep, but awakened just then, bathed in the reddish yellow glare of the forty watt electric lamp. Saleha Begum, his wife, with a hint of saliva at the corner of her lips, rusticity writ large over her face, and stammering speech.

"Polly's ma, where is my lungi?" Today is the fifth day of October. He usually addressed his wife as Saleha during the first part of the month and called her Shelly when he travelled in a ricksha. But his disgust and irritation tonight made him break his own rule.

To avoid Saleha's sleepy smile, Anwar Ali faced away from her and began to put on his lungi. Grudgingly he thought, "This girl has gone to college, if only for a year. She even had a love affair with him before their marriage. Then why is she so unsmart, so entirely devoid of charm?" No undulations beneath her sari in the region of her breasts or buttocks, always ambling about like an oblong pillow.

"Quite late in the night, isn't it? What time is it?" Saying this, Saleha Begum got up and went to the small courtyard.

"She will now discharge about a gallon of urine," thought Anwar Ali, "sitting squat with her ugly feet resting over two bricks." He had never liked women who urinate repeatedly like this, or spit in blobs. But what could he do? Women like this can never rectify themselves. Let her piss to her heart's content. Meanwhile he would cast his mind back over the events of the evening. With one hand on the trousers hanging on the clothes stand and another holding his damp, yellowing underwear, he concentrated on resurrecting the gala evening of the marriage ceremony.

No complete picture of either the festivity or any of the beautiful women appeared in his mental vision. The ceremonial events of the marriage that took place under bright lights, now appeared as faint impressions, mostly torn in pieces, winking along the reddish lines of his dreaming eyes. He wondered, perhaps it would have been better if he had not responded to the invitation at all. How intimate a friend was Kaium, after all? He would not have known about the marriage if by chance they had not met in the stadium. They had been at college together for two years, worked for the same union, and got somewhat close while organizing a strike together. Son of a rich man and a meritorious student, everybody had wanted to befriend Kaium. But who would have missed Anwar if he had not attended the marriage? However, by going there, he had been able to meet some old friends.

Who could come closer to Kaium? He used to have some sort of a competition with Hafiz on this score. Finding Hafiz among the invitees, the ten year old jealousy was revived. When they had just entered college, Hafiz was a rustic youth. The regional tones of his accent used to be jarring to his ears, he could clearly remember. They had observed Twenty First February Day during their student life by collecting subscriptions. Now Hafiz taught Bangla in a local college, still faithful to his commitment to Twenty First February. The fellow was garrulous, talked too much. The beautiful women gathered at the marriage appeared and disappeared before his eyes, but Hafiz went on reciting his autobiography without any pause, "As for myself, you know, I avoid these functions in general. I am nothing but a professor and I spend my time in studies only. I don't like this hilarity. I left politics as soon as I got out of the university. Almost stopped writing too. But radio and television people are always after me, it is only on their insistence that I still write songs, only songs ..."

Anwar Ali still had one hand on his trousers, and was clutching at the soft underwear with the other. Songs of Lata Mangeshkar were blaring at full volume in Ahmadia Restaurant. The autobiography of professor and lyric poet Hafizur Rahman was being played out on a human tape recorder. Anwar Ali had cast his glance here and there, where are the girls? It was essential to have a close look at a few charming girls. He would never get the chance to see so many beautiful women together. He had occupied a vantage position, the best possible spot. Chairs were strewn around the deep green lawn. Some people were seated, some were strolling about and conversing with different people. Special traffic police were on duty outside, manning everybody with smiling faces. Men and women were laughing hilariously at the slightest joke or even at words without any wit or worth. Some ladies were entering the balcony across the lawn and going into the rooms. That place was also clearly visible from where Anwar Ali was seated.

At one end of the lawn, beneath a lighted krishnachura tree, a few dedicated men and women, deeply engaged in discussing culture and socialism, had formed a cosy corner for themselves. Anwar Ali craved in his mind to join the group as one of them. These women knew how to beautify themselves with a few deft touches. How attractive was their way of talking, how worthy of emulation their voices and manner of speech. It was one thing to listen to imitation outside, and quite another to enjoy the original – there was no comparison at all. He was itching to go and join them, but he did not know any of them, so how could he intrude?

"Your bhabhi inspires me a lot, you know, in these matters. My mother-in-law belongs to a highly aristocratic family of West Bengal. Very cultured people, related to Sayeed Badruddozah's family. You must be knowing my second brother-in-law Sahriyar, Sayeed Sahriyar Hossain – appeared for the CSS this time, got the civil service itself, having his training at Lahore – he is also very fond of music. You may have heard my latest song, it has become very popular, it was recorded practically at his initiative. Khondkar Rafique Ahmad has lent his voice, quite a hit song – *Ogo bondhu, aamay tumi dile ogo keyar kaantar shaaj* ... that's how it goes" ... The recitation of Hafiz's autobiography came to a sudden halt as Kaium approached them along with a young man. The young man was well-dressed and quite handsome, with sharp features. When Kaium praised the literary achievement of Hafiz while introducing them, Anwar Ali experienced a pricking pain.

His name was Iqbal Hossain Chowdhury, First Secretary in the Pakistan embassy of a West European capital city. When he was a student at the Dhaka University, thirteen to fourteen years ago, he had often delivered speeches at Amtala, being inspired by left wing politics. Moreover, he used to sing Tagore songs and, as per the prevailing trend, wrote fiery poems. Reading one of his poems, titled, "Aamra Shurjota Aanboi," in those days, Anwar Ali had been in high spirits for at least three days. Ex-poet Iqbal Hossain Chowdhury provided fresh inspiration that day to Professor Hafizur Rahman. The main organ used for reciting his autobiography, the tongue, was metamorphosed into a tail, and the hairless, small tail worked delicately on the sound waves produced inside his mouth, so that the following stream of words came out in a continuous flow, "I am familiar with your name since long. If you don't mind my saying so, you were wrong to give up writing. Rather, may I be allowed to say that you committed a crime? We have been gifted with an A class diplomat, no doubt, but at the cost of an A class poet."

Anwar felt a little sore in his lips watching Iqbal with his readymade European smile. The incoming flow of people continued unabated. Kaium went to the gate to receive a famous politician clad in sherwani and walked to the lounge with him and his three to four escorts. The gentle laughter of the cultural corner suddenly became louder and more abandoned, creating a sensual resonance in Anwar Ali's body. Kaium came to them once again. Hafiz's tail wagging was still continuing, "I tell everybody, whatever others may say, and I say this all through, even to my students, that our art and culture survive to this day only by virtue of a few enlightened people in our foreign service and civil service. The attitude of our political bosses, at least as far as art and culture is concerned, is not very, I mean ..."

"Not very agreeable." As Iqbal completed Hafiz's sentence, Kaium introduced Anwar Ali to Iqbal's Punjabi wife. "We have been friends since our early youth."

Mrs Irshad Hossain Chowdhury smiled in an attractive manner with veiled suggestions emanating from the pupils of her eyes and the prominent undulation of her bosom. "Well! Did you attend the same school?"

The peculiar accent of her Bangla was pleasing, but not infatuating. Kaium said, "No, we were together in college. We subscribed to the same political views. We were deeply involved in politics during our college days."

"Is that so?" In that sweet voice, in the corner of her beautiful eyes and her fully blossomed lips, there appeared an expression like that of a film star, "My god, I am afraid of politicians. Politics terrifies me!"

Kali, son of Anwar Ali and Saleha Begum, was sleeping with one of his legs lifted over the frail body of Polly, their daughter, sleeping by his side. Their mother shoved them to one side after arranging their limbs in proper position. The children remained in deep sleep. A couple sang just a few lines of the title song of the film *Arman* in duet and stopped suddenly. Saleha said something in a husky voice. Anwar Ali listened to her, and simultaneously, the murmuring voice of Mrs Irshad Hossain Chowdhury rang in his ears, a voice he had heard only a few hours ago. Hafiz was overwhelmed by the satisfaction of talking against the government before such a highly placed government officer. While Anwar Ali was contemplating what to say in reply to Mrs Chowdhury, the attention of the beautiful lady was diverted elsewhere. He heard Hafiz speaking in his ear, "I don't care about anybody! Did you notice how I condemned the government through my sweet talk?" Anwar had now completely forgotten Mrs Chowdhury – what did she look like? He had examined her closely and from different angles, and now she was completely obliterated from his memory! How does one cope with age advancing so fast? Anwar Ali sighed heavily and the festive mood was blown aside to some extent.

Saleha Begum placed two pillows side by side. "How warm it is! What sultry weather!" She sprinkled talcum powder over herself. Saleha was coming out of the shadow of drowsiness and was becoming sensuous – pure lust getting hold of her. She continued in a husky voice, "Your friend is very rich, isn't he? Is it their own house at Dhanmandi? How did the bride look? What gifts did the bride's father give your friend? You are good for nothing – had I been there, I would surely have known all this. Did a lot of people come? What was the menu?"

As he prepared to get into bed, Anwar Ali gave precise and satisfactory answers to his wife's string of queries. Now all was set for their regular sexual activity before sleep. He would make love now to this woman for at least twenty minutes. He was afraid that Saleha may spoil the mood of his rare and precious evening. However, the memory of the beautiful women he had seen would provide him the real pleasure, Saleha was just a token medium.

As Anwar Ali unbuttoned his wife's blouse and was about to unhook her bra with a practised hand, she said in a routine, seductive voice, "No, no, let it be, not today." At the same time she snuggled closer to Anwar. But Anwar's blood had congealed, and a cold film began to spread over it. His unresponsive body seemed to say, "What happened, why am I devoid of any desire today?" Some days he read pornography during the day in his office, and in the night this same female body felt quite fresh. He grudgingly thought, they can't learn the tricks, however sexy they may be – these Saleha-type women.

Look at Parvez's wife! She didn't have much education, but her style of talking, the seduction in her eyes! He had been introduced to her at the fag end of the festivity. He was about to leave, when Parvez touched Anwar Ali's shoulder, "I have been tracking you since long. You have put on a lot of fat, Anwar. Difficult to recognize me, is it?" Then he introduced Anwar to his wife standing close by, saying, "My school friend. We passed matriculation from the same school, then studied in the same college. Passing out of college, I went on to do engineering, and he went to the university."

Anwar Ali, in fact, had not gone to the university. He had failed in the college examination, and passed his BCom from another college. His friend's wife's expression suggested that she was quite talkative. But she was observing the cultural circle in an absorbed manner. "You are his childhood friend? Such a long friendship, but you have never come to our house, how strange!"

Anwar concentrated his total attention to paint a permanent picture of her in his memory. He devoured with his eyes her entire female body, noting the cut and colour of her blouse, the patterns on her Jamdani sari, the red round bindi on her forehead, the fine bangles on her forearm, her fair fingers and the colour of her nails.

"You got married long back, didn't you? How many children do you have? Come over some day."

Anwar Ali noted down Parvez's address, replied to his questions and mentally drafted a well-knit response to Parvez's wife. "Really, a friendship of so many years. But he and I have not met each other for a long time. Yes, I shall come. Some day I shall come and disturb you."

But before he could overcome his hesitation and utter the carefully composed sentence, Parvez's wife said, "Why don't you come with your missus some day – come any Sunday. Please come. I shall be highly displeased if you don't come, remember." Parvez walked away with his wife at his side, taking out his car keys from his pocket and toying with them in his palm. Anwar Ali was unable to conduct the well rehearsed dialogue. Will he ever get such an opportunity again? A mild perfume was exuding from her body. The perfume was very refreshing and very faint. Only sometime ago she was talking to him from such a close proximity, but now it seems to have happened long back. Again, still closer, much closer and within his grip is Saleha's breast, but even then why is he unable to feel her? Was he wearing thick rubber gloves on his hands that were holding the pair of Saleha's tits like two airless balloons?

"Please come. If you don't, I shall be highly displeased, remember," he could distinctly recollect the words, the aroma reached his nostrils, but the festivities and the women remained far away. The saline vapour of Saleha's sweat wafted from her hands, her breasts and her face, and clouded the room. Her swelling pair of breasts were as if at boiling point, but who would remove the shock proof gloves from Anwar Ali's hands?

The restaurant loud speaker was now blaring, *Awara hoon* ... Happy people were returning from the cinema, each of them now the hero of the film.

Some of them were singing the hit songs of the movie. A loud whistle was heard, just once. Apparently, there were not many females among the crowd.

After a momentary silence, the chorus of voices became louder and louder. Had something untoward happened in the gambling den? But the tone of the chorus suggested that the people were rejoicing over something.

That other place also hummed with various sounds. There were so many people present, so many women. But how gentle, how pleasing the sound was! The tape recorder was playing in a subdued tone — mostly western music, some Tagore songs in-between. *Esho aaamar ghare esho, aamar ghare* ... Listening to this song, a lady had remarked, "Very appropriate at a marriage ceremony, isn't it?" Who was the lady? ...

The combined shouting of many voices submerged the lone voice singing, *Awara hoon* ... The disc was changed, but the words of the song were not audible. What was the reason for so much jubilation among that crowd?

Anwar Ali tried to make sense of the noise by pricking his ears without changing the position of his body. From the mouth of Saleha, hot with desire, came an irritated remark, "What is the matter so late in the night? What are those damned people shouting so much about?"

"Damadam mast kalandar ..." a deep voice belted out the hit Hindi film song, and the crowd broke into a wild fit of laughter. Anwar Ali's limp hand fell like a block of wood on his breast that had turned cold because of the noise outside. He sat up, "Let me see what those people are so jubilant about at the dead of the night."

There was a narrow balcony outside the door, and steps down to the lane. At the end of the lane was a small gathering of people. People of every age, including a few boys. They did not seem like they belonged to any family or household, nor even to a barrack or slum. They were those who carried loads in the market, sold cinema tickets in the black market and pushed carts or pulled rickshas on the iron bridge, for their livelihood. They spent their nights sleeping on the sidewalk, or on the veranda of one house or the other.

Anwar Ali called out to one of them and asked, "You, boy, what is the matter?"

The boy looked at Anwar Ali, then shouted at the top of his voice,

"Damadam mast kalandar." The entire scene was clearly visible by then. Near the entrance to the lane, close to Khijir Ali's bakerkani shop and below a lamp post, a dog and a bitch were engaged in coitus. The crowd was giving vent to its exhilaration on seeing the sexual act. They were cheering the dog in various ways. From the gambler's den on the ledge of a house on the main road, somebody was singing a line in parody of a popular song, "In this month of October, two dogs slumber ..." From the same group another loud voice was heard, "You bastard, go and fetch a pinch of salt, you rascal. Sprinkle some salt, I tell you." Intimidated by this loud voice, the rest of the song faded away. But who would go to fetch salt? Nobody wanted to leave his vantage position. The gambler's den was located such that the amusing scene was visible even as they played cards.

A big pan of shahi halim, meat broth, could be seen, on a four wheel push cart. A local man sold halim at the Rathkhola crossing daily from evening to nearly midnight. At about one every night, he would wheel his pushcart to this alley, park it there, and go home. Since the entrance to the alley was blocked by the crowd, he too joined the revelry out of compulsion, leaving his pushcart at the end of the alley. He was serving the halim in small earthenware pots – the dregs of the broth contained not even a small piece of meat. People were sipping at the nearly cold broth, availing of a concessional rate. The boy who sold paan, bidi and cigarette in front of the Ahmadia Restaurant, whistling to the tune of recorded music, was also sipping the broth, standing close to the gamblers' ledge. An autoricksha driver, one of the gamblers, looked at the canine couple while playing his card, and kept shouting at the boy at one minute intervals, "Hei, you fucking bastard, why don't you give me a cigarette?" But the cigarette vendor, who had the tray of paan, bidi, and cigarette hanging from his neck, was holding the pot of halim in one hand and an aluminum spoon in the other. With both hands full, how could he pass on a cigarette?

"Here you are, Anwar Saab." Turning around, Anwar saw that Nasrullah Sardar was looking out of his bedroom window. Once upon a time, Nasrullah Sardar had been the leading man of the locality. Nawab Salimullah Sahab had himself conferred the crown of the chief to Nasrullah's father in the year 1907. Nowadays, though, Nasrullah was not much sought after. As Anwar Ali came closer to his window, the one time chief grumbled, "Look at the pigs, what they are doing. What can one say to these shameless, uncultured people, tell me! So many gentlemen live in this locality, there are ladies and children inside, and look at what fun the harlot's sons are having at one o'clock in the night, just look at them!"

Then Nasrullah too came out of his room. The position was as advantageous for him as it was for Anwar Ali. The whole scene could be seen clearly from here. "Has there been any retrenchment in your office?" he asked Anwar in a friendly tone. "Is 303 among those being dismissed?"

"Yes, our chairman is at the top of the list. He has amassed a fortune already. What good will come of it to catch him now?" But Anwar Ali was not prepared to waste his time talking to him. This fellow begins to talk about himself given half a chance. A comparative assessment of the virtues of the British officials during Nawab Safiullah and Nawab Habibullah's times with those of the present batch of Pakistani officers formed the background of his autobiography.

With a bucket of water in one hand, and small glasses and a kettle over a small portable coke oven, a tea vendor sneaked in and out of the group. Muttering to himself, Nasrullah retired to his room. He cast a last look towards the copulating dog couple and slammed his window shut.

Immediately after Nasrullah's window was shut, a small piece of brick struck the body of the dog. Affected perhaps by shame, or fear, or both, the canine couple started moving away little by little. But it was impossible for them, in their present condition, to disengage. They may not have been inclined to do so either.

Clusters of small clouds were floating about like grazing cows all over the autumn night sky. A reddish yellow moon was shining above a thin veil of transparent mist. Anwar Ali felt like giggling as a gentle breeze came along with the moonlight and titillated his senses. He was lucky – his chain of thought was broken as a shrill voice was heard from the gamblers' den, "Oh my childhood friend!" The crowd broke into a loud laughter. Anwar Ali had also seen the film with his wife, and they too had laughed at this dialogue.

The other street dogs had gathered in a group on the other side of the main road. Some were lying in a relaxed manner, others were standing and barking, perhaps also laughing. A lonely dog sighed heavily from some undefined anguish, incomprehensible to human beings, maybe even to the other dogs. A sentimental dog stood on a pushcart parked at the main road crossing, a little removed from the festive arena, and looking up to the fond face of the pleasantly shining moon, wailed piteously at short intervals.

"Jumman Ali, you, Jumman Ali." Men and dogs alike looked back on hearing a new voice. Tota Mian, owner of the bread shop, was shouting for his servant boy. "You fucking bastard, what are you doing standing here? It's one o'clock in the night and you bastard, son of a harlot, are enjoying this fanfare? Which father of yours will open the shop in the morning?"

Jumman Ali said in a cajoling tone, "So what? I have packed all the bread, I have."

"You motherfucker, if you watch this cinema show all night, will you be able to open the shop in the morning?"

It did not appear as if Jumman Ali cared much. But he looked at the dogs for one last time and reluctantly went away with Tota Mian. Someone among the gamblers remarked, "Jumman Ali saw the cinema show of the dogs all right, now you are going to enjoy the cinema with Jumman, and who is going to see to it?"

Another piece of brick fell close to the dog couple. This missile had been aimed at the electric bulb of the lamp post. It hit the post with a metallic sound and rebounded. Radiating a damp, misty light, the bulb went on glowing.

Entering the room from the balcony and closing the door, Anwar Ali called out in a full, throaty voice, "Saleha!"

In a sleepy, voluptuous tone, Saleha said, "What were you doing so long? What's happening outside, tell me!"

"I went towards the road crossing and saw a lot of people gathered there." Lying down on the bed, Anwar Ali murmured, "My Shelly," and drew his wife close to him.

"What are they shouting about so much, tell me, please!"

"What am I to tell you Shelly, they're enjoying the goings on between a dog and a bitch, the bastards ..."

The words came out in a lascivious trickle from the lips and throat of Anwar Ali, now hot with desire and excitement.

"The Festival" was originally published in Bangla (Bangladesh) as "Utsab."

Fullmoon Night
by Gautam Sengupta
translated by Jayati Dasgupta

Like any calamitous happening, this one too had started off in a very ordinary manner. What it boiled down to, presuming of course that the actual reason behind all this is the one that is being assumed, was apparently rather commonplace. The parents were given to returning home late every evening and this made their daughter feel resentful. Well, that's quite natural. Who on earth likes it when she has to let herself into an empty flat every day and then sit around all alone?

It was not as if Jiji came home directly from school. Four days a week she attended tutorials, and she took dance lessons on Wednesdays and music on Saturdays. She was learning to draw and paint too, but that was at home on Sunday mornings. On that day, when she entered the house after her dance class, could it have been the note on yellow post-it stuck to the fridge that caused her temper to flare up? It must have been, otherwise, why would she have crumpled it up and flung it with such force that it went under the sofa, rebounded off the wall and emerged again?

Yet, the note contained just mundane stuff. It said,

> My dearest Sonai-sona,
> Your sandwiches are in the hotbox. Wash your hands
> well with liquid Lifebuoy and eat properly. If Mitra

Auntie calls tell her we will be late. When Subal comes
with the clothes give him twelve rupees. The money
is under the phone book. Be a good girl, my pet.
Yours lovingly,
Mum-mum Ma.

If the note was the source of her irritation, then, either after reading
it or earlier, she would have tossed her bag away from her shoulder
aiming it towards her bed – probably stooping a little in the process
in imitation of the style of her most favourite Azhu. The bag, being
heavy, would have brushed against the door and fallen right next to
the box containing Jiji's new Reebok shoes, close to the wall that has
the mirror on it.

Whether she made a face at her thammi's picture fixed next to
the mirror or spoke to her of her terrible vow is difficult to say. But it
could very well be that she had not taken a vow at all.

Fixed to the wall opposite to Thammi are the ever scowling Azhar,
the black clad Jackson and Sachin with a tiny stud in his ear. Her eyes
may have met Jackson's in the mirror. Perhaps it was then that Jiji
remembered she had to return Rimpi's cassette. She hadn't gone
towards Rimpi's house that day, though. Rather, she had walked in
exactly the opposite direction, leaving the Buddha temple on her left.
Later, when her walkman was switched on these words could be clearly
heard – "Did you even stop to notice the crying Earth, the weeping
shores ...?"

It's true, things had been very different as long as Thammi was
there. At the sound of Jiji's footsteps on the stairs she would open the
door and be ready to welcome her. Thammi would hug her as soon as
she entered, take her bag from her and remark – "This is hardly a
school bag, it's more of a stuffed sack, I'd say." Jiji would rush to
change and wash, and soon she would be snuggling close to her

grandmother. Thammi would feed her rice and bananas mashed with milk, chikon-chire or some other delicacy. Stroking Jiji's hair she'd say, "Your Mum-mum Ma will be late in getting home."

"What Mum-mum Ma, she is No-good Ma," Jiji would respond with her face in Thammi's lap.

"You mustn't speak of your elders that way, my precious, it makes god angry." Thammi would remonstrate. Then she'd start telling her stories — fairy tales and legends of Buddhu-Bhutum, Ashoka sashthi, Chapra sashthi.

On that day Jiji evidently hadn't even washed. The bathroom was found to be absolutely dry except for some Coke spilt in the basin. So one can imagine that she had drunk some from one of those Coke cans her father had around to go with his rum, and had poured off the rest. Later the empty can was spotted lying on the sofa.

The reason why she left the house is not clear to this day. Was it because some strange breeze had drifted to her from an unknown shore bringing with it a whiff of Thammi's person mingled with the aura of her tales? Maybe she had felt — What do they think they are doing? What do they take me for? Maybe she had wanted to teach her parents a lesson. Had some nameless exhaustion or excruciating boredom invaded her, or was it that an undefined emptiness inundated her being urging her to make her way down the stairs? Perhaps she had drifted on, like one entranced, with the moon overhead, towards some elusive land of dreams.

For the sake of this narrative, let us assume that after walking absentmindedly for quite a while, all of a sudden, she stopped in her tracks. Her halting made her conscious of her surroundings. She realized she had never before come to this end of the lake. Huge concrete pipes were lying on one side and on the other, the waters of the lake stretched out dark and deep. The reflection of that large moon on the water reminded her of her father, her babi. It was Babi who had mentioned that morning that it was Buddha Purnima. Standing there in the moonlight, as she brushed her hair back with her hand, she started to feel scared and wanted to turn back. Around this time Nelo had spotted her.

In fact Nelo was not supposed to have left the shelter at all. He knew very well that Lottery Papu's men were after him like mad dogs. If they laid their hands on him, he would be done for – khalas. He had no clear idea as to what it would feel like to be khalas, but since his experience in these matters far outweighed his years he had managed to come to a conclusion. It couldn't hurt all that much, he decided, it would probably be just a bit more painful than when he had had his face bashed in by Raju's gang and was left bleeding by the railway track.

Nelo did know that the "public" was very scared of dying – he had observed this so many times. Only a few days ago as they dragged Madna away to be butchered he had cried so much. Madna, with that great Bachchan-like body of his, had snivelled – "Ustad, please let me go, I beg of you." Right at the end that bugger had even wet his pants! Nelo pondered over this entire situation leaning against a large pipe, smiling to himself and pushing his tongue out through the gap that a broken front tooth had left.

Nelo had to go out to buy himself some "maal." Having procured it he was heading straight for the shelter, following the usual path. On the way he happened to see the pipes lying there in the moonlight and felt an urge to take his first puff right there, and once he had settled down something kept him glued to the spot. Actually, that day from the very beginning the drug had come on very strong and taken him soaring. The fix was, to put it in Nelo's terms "full-tight, full-chakas." According to Nelo this stuff, this essence of leaves, was the king among intoxicants, fit to blow one's mind. Problems cropped up only if one ran out of supply when it was time. Once, when he was in a police lockup, Nelo had experienced that trouble. It had begun with yawning, his nose and eyes watered next and then came the pain. And what a pain that was! It had seemed as if all his bones were being twisted out of shape and would soon break out through his flesh – "Oh guru"! Later he learned that such a state was called "Turkey." Billu had told him so. It was Billu who had got him addicted to this stuff, last year in jail. Initially he used to throw up sometimes, then such minor discomforts passed.

Billu may not be educated, but he sure knows a hell of a lot. According to him all these intoxicants were developed by "sahabs," Westerners. That must be true, for sahabs are a smart lot. As Nelo was considering all this with his eyes shut, images started forming in his mind. Stretched out on something like a 70mm movie screen was a torn yellow mat. A man was cowering on it and moaning – that was Nelo's father. Another man, wearing shoes, had just kicked him hard – that was Nelo's uncle, his father's younger brother. There was a woman too, she was laughing away holding on to the uncle's shoulder and was brushing back her hair with her free hand from time to time – that was Nelo's mother.

Each and every day these scenes replayed themselves behind his closed eyelids, so much so that he had all of them by heart. He knew exactly what came next. The man he called uncle would unzip his trousers and urinate on the man called father. That would make the woman called mother laugh even harder. Then she would go and get into a taxi with the uncle, brushing back her hair again with one hand. A while later, that father fellow would slowly get up and set right his lungi, then finding no one else at hand he would send his fist crashing into little Nelo's face, breaking off a front tooth.

The free show that was playing on and on in his mind made him think back on those times, stirring up all those memories that set his brain afire. It was happening inside his head – he could feel the heat turn scorching, the pressure building. He reached into his pocket for the stuff. He knew he'd need some more of it to douse the blaze. Some light fell on his face to distract him at this point. He opened his eyes to a huge moon, which seemed to hover right on top of him, focusing all its brightness into his sight. He uttered some choice four letter words through clenched teeth and turned his face to the left to avoid the glare. At that very moment he spotted Jiji. He spied a female form in jeans standing all by herself, holding a walkman in one hand. With the other hand she was brushing back her hair in exactly the same manner as the woman called mother.

The police station had been in a state of ferment from early that morning, because of the rape and murder of Antara (Jiji), the only daughter of professor and poet, Dr Mallinath Sarkar. A peace march had been organized which had completed its course. All the evening papers had reported the news in detail and as a result the phone at the police station was ringing almost constantly. The officer-in-charge Chakraborty Babu had only recently assumed office. After a great deal of effort he had managed to secure a transfer from Coochbehar, but before he could even settle down this troublesome case had cropped up. He examined all the rings on his fingers over and over again – a pearl, a gomed and the others. It's time he wore a coral too, he decided and directly called his astrologer's home in Bagbazaar.

The next in command, Paresh Saha, had been around for a long time. He had gone out to take a look around and feel the pulse of the locality. On his return, finding the OC busily talking into the phone, he decided to wait at the door and kept picking his teeth with a matchstick. As soon as the conversation had ended, he fished out a tiny piece of betel nut from between his teeth and flicking it away, entered the room.

Pulling out a chair for himself, he enquired, "Have you taken a look at the body, sir? It's really in bad shape. The left one has almost been ripped off."

"Really ridiculous," Chakraborty Babu commented, "watching all that awful stuff they show on television these days is taking this country into an abyss."

"She had been gagged firmly. But this is not the handiwork of a gang, maybe two people are responsible or even just one. There must be some old grudge at the bottom of this."

"Who could have a grudge against so young a girl?" Chakraborty was not convinced.

"Don't you take her for a mere kid, sir," Pareshbabu smiled knowingly, his right eye drawn to a slit. "You have no idea what these girls from the south are like, hussies all of them I say."

"No, no!" Chakraborty Babu shook his head. "How does being from the south or the north matter in this case?"

"Oh yes, sir, surely it does. Why, no girl from Barasat, the area where I live, would stand in a dark place all on her own, that too as late as eight in the night. There must have been some prior involvement in this case, just you wait and see. All that I have seen in this area in all these years is enough to turn one's stomach." With that he got up to leave, toying with another matchstick.

After Paresh Saha's departure Chakraborty Babu suddenly remembered that today being a Wednesday, his daughter would be going for her music lessons. His daughter, Nandita, was in her final year. No, there was no need for her to go all the way from Salt Lake to Tegharia just for a music lesson, he decided. There is that dark stretch in between, on VIP Road. He couldn't think any farther. The Omega on his wrist showed it wasn't seven as yet. He called his wife.

"Listen Rani, has she gone out?"

"Who?"

"Your daughter of course. Has she left?"

"No, but she is about to. Why ..."

"From now on she'll have lessons at home."

"Goodness! Why? You know very well Jayanta Babu does not go to any student's place to teach."

"Then she'll have to learn from someone else. The main point is that she will not go anywhere by herself – nowhere at all. Is that clear? It's my order and it is final."

"Tell me what has happened."

"Why do you have to know? What can you do about it?" Chakraborty Babu got irritated. "She mustn't go out after sundown, just get that straight." He banged down the receiver without bothering about any further reaction from the other end.

Jiji's place is overflowing with people. Even the flat next door, Monica's, is filled with them. Jiji's father's brothers and his friends are in Monica's sitting room, while her mother Binata's family and colleagues are in their own flat. Binata is sitting on the floor with her back against Jiji's bed. Her sister is holding her hand. In front of them, on Jiji's writing table a photograph is kept propped up against the thick Oxford dictionary. Jiji's uncle will soon be taking it away to be laminated.

Jiji's father had taken the photograph when they were holidaying last year. This was just prior to their setting off to visit the Elephanta Caves. On the left Jiji can be seen laughing in a pink polka dotted dress. Binata is mid frame in sunglasses, with a scarf covering her head. She has her arms around her daughter and a half-smile on her lips. The wind blown pallu of her sari covers most of the area on the right. If one looks for the details one can see that it is worked in batik and can spot parts of the old building of the Taj in the background.

Jiji's kakima, the wife of her father's younger brother, is managing the kitchen. Jethima, the elder brother's spouse, troubled by gout, has stationed herself at the kitchen door on a round mora. Mallinath is moving around from one flat to the other wearing a saffron kurta over a pair of ochre corduroy trousers with a cup of black coffee in one hand and a cigarette between the fingers of the other. Meeting him at the door, his old aunt breaks into sobs. "Be strong Bhola, don't lose faith, this is god's way of testing us." Throwing down the cigarette and crushing it underfoot Mallinath mumbles to himself, "God, my foot!"

Mangoes are being sliced for the visitors. There is also some coffee and sandesh. Not that people are really eating anything. Once in a while someone picks up a sandesh or a piece of mango. "You are cutting the mangoes too small, Namu," comments Jethima.

"Oh don't worry Didi. I'll put some forks alongside."

"Where will you find so many forks or spoons in this melee?"

Sarama, the maid was washing the cups. Without looking up she says, "There are some spare ones on the upper shelf of the showcase."

Jethima says, "You concentrate on your job, Sarama."

All those who are arriving are bringing along fruits, sweets and flowers. Binata's fridge as also Monica's large BPL are nearly full. Sarama thinks, "My children are perpetually on the lookout for things to eat, so I might as well take some of this home. On their own they are not likely to let me have any. They are ready to throw away but not to give away." Then she is suddenly reminded of Jiji. It seemed as if it was only the other day when that little girl in red shorts would follow Sarama around the house. All of a sudden she had shot up to become tall like her father. "Oh, what a pity" – Sarama's eyes brim over with tears.

Jion, Jiji's little cousin, is having the time of his life. He has extracted a Barbie doll from the showcase and is giving it a bath in the small, blue basin at the far end of the balcony. No one is forcing him to eat or to wear shoes, they are not even preventing him from playing with water. It would be great if things could be this way every once in a while. Pressing his finger against the mouth of the tap, he sprays water on the doll's face. He is aware that his Ji didi has been killed by some awful men, but that doesn't make him cry because he is sure He-man will soon be here sword in hand. He will have a dishum dishum fight with all the bad guys and bring Ji didi back.

On the third day after Jiji's incident Nelo was killed in front of Jamai's old teashop in the narrow lane behind the market. At a quarter to six in the morning he had woken Putia for a supply of drugs, and was coming back by the shortcut when a gang of eight had surrounded him. They were armed with swords, pipe guns, choppers and revolvers. They had fired four shots aimed at Nelo's head, one of which missed its mark and got lodged in the back wall of the market, creating a new landmark so to say. Then they kicked Nelo's body out of the way and left it lying by the drain. They then headed off towards the railway tracks, making their way through the market, singing "Pardesi, pardesi" in chorus. It goes without saying that the shutters were downed in the market immediately afterwards. In the days to follow one or two other cases of murders occurred by way of retaliation. Gradually things became calm again, as usual.

The lights that were put up around the lake after the tragedy have gradually disappeared. Some have been stolen, the others were broken. The same old darkness has once again descended around the lake. As a result one and all, from love struck couples to the police and the patty sellers, are at ease. Things have returned to what is considered "normal," and so it is all rather peaceful. This year Buddha Purnima has moved forward by five days. Once again the moon can be seen rising as a huge, dull yellow disc. These days Binata stays in Jiji's room. No one has come today, she thinks to herself. It's her daughter who has gone for ever, the pain is hers, the rest of the world is hardly bothered. On that date they'll all turn up together, bearing flowers.

There is no one in the flat this evening other than Binata. She left her job almost nine months back. Nowadays she spends the greater part of the day in the library of the mission. She even goes there in the evenings sometimes to listen to talks on Gita or the Upanishads. Her guru has advised her to spend more time in meditation. Yet whenever she tries to meditate that one face constantly pervades her consciousness, making her unable to continue. She rearranges her little Jiji's books. She unfolds Jiji's clothes and buries her nose in them, only to fold them all over again. She had considered asking Sarama's youngest daughter to come to stay, but it didn't materialize as Mallinath had objected vehemently.

Quite a few have advised her to have another child. Thirty seven is not too old for that, they say. Who knows, it could be true. But she can't even bear to think that way, such things somehow seem far too distasteful. Actually all her physical desires have shrivelled up from the very roots and have died away. One night, going out of her room, Mallinath had called her a frigid bitch. On another occasion he had almost slapped her. She understands that if things continue this way it will be difficult to make their relationship last, and yet she just can't rekindle the slightest interest in herself.

She has been sitting quietly all evening holding a top of Jiji's close to her heart. Thoughts arise — what if the doorbell rings one day and on opening the door her little Jiji runs into her arms ... The tears well up once more from the very depths of her being. She raises her face to find the moon glaring — insolent and malevolent. The moonlight is pouring in, engulfing every nook and cranny. She carefully wipes away her tears with the end of her sari, then shuts every window and draws every curtain till everything is covered.

Mallinath spends his days teaching, at seminars and at addas. These days he is unable to write much of poetry. Whatever little he writes is only a rehash of all that he had written earlier. If ever Jiji comes to mind he tells himself that for one who is alive it makes no sense to grieve for those who are no more. He knows, doesn't he, that life is nothing but a huge kaleidoscope, that brings forth different patterns at every shake and turn. Man is a mere observer. The most he can do is write about a few of these and that's all there is to it. In this context, there is no point in being either happy or sad.

The adda he and his friends had indulged in, Thursdays and Saturdays, at the Coffee House, has long stopped. These days they have "fullmoon night get-togethers," which all of them take turns to host. The fact that for the last one year Mallinath hasn't been able to have it at his place because of Binata's intense objection makes him feel uncomfortable attending these sessions. But today they had a special one at Badal's place in Salt Lake. Badal is Mallinath's childhood friend, and what was being celebrated was the twenty fifth anniversary of the publication of *A Supernatural Travelogue*, Badal's first book of poetry.

Two varieties of Scotch were served – Blue Label and Black Dog, plus some Gold Reserve which had been specially brought for Mallinath. He had sat in one corner with his eyes shut, listening to the reading of Badal's old poems. How quickly the years have gone by, he thought. He could still so easily recall their journey by tram to College Street and beyond, after collecting the first copies of Badal's book from Durlabhda's press. Oh dear, he really was getting old.

In the taxi on his way back he realized he had had a little too much to drink. Midway down the bypass, near the massive statue, he took out his handkerchief to wipe away the sweat on his face and caught sight of a demonic moon chasing after them. It reminded him of the god Tezcatlipoca who, as myth has it, has the power to charge the whole of nature with hostility when he hovers over the earth.

As the taxi driver handed him back the change he felt some difficulty in breathing. He leaned on the shutter of a shop across the road from his home, the one from which he bought cigarettes and at one time used to buy Cadbury's chocolates for Jiji. Gradually he slid down to a sitting position. Was it a heart attack coming on? He shook his head rejecting the possibility – he had a feeling he was not going to go that easily. Then suddenly he saw Jiji standing there in her white round necked T-shirt, her head tilted a little to one side. She was smiling and saying, "Babi, Sachin is greater than your Gavaskar."

"What's all this nonsense?" he blurted out, trying to raise himself up with all his strength. At this point the sky spun like a top before his eyes, carrying the moon along with it.

Robi, the caretaker of the building opposite the shop, Akash Deep, had come up to the terrace with his newly wed wife. She was from Belda and had come to Calcutta for the first time. She was still very much in awe of the city, which appeared to her like a gigantic movie set with so many tall structures looming all around. She was the one who spotted Mallinath lying there on the roadside and drew Robi's attention with a poke aimed at his midriff. Robi bared his teeth in a grin. "Oh that's our Mallibabu. He must have downed too much liquor. Not to worry, he will make his way home once he comes to." Then, drawing her to himself with an arm around her shoulders he asked, "Well dear, does a moon this big ever appear in Belda?"

Robi's wife couldn't think straight anymore. The moon, like a brass platter, high above the massive buildings, unearthly in the enveloping darkness, made her wonder – maybe in Belda the moon is never this big. She rubbed her face on Robi's chest. Everything seemed glorious to her in that fullmoon night.

"Fullmoon Night" was originally published in Bangla (India) as "Purnimaar Raat."

Jhatpat
by Suvarna
translated by Kamal Sanyal

Jalgaon roads
beautiful and shapely
come hurtling
to embrace me.
Someone is rolling
a hoop there ...
Someone? Who is it?
Oh, I know –
It's Diwakar!

I am in my study, reading. Suddenly a memory jogs my mind. The roads of Jalgaon! And on those roads, Diwakar. Rolling a hoop. Shall I continue reading or think of Diwakar? In other words, shall I read a story written by someone else or shall I think about the story my memory will weave around Diwakar and me? In the end, the book remains in my hands, unread. My mind has flown to Diwakar.

Diwakar! Diwakar! Come to me. Come near me. It's me, Ramya, calling you.

A boy of twelve or thirteen years, beautiful, delicate, charming. That's Diwakar. And a girl of ten or so, naughty and obstinate. That's me, Ramya.

Diwakar and I. Where and when we met, I don't remember. It could have been in his house or under a tree. Or perhaps on that heap of sand in front of our house. No ... I can't recall. What was our relationship? My relationship ... with Diwakar?

Can it be called a relationship at all? It would be true to say that I built no relationship with Diwakar. So none was broken. But something definitely happened between us. As a matter of fact, I left after a fight with him. But that was only on the surface. In my heart of hearts I liked Diwakar. While it is true that I did not experience any great thrill in the middle of the night recalling his words, I liked listening to those words. I cannot pretend that I didn't.

Perhaps it was because I was only ten then. One day Diwakar told his sister Divyalata, "When I grow up, I will marry Ramya." When I heard this from her, I was annoyed and went to have it out with him. Later, we all started playing Jhatpat, as usual.

Diwakar's two upper teeth protruded slightly. This was not obvious except when he laughed. This little slip on the part of nature only enhanced his good looks. Actually, I liked Diwakar very much indeed.

There was this game — Jhatpat — that we children played a lot. It was something like playing Catch. One of us would be the Den. While the Den counted to a hundred, the rest would run away in all directions. We used to play in the compound of Diwakar's house. The compound was very big and had a railing all around. We would climb up on the railing during the game. The Den would touch a player, who in turn became the Den. Whenever Diwakar was the Den, he would finish counting to a hundred and run up to where I was sitting on the railing. He would tap me on the head or shoulder or hand. I would then get down, but instead of running away from me he would just keep standing there. I would tap him and say Jhatpat because I was the Den now. Then I too would stand there instead of running away. You had to say Jhatpat every time you caught someone.

The two of us would then continue to play with each other, quite forgetting the other children. In my later life, I have longed for the male touch. I have experienced fulfilment. I think Diwakar was at the root of both the longing and the fulfilment. It is possible that I went to other men looking for Diwakar in them.

Diwakar was tall and older to me by two and a half years. His hair was curly. I loved to watch his curls blowing in the wind. I would tease him – "Diwakar, look how untidy your hair is." He would get angry and pull my plait. He would yank the ribbon from my hair and move his fingers round and round on my head. Then he would say, "Look at your hair now! So untidy! Now, will you tease me?"

Diwakar's father was an advocate. His elder sister went to college. So she must have been the same age as my sister who was also in college. My father is still alive and is eighty seven years old. If his father is alive he would be around the same age. How I wish I knew if his father is alive or not.

Diwakar lived in a two storeyed house. It was right opposite the Jalgaon City Civil Court. Diwakar's younger sister was a nice girl. Though Diwakar was older than her, Divyalata never called him bhai – it was always Diwa or Diwka ... "Eh, Diwka, ikde ye" ... They spoke Marathi. We did not know Marathi so they spoke to us in Hindi. Later I came to know the language quite well and the credit for this must go to Diwakar.

I learnt to speak Marathi, but that was in the last six months of our stay there. Then we had moved house and I lost touch with Diwakar. Now I think that Diwakar would have been very happy if I had talked to him in his mother tongue. And I would have been happy to see him happy.

It's raining. I always remember Jalgaon when it rains. Rain is the memento given to me by Diwakar. I used to stay indoors when it rained, but I always sat near the window. I would feel one with nature, an inexplicable sensation of being united with it would come over me. Then I would want the rain to stop and Diwakar to come. And he always came, as soon as the rain stopped. Diwakar and Divyalata came to our house to play with the hoop.

Rain! Rain! What an extraordinary thing is this water called rain! It unites not just our earth but the entire universe. I feel that the incredible phenomenon of the birth of life must have taken place when the earth and sky joined together in torrential rain.

It's noon. Still lost in my thoughts I eat and go in to take a nap. Outside, the rain continues to fall. As soon as the rain stopped we would run to the garden with the hoop. Do you remember the games we played there, Diwakar? Was there a slide? Swings? A seesaw? I cannot remember. I know we did not play Jhatpat there. All I remember is that I used to be impatient to go to Diwakar's house and play Jhatpat.

As I remember those days something happens to my mind and my body. I want to recreate the fleeting and indistinct touch of Diwakar's fingers. Why didn't my entire being get contained within his tiny fingers? I want to ask him – "Diwakar, why didn't we hold hands and run in the garden? Why didn't we, standing under a tree and watching a bird, become a little Paro and Devdas and sing, O albele panchi tera dur thikana hai ...?"

I know only too well what I have lost in losing Diwakar. What we had between us at that time was real friendship, true love. Love? At that age? We not only did not know the meaning of the word, we had never even heard the word itself. How could it have been love? But it was. It was love that longed for the fleeting touch of Diwakar. May I call you Diwa? Like Baby called you? And you called her Baby instead of Divyalata – I remember that. I want to talk to you, Diwa. To tell you about all the ups and downs in my life. It's possible you have forgotten me. To be truthful, I cannot say that I have thought of you night and day since we parted. But I must tell you one thing. Whenever I have had a love affair, I have thought of you. Your words would echo in my ears and I would ask myself, Why did Diwakar say that? Did he have the same feelings for me as I have for Mr X? Or Mr X has for me? That was all. Then I would drown myself, body and soul, in the love I had for the man. You would recede. But you were never forgotten completely. Yes, I did marry. You too must have. My marriage fell apart. I hope yours is intact. I have no children. I have been unhappy from the point of view of love, family and children. I hope you have been happy. If you have, I must have been effaced from your memory.

There have been many ups and downs. If and when we meet we can talk about it. Can we, after forty years? Will we ever meet? Many dramatic changes have taken place, many love affairs too. So many tempestuous events that I have had to go back again and again to find out who I am, what I am, why I made so many mistakes, where I got lost? At those times your innocent face would appear in front of me. Today I want to weave a garland of stars around it. I want to light glittering lamps around it. Alas, I don't know how to paint, or else I would have liked to paint rainbow colours in the picture and look at you in it, pulsating with life.

After running fast and hard, you would suddenly stand still. I regret that I never stood by you and felt your warm breath. I want to relive those days with you. I want to be with you, to ruffle your hair, to hold your hands, to sing with you, to sit on the branches of a tree with you and talk. Not the you of today but the you of forty four years ago. To hear those words of yours once again and get annoyed and say, "You are a bad boy ..."

Where are you, Diwakar? In Jalgaon? Do you live in the same place? Is the railing still there or has a multi storeyed building come up there. What are you now? If you are an advocate you must be practising law like your father did in Jalgaon. You must be wearing a black gown to court. What do you look like? But maybe you are not a lawyer at all, perhaps you are working in a company in Bombay or Pune. You could be in America. In that case the change would be so great that I must have become an insignificant person in your life. I would like to. believe, though, that staying in a foreign land you remember your motherland intensely. And that when you do that you think of your childhood in which I had a place. You would remember my name. Am I right? I want to be sure about this. I want to meet you to find out if this is really so.

Tell me Diwa, where do I go looking for you? I must go to Jalgaon. I shall ask someone where the Civil Court is. If it is in the same place, well and good. If not, I shall go to the old place and ask the rickshawalas. All over the country there are rickshas now, so they must be there in Jalgaon too. When we were young there were no rickshas. There were either cars or victorias, which were pulled by horses. When we first went to your city we rode in a victoria from the station. We had come from Ankleshwar, which in those days was a small village. We were very impressed with urban Jalgaon. Specially its beautiful roads — even today I cannot forget them. So when I reach the court I shall look in front of it. To see whether the old house is there still or is it now a block of flats? If the house is there, I will have no difficulty in finding you. If there are flats, I shall ask the chowkidar or a flat owner. Someone is bound to give me your address. It is possible that you stay in one of those flats.

Then what? You would be there and your wife and children. Perhaps your father and mother too. What will we do then? I have a thousand questions to ask you. Would you be interested in knowing anything about me? Actually I would like it, if your wife has no objections, that the three of us go out for coffee. Would you like that? There is one thing that bothers me — suppose you have forgotten my name! If you have, I shall be really hurt! I'll feel humiliated.

What do I want to know? Shall I tell you, Diwakar? I have been in love more than once. Have you too? When did you fall in love? Were you able to marry her? Or are you married to some other woman? Have you been faithful to your wife after marriage? Or are you in love with someone else? Do not be afraid, Diwa. Your marriage will not be affected in any way because of me. I just want to talk to you.

If I go to Jalgaon, do you think you will recognize me? I wear glasses now. Do you? I used to wear frocks and skirts when you knew me. Now I wear salwar kameezes. You should be fifty six now. I am fifty three. I want to erase the last forty four years. Where are you, Diwakar? Just once, tell me where you are. I have not fallen in love with you in my usual way – I am engulfed by you. I long for you, I crave to have just one glimpse of you. Even a little information about you will be enough. I am eager to know if you felt the same way as I did those days. Let this torrential rain stop. Let Diwa and Baby come over with their hoop. Let us all go into the garden and play with it. This question that has cropped up in my mind will not let me rest in peace till it is answered.

What was our relationship? How deep was it? How trivial? At midnight, when Radio Ceylon broadcasts "Bhule Bisre Nagme" and plays one of those very old songs, I feel the same emotions that I experience when I think of you. The stars around me glitter. The strains of the sitar play in my heart followed by the melody of the shehnai.

One such song is *Chandni raat mein jis dam yaad aa jate ho tum, roshni ban kar meri ankhon pe chha jaate ho tum.* I yearn for words such as these, to join us for ever and ever. A few moments when only two names matter – yours and mine.

I am impatient to relive those moments. There has always been a doubt in my mind. I am alone and have to answer to no one. But

Diwakar? What if he is married and has a family? I want to relive a few moments of my past, to get answers to a question or two. Suppose even that turns into a spark?

For two long years I have lived with this doubt. It is easy to go to Jalgaon — it is not far. What if his wife disapproves? I certainly don't want to snatch Diwakar from her. Nor do I want to enter into a physical relationship with him. All I want to know is whether he remembers the name Ramya. Forty four years ago there were some moments which belonged to us. No third person had any place there. Do I have no right to desire Diwakar's company just for those moments? What is wrong in my going?

Believe me, for two years I have lived with this conflict. Thrice I bought the ticket and I cancelled them twice. The third time I came back from the station. I have lost count of the number of times I have packed my suitcase, and unpacked it. Indecision has dogged me. One part of me always asked, "What was there between Diwakar and you? Nothing." The other part said, "Whatever you had with Diwakar you have never had with anyone else. And what was there between the two of you was the truth."

Two more monsoons came and went. But I was unable to free myself of the wavering. Finally one day I bought a ticket to Jalgaon, packed a suitcase and reached the station. The train was three hours late. Doubt raised its head again.

"There is still time. Should I go back?" But I found myself unable to move. The train arrived and I am in it. It is moving and my imagination runs ahead full speed.

Jalgaon. I get down. Everything happens just as I had imagined. The City Civil Court is where it used to be. A ricksha takes me there. Diwakar's old house is gone and a new ten storeyed building stands in its place. The compound is big, the railing is there but it is a new one. I enter through a door. It is dusk and there is a soft light all around. My heart is beating fast. I go to the chowkidar and learn that "Diwakar Patil is an advocate and lives on the seventh floor." I go up in the lift. There is a nameplate at Flat 7/C. "Diwakar Patil, Advocate, Civil Court."

Who will open the door? Diwakar? His wife? His son or daughter? What kind of reception will I get? I ring the bell. In a few moments a boy of twelve opens the door. "Who do you want?" he asks in Hindi. His voice comes back to me through the centuries. I know that voice. I stand speechless. The child asks again, "Who do you want to see?" I want to say "You." Instead I say, "Diwakar Patil."

"Please come in. Papa is on the phone. My aunt from America is calling." Saying this, he goes to play cards by himself. Aunt? Who? Has Baby gone to America? Or is it the elder sister whose name I do not know? Or both of them?

I sit on the sofa. The child is engrossed in his game, oblivious of me. A voice can be heard from inside. A few words in Marathi, a few in English and the rest I cannot hear. I stand up and go to the child.

"May I play with you?"

"Which game do you know that can be played by two people?"

"Whichever you know. Teach me."

"Rummy ..."

We start playing rummy. I do not want the game to end. I want Diwakar to come out soon. I realize I have not asked the boy his name. "What is your name?"

"Ramyanshu, who is it?" Diwakar comes out. At the same time, the boy replies.

"Ramyanshu."

Ramyanshu! What an unusual name! Hardly any Ramayanshus around.

This is the critical moment. What will be his first reaction? Will he recognize me? For a moment I think of removing my glasses, but I do no such thing.

Diwakar goes and sits on the sofa I had been sitting on earlier. "Have you come to see me? What can I do for you?" Before I can reply, he says, "I have seen you somewhere before. Have you been here?" I put my cards down and remove my glasses.

"My name is ..." But Diwakar does not let me finish. "Ramya?" he says. "You? Where have you come from?"

"I thought you wouldn't recognize me."

"How can that be? For a moment I was out of my mind." He is talking in Hindi. I look at him and then at Ramyanshu.

Just then the doorbell rings. Ramyanshu runs to open it. A little girl of around ten stands there.

"Papa, Bhavya and I are going down to the railing to play Jhatpat."

"Jhatpat?" My ears prick up. I look at Diwakar. Diwakar says in a natural voice, "You see Ramya, both Ramyanshu and Bhavya love to play Jhatpat."

"Really?" I feel like telling Diwakar – Let's go and play Jhatpat for a while. But of course, I do not say anything. The children run off to play. Almost immediately the doorbell rings again and Diwakar opens the door. A beautiful and dignified woman walks in and smiles at me. I smile back. Diwakar says, "Who do you think this is, Vithika?" Without saying a word Vithika laughs aloud. I become a little self-conscious. My first impression of Vithika is that she is clever and different from most ordinary women. She says, "How do I know? Have we met before?"

"No."

"In that case, Diwa, give me some hints."

Baby's words resound in my ears. Diwa, Diwa ... I say to myself, how sweet it sounds, abbreviated.

Diwakar says, "Jhatpat, Jhatpat."

Vithika smiles again. "Jhatpat ... oh, Jhatpat! Ramyanshu, Bhavya, Jhatpat ... what about Bhavya? Jhatpat? No, I can't ... give me another hint."

"Something to do with Ramyanshu."

Vithika claps her hands and says, "Oh, Ramya! So that's who she is! Your childhood friend! What brings you here, Ramya?" She comes up to me and takes my hand. "It's a small world, Ramya. A small world indeed. Welcome!"

I am petrified. My heart is beating fast. Diwakar remembers me so well that he has named his son after me! And I had thought he would have forgotten my name. And this woman, Vithika. What a marvel! How open hearted! Not an iota of envy in her! What a wonderful woman. How fortunate Diwakar is.

"I am so very happy to meet you two," I say.

"Me too." Vithika says. "I still can't believe you are Ramya! I am very surprised but happy too. Diwa, why don't you say something?"

When I hear Vithika call him Diwa I am agonized. Why hadn't I ever called him Diwa? I want to hear what Diwa has to say.

"Aren't we going to offer Ramya some tea and snacks?"

"But of course," Vithika starts towards the kitchen.

"Just plain water, please," I said.

Vithika brings the water and says, "Ramya, have dinner with us."

"No, let's all go out and eat. I don't want you to bother."

"No bother, really. But let's go out. What do you say, Diwa?"

"Whatever you two decide."

"There is one condition, though," I say.

"What condition?" Vithika asks.

"You will be my guests and ... along with Ramyanshu we shall take Bhavya too."

"No problem," says Diwakar. "No problem at all," says Vithika, and laughs. I am familiar with her laughter by now.

Just then, the doorbell rings. Vithika goes to open the door. I think, there is so much I want to say and Diwakar is absolutely quiet. Why?

When the door opens Ramyanshu and Bhavya are standing there, holding hands. I want to take their photograph. They walk in. I can't take my eyes off them. Suddenly I want to look at Diwakar. I want to go down and run through the roads of Jalgaon. The roads, the rain, Diwakar, Baby, me ... oh, why didn't I ever hold hands with Diwakar and run down the road? Should I tell Diwakar what I am going through? Let Vithika know ...? Someone is playing with a hoop on the road ... who? Ramyanshu? Yes. No. No. Only Diwakar. Only Diwakar and the rains, on the lush green maidan ...

"Why are you quiet?" Vithika asks.

"Nothing, really."

"You are remembering your childhood! You and Diwakar also played together like these two." She has read my thoughts. "It's good you invited Bhavya for dinner. Those two are inseparable."

"Really?" I can't help asking.

"That surprises you? It shouldn't!" She laughs again.

"Let's go. Are you all ready?" Diwakar starts looking for the car keys.

"Here you are," Vithika throws them at him and he catches them.

"Don't we have to inform Bhavya's mother?" I ask.

"No. They will understand. They live on the ninth floor."

We all go down in the lift. Walking past the railing, we go to the parking lot. Diwakar opens the car door and we all get in – Vithika and Diwakar in the front, Bhavya, Ramyanshu and I at the back.

"Why are we in a car?" I wonder aloud. "I want to run on the roads, not alone, but ..."

Vithika says, "The roads of Jalgaon are really beautiful but there is no end to the traffic. It's impossible to walk. Such crowds, cars, scooters, bullock carts, buffaloes. Would you believe it, Ramya, often I think of walking down the lush green roads holding hands with Diwakar ... but do you think these crowds would let us do that?"

The car comes out of the parking lot and passes the railing. I look at the railing. Vithika laughs and taps Diwakar. Diwakar taps her in return. I don't know what is happening to me. I look out of the window. I stare at the cows, the cars, the people. I smoothe my hair. Why doesn't anyone ruffle my hair? Why doesn't anyone say, "Will you dare to tease me any more? Look at your own hair!"

Next to me Ramyanshu and Bhavya are playing Jhatpat and tapping each other. Vithika looks at them and says to Diwakar, "Why are you so quiet?" She pulls his hair and taps him again. I too want to say Jhatpat and tap him and run my fingers through his hair. I want to tease him – "How untidy your hair is!" I raise my hand to touch him and stop. I smoothe Ramyanshu's hair instead. With one hand on the steering wheel Diwakar tidies his hair. Vithika ruffles it again and Diwakar pulls at her hair. Both of them laugh. I join them. But I look out at the lush green roads.

I was sitting by the window. My hair was blowing in the wind. I realized that I was still in the train. We would reach Jalgaon soon. My uncertainty still dogs me. Maybe I should just go back from the station. After coming all this way? I don't understand myself. I don't know what to do. Do you? Why don't you help me solve this dilemma? Why can't you tell me what to do? Each moment of my life is full of doubts. One part of me says, "What's wrong? You are not out to destroy someone's home. Why be so afraid to fulfil an innocent desire?" The other part argues, "Suppose this innocent desire turns Diwakar's life into hell? Or what if he just doesn't recognize me? Even if he does, suppose he thinks I am insane? Let him. I am ready to pay the price. But to have come all this way and then to turn back ..." I shall never be able to muster this courage again. But suppose Diwakar's wife turns this simple incident into a huge problem?

You will have to tell me what to do. There is very little time before we reach Jalgaon. I shall do exactly as you say. Should I get down at the station and go towards his house or should I catch the next train back?

The train is running at full speed. I am sitting near the window. I touch my flying hair softly. I look out of the window. I ask myself if Jalgaon station has changed a lot. And I await your decision.

"Jhatpat" was originally published in Gujarati as "Jhatpat."

She Too is Ahalya
by Usha Mahajan
translated by Pamela Manasi

Leaning back, she peered at him again over the rim of her spectacles. He still seemed engrossed in writing. Seemed because, sitting at a distance, she was unable to gauge whether or not he had actually written anything on the sheets of paper spread out before him. But the pen in his hand was constantly visible and every now and then he looked out of the window and stared into the void for a while.

Reclining in her old cane armchair, basking in the sun, she couldn't even see him properly. The glare of the fading sun was directly in her eyes, though it didn't reach his room. He was sitting slouched, with his elbows on the table near the window, so she could see only his back and right profile. The sunlight filtering diagonally through the window bars fell in stripes across his chest, arms and face while the rest of his body was steeped in the darkness of the room.

He shuddered.

Ajju looked like his own silhouette, shrouded in mystery.

Something had definitely happened. He had been distracted ever since he had come back from Ira's. She wanted to walk up to him, caress his back, take his face in her palms, turn it towards her and ask, "Ajju, what's the matter with you?"

But there no longer existed that natural bond between her and her young son, by which she could ask him anything unhesitatingly and he could reply! How and when such walls of silence rise between parents and children, is a mystery in itself. This was the same Ajju who as a baby, taking one of her breasts in his mouth, used to knead the other with his tiny hand. Whose pee-potty she had cleaned, whose naked little body she had bathed for years. And here she was today, trembling before asking him one little thing, as if ...

The last time he had been quiet like this for days was when he had lost his job. It was from his friends and Ira that she had learnt that he had chucked up his cushy job after an altercation with his employers. How perturbed she had been! What could have caused the discord? He had always shared a good rapport with them, almost friendly. Ira had told her, "Biji, he had become too thick with them. So much so that they had begun to dominate him completely. He had no freedom in work For how long could he have been a puppet in their hands? You don't know Biji, too much intimacy isn't healthy for any relationship."

She longed to ask Ira, "Your relationship with him too is getting quite intimate. Where is it leading? Tell me."

In fact she failed to understand their relationship. She had seen this girl visiting their house for the last five or six years now. Sometimes alone, sometimes in the company of Ajay or their mutual friends. Ira lived all alone in this metropolis. No parents, no siblings. She had her own flat. Whenever Ajay disappeared from home for a few days, it was her telephone number that he left behind. They didn't even feel awkward in admitting that they stayed together under one roof for days on end. They openly declared that they were in love but there was no question of marriage. First they had to test each other.

After a whole lifetime she still did not know what this loving and testing each other meant. She had got married when she was still playing marbles with her friends in the lane. She had been sent away with a total stranger as his bride. He could treat her as he liked. He was her god, her pati parmeshwar. And that is how she had viewed him till she became a widow. Year after year she had fasted for his long life. One after the other, she had given birth to seven children. It had never ever crossed her mind that a woman could have qualms about surrendering her body for her husband's pleasure as and when he desired. Whether looking after the house and rearing children was an act of slavery or of duty, she couldn't tell. She could neither perceive nor feel any difference between the two.

And now, this Ira and Ajay! Where do they find so much to talk about? They argue like mad over trifles. And what is this dejection and loneliness he writes about in his stories, filling page after page?

And Ira! She keeps making such absurd paintings!

She claims to capture the subtlest emotions of a woman in her paintings.

Once Ira had taken her to an exhibition of her own paintings. It was in a big hall, full of huge canvases. Of women in various forms. Women floating on still waters, women suspended upside down from the heavens, women impatient to fly away like wingless birds, fleshy women with the horns and eyes of beasts, dauntless Durga-like women, stern unrelenting Kali-like women destroyers. Women, women and more women.

Has woman really become so important in today's world?

"You won't understand Biji, in your time women were anaesthetized by man to suit himself. A woman was only ..."

"But still everything was going on fine."

"Fine! Frustrated women with thwarted desires! Intent on getting from sons what they didn't get from their husbands. What else is all this bride burning we hear about? What is it if not the pent up resentment of women who have been repressed for centuries?"

"All right. At least your generation is fortunate to be free to do what you like."

"Free? Our generation? The lot of women in this country is not going to change in a generation or two. What freedom, Biji, till man doesn't change his attitude?" Laughing bitterly, Ira had extended her hand to her for support, "Come, take a look at this painting of Ahalya. Do you know what Ahalya means? A woman with a famished heart and body ... whose mind and body have not been stirred ... or nourished. A neglected woman. Turned to stone for ages. Anxiously waiting for the touch of a maryada purushottam – an ideal man."

Ideal man?

She had known only one man. In the form of a husband. She had never wondered whether he was ideal or not. He was a man. She a woman. That was all. When had she ever thought of the needs of her own mind and body! When had anyone ever tried to find out what was in her mind! There was never any consultation or advice. When had she ever been thought worthy of it! And physical desire? He would come in the dark, take his due and leave. That a woman too had the right to enjoy sensual pleasures, was something she never even dreamt of. But still there had been moments when she became aware of her own body. Her cousin brother-in-law Nikka, who was only two years younger than Ajju's father, would invariably touch her fingers while taking the store keys or a glass of lassi from her. How her heart used to flutter! Light eyes, curly hair. How good looking he was! Many a time she wanted to ...! Shame! Her conscience would reproach her. It was a sin to dream of a man other than her husband. But what could she do about the actual dreams! Those dreams had made her realize that the foul smell emanating from the mouth of Ajju's father turned her pulsating body into wood. What control could she have over the dreams that visited her while she was asleep! Hadn't she seen Nikka bending over her, so many times, in her dreams? Bending ever so gently and tenderly as if it were an act of veneration. Her heart would fill with disgust as soon as she woke up, her body drenched in perspiration. She had committed a sin. She would try to hide her face from everybody the whole day lest somebody guessed it.

And this Ira! She has neither shame nor modesty.

She had been quite disconcerted the first time she saw Ira. No hello, no words of greeting. Puffing at her cigarette, she had walked straight into Ajju's room after throwing her a casual look, as if she was not Ajju's mother but some unwanted entity, a ghost. Probably Ajju hadn't even told Ira that she was his mother. What did he care for her? She might as well not exist! She looked after his house even at this age and despite all her physical afflictions because he was her son. But did he understand the duties of a son? This is how men treat their old parents. They understand only one kind of relationship with a woman because ... well, even that would be in order. One should get married and set up house. But no! Whenever she mentioned it, he said, "What's the hurry?"

Why doesn't he bring her home legitimately ... this Ira, who comes here as if the place belongs to her? She wouldn't object to that, now that Ira was quite fond of her as well. Sometimes she came even in Ajay's absence. She had become so close to her that she had started sharing her secrets with her frankly, like a friend. "Would you believe it, Biji? I was so very innocent. Absolutely foolish. I wasn't even eighteen when I got married ... my parents saw the upper class family he came from and the man's status and bestowed him on me, lest he slipped out of their hands. He was double my age. He didn't understand my desires, nor did he ever let me do as I pleased. In my parents' house I had been a free bird. There were no restrictions. But in that house ... I had to watch my every step. Don't do this, don't do that. A whole regimen of rules and regulations for me alone. The slavery of my in-laws on the one hand and on the other, the demands of my husband. Whenever he wanted ... to tell you the truth, Biji, I detested him. I used to feel repulsed! Yet I put up with everything.

But when he started raising his hand I went back to my parents' house and never looked back. They had to come to me to get the divorce papers signed. Good riddance! My only regret is that he didn't give me a child."

This was the limit of brazenness!

Last week Ira had come and squatted on the floor beside her, placing her head on her knees. Then taking her hand in her own she had looked deep into her eyes and said, "Biji, I've made a new painting ... of a woman ..."

She often talked incoherently like this but the way she said, "At last my wish has come true ..."

She had already begun to suspect from the way Ira was walking. She gaped at her, astounded. Ira didn't seem embarrassed but she felt too distressed to ask if Ajju was the ...

When Ajju came home, she had somehow mustered the courage to ask him.

She was destined to suffer all this in her old age, at the hands of her youngest born. Still, she consoled herself that whatever it was, the girl wasn't bad. At least she cared for her. She had adapted herself so much to the changing world that this too could be endured. Feeling that Ajju might hesitate to talk about it, she herself had suggested that now the two of them should get married soon.

She had goaded Ajju to go to Ira's. At a time like this, Ira needed an assurance of security from both the mother and the son. She would bring Ira home as her bahu after a simple Arya Samaj ceremony. She would have gone to Ira herself, but climbing up and down the stairs aggravated her pains. She had given away all her ornaments and jewellery to her married children one after the other. Only her necklace with a guinea pendant remained. Placing it in Ajju's hand, she said, "Give this to bahu on my behalf." Ajju had gone to Ira's house yesterday and returned only this morning. Since then he's been sitting like this at his table. He doesn't brook any disturbance while writing.

But was he really writing?

He hadn't even told her what transpired between him and Ira. What did she say on seeing the necklace? When is she coming to visit her? What will she do with her apartment now?

How anxious and eager she was to know all this!

But this son of hers! What kind of a writer is he! What men and women and their sorrows does he write about, when he can't understand the sentiments of his own mother, the tumult in her heart. He is concerned with only his own grief. So self-centred!

Her heart softened yet again. There is definitely something amiss. She can't bear to see him dejected like this. What could have happened at Ira's that ...? Any disaster? Any mishap?

Oh! The pain in her knees! It is so difficult to stand up after sitting for some time. Placing both her hands on the arms of the chair, she rose to her feet slowly.

Her weak eyes turned towards his room. Resting his head against the back of the chair, he had probably closed his eyes. She felt a surge of affection for him.

Her corpulent body swaying, she approached her son.

The sound of her footsteps disturbed his reverie. He got up in a flurry and found his mother standing right in front of him.

"What's the matter Biji?"

She hadn't reckoned with confronting him at such close range and stuttered, "What has happened to you that you ..."

He stood up as if he too had not counted on facing her. With eyes lowered, he whispered, "You won't understand Biji."

Suddenly, opening the drawer of his desk, he took out the car keys. Then, fumbling in his shirt pocket he fished out something and throwing it on the table, said, "She returned this."

He swiftly turned to leave the room but exploded before closing the door, "She says the child is hers, hers alone ... that I shouldn't try to claim it ... bloody bitch! She's not a woman but a slab of stone."

Dazed, she held on to the chair vacated by him and watched him go. Her torn heart didn't know who it was crying for, Why won't I understand, son? I understand everything. You as well as her. How can I blame even that slab of stone? You too must have failed to be the maryada purushottam whose touch could have infused life into that slab of stone.

"She Too is Ahalya" was originally published in Hindi as "Ahalya Yeh Bhi To."

A Piece of Wall
by Bolwar Mahamad Kunhi
translated by K A Parthasarathy

> Burning the house with my own hands
> Stirring the ashes;
> If you are willing to burn your house
> You may accompany me.
>
> Sant Kabiṛ

Roti Pathumma, who made a living by supplying rice rotis to five military hotels — three near the bus stand and two on mosque hill — saw Devaraj Urs in her dream one night. "What are you thinking of, Pathumma? It's been eight years since I gave you a piece of land and you seem to be in no hurry to build a house on it! Kanalakka, the milk vendor Karmeen Bai, and the fish stall owner Podiatta also received sites at the same time as you, and they all built their houses long ago. If you continue to be indifferent I will transfer your land to someone else. Take care," he warned. Pathumma was shaken out of both her dream and her complacency.

It was a full eight years ago that she had been granted a five cent plot of land on the right slope of Muthupadi mosque hill by the then chief minister, Devaraj Urs himself, at a grand ceremony held in

Mangalore's Nehru Stadium. Many of her friends had been trying ever since to persuade her to build a house. Sitarama Bipadithai, the village accountant, put it to her bluntly, "Don't think you can afford to sit tight just because you have the ownership papers in your hand. Overnight, if someone were to plant four poles on your site, cover them with a thatch and light his stove there, you might as well throw your ownership papers into that fire. If you don't start building the house now, I will report the matter to the district collector. Don't come running to me if you lose your site. Is that clear?"

Pathumma, a widow of about forty with no one to support her, earned a living by making rice rotis in a half-built roti factory behind her distant relative Kasim Byari's house. She paid him a monthly rent of fifteen rupees. Kasim Byari's sister Saramma's son, Samad, had joined her as a child labourer some six months ago, on a weekly wage of seven rupees. Every day, Pathumma would grind five or six seers of rice, spread the dough on a piece of muslin stretched across a wooden board, pat it out into rotis and toast them over red-hot coals. In the evening she would dispatch the rotis to the hotels. In this manner she made enough to clothe and feed herself. Her services were always in demand when there was a special event in the village – a marriage, a thread ceremony or a feast for in-laws. Her rotis, cooked and puffed over coals, were soft as petals and sweet as jaggery. The people of the village had bestowed upon her the sobriquet "Roti Pathumma," almost like a Padma Shri.

Every now and then, the villagers would prod her to build herself a house, most of them out of sympathy, some out of jealousy. But Pathumma remained unmoved until Devaraj Urs himself appeared in her dream that night and gave her the warning. That shook her out of her slumber.

After her morning ablutions, she offered namaaz. Next, she took the holy Koran from the shelf in the wall and, extracting two ten rupee notes hidden under her pillow, placed them between the opening pages of the Yaseen Sura. With the Koran on her lap she recited the entire Yaseen Sura from memory. After offering the customary concluding prayers to the holy book, she placed it back in the cupboard and set about her daily work.

In the evening, on her way back home after distributing all the rotis, she bought a porcelain pickle jar for seven rupees. Late that night, when her neighbours had all gone to sleep, she dug a hole in the earth under her mat just big enough to conceal the jar. Satisfied with her work, she washed her hands and took out the two ten rupee notes from the Koran. She touched the notes to her eyes and sent up a prayer, "Merciful Allah, grant that these two notes may grow into two thousand rupees and please help me save enough money every week." She placed the notes in the jar and closed it, then covered the pit with a square sheet of tin that she had located in the morning, and spread her mat over it. That night she dreamt that there stood on her plot of land a house as beautiful as the one Annu Gowda, the honey seller, had built.

From that day onwards, she made it a habit every Monday to add ten or twelve rupees from her weekly earnings to the savings in the jar. She vowed that with Allah's mercy she would build a house for herself, even if it took a hundred thousand years. She did not reduce the size of her rotis or their thickness by even a fingernail, but she worked longer each day and ate a fistful of rice less.

Thanks to these changes, by the time Ramzan came around next, the notes in the pickle jar had added up to three hundred and fifty rupees. Pathumma was elated.

Her treasure jar, which was more than half full, contained ten to twelve times more one and two rupee notes than five and ten rupee notes. As a timely measure, Pathumma went to three different shops and exchanged the small notes for three one hundred rupee notes and one fifty rupee note. She rolled these large denomination notes and the few others left in the jar into a tight wad, secured it with a piece of string and put it back into the jar. Although it represented a whole year's savings, it now took up so little space at the bottom of the jar that it could barely be seen. All manner of thoughts that she could have done without began to come rushing to her mind.

Her legs started to tremble whenever she crossed the threshold. What if someone were to break into the house in her absence and steal the jar? Worse, she began to suspect Samad's every action.

At this troubled juncture, Pathumma hit upon a brilliant solution – she would convert her savings into gold ornaments which she could wear next to her skin all the time.

Sreenivasa Achari lit agarbattis to the Dhanalakshmi – a B Saroja Devi lookalike – smiling down from the Parimala Agarbatti calendar, folded his hands to the goddess, and reverently touched the strongbox and then his eyes. When he opened his eyes the first person he saw was Pathumma.

Pathumma was not a complete stranger to Sreenivasa Achari. He recalled that some twenty years ago he had made the gold studs that still adorned her ears. He could not easily forget the woman who had pawned those same earrings to him for fifty rupees when her husband, a coolie in a saw mill, was crushed to death between two large logs. She had repaid the loan and redeemed the jewels earlier than promised.

There was a wooden bench propped up against the wall near the platform in the Muthupadi Achari's shop and whoever came to see him, whether maharaja or beggar, on whatever errand, had to be seated on this bench. That evening, the first customer to enter the shop after the lamp had been lit at sunset was Roti Pathumma. "Sit down," said the Achari, pointing to the bench, but she remained standing and he continued to be engrossed in his work.

Achari's shop was famous not only in Muthupadi village but for fifty to sixty miles around. If there was any honesty in transactions involving gold, it was to be found only in Achari's shop. True, he would not forego his profit, but though he might inflate his labour charges by some fifty paise, he would never cheat on weight. He was not one to indulge in discussion or empty talk. If a client argued needlessly, Achari would bluntly ask him to take his custom elsewhere. Mention of Achari's shop was bound to come up during marriage negotiations. If the bride's father were to let it be known that the jewels had been made by Achari, the girl's horoscope would definitely be found suitable.

Pathumma coughed gently. "Sit down," Achari said again, without looking up from his work.

She lowered herself gingerly on to the edge of the bench and took out the purse tucked at her waist. From it she extracted the wad of notes and placed it on the glass counter in front of Achari. "Give me something for this money," she said.

"*Something!*" His eyebrows rose. In all his forty years as a jeweller, no man had dared to speak so plainly and haughtily to him as this roti-selling woman here.

He looked her up and down. All that was visible outside her burkha were her dark fingers roughened through constant contact with hot coals, her equally dark, oval face, and her teeth red from constant betel-chewing. Her guileless eyes evoked pity in the jeweller's heart.

He picked up the notes she had placed before him and counted them. Four hundred and ten rupees. He took a silver anklet from the cupboard on his left, turned it around in his hands, frowned as though he found it unsuitable, and put it back. "You can get a child's finger ring in gold," he said, and then turned to her with awakened interest. "Whom is it for?" he asked.

"For me," she answered immediately and went on to add, "I don't want a ring. It will probably turn black on my finger. Give me something else."

"Is it all right if it costs some ten or twenty rupees more?" he muttered to himself and without waiting for an answer, he took out a silver waistband from the jewel box on his right and showed it to her. "How do you like this?"

Roti Pathumma's eyes lit up. A waistband would be just right. She could wear it round her waist and also cover it with her sari so that nobody would notice it. And even if someone did, so what? She had paid good money for it, after all, not stolen it. She could buy the waistband now, she reckoned, and something else next year or perhaps exchange it for a gold chain in the same shop.

"If I bring this back to you in a year's time, will it fetch me all that I pay for it now?" she asked.

"How is that possible?" he replied matter-of-factly. "This is a silver item and if you resell it, you will get only half the amount you paid for it."

Suddenly the silver waistband seemed to Pathumma like a python that was trying to swallow her.

"In that case I don't want it," she said. "Give me something that I will not make a big loss on when I resell it."

"So you want to buy something just to sell it next year," remarked Achari with gentle sarcasm. Pathumma's face fell. Achari was in a dilemma. She was the first customer to come to the shop after the lamp had been lit that evening, and he had already counted her money. He could not turn her away. That would be an affront to Goddess Lakshmi.

"Look here," he said, "if you buy something today and sell it tomorrow, you will always lose something. Labour charges and the allowance for wastage will always translate into a loss. If you want all your money back you will have to put it in a box and place it in the locker here."

Roti Pathumma's eyes lit up. She looked lovingly at the locker, the solution to all her problems. " Would you please do that for me? Put the money in the locker. I'm not interested in any jewellery now. I'll come to you when I need something. You can give me the money then."

Oh ho! So that's how it is, thought Achari, heaving a sigh of relief. He nodded his head in understanding. This was not the first time he had been requested by a villager to safeguard money.

But when Roti Pathumma went on to give him a detailed account of how Devaraj Urs had given her a site and of Samad's disquieting behaviour, he demurred.

"This cannot be done," he said. "Nowadays, the law requires that I hold a licence to accept other people's money for safekeeping. There are banks now for this kind of thing. Go and open an account in a bank. They will even pay you some interest on your money."

But Roti Pathumma had made up her mind. She told him repeatedly that she had greater faith in his locker than in her relatives, and that it was his duty to help her like a father would help his widowed daughter. She rapidly put forth whatever argument came to her mind till Achari was forced to yield.

"All right. If it is of help to you, I will keep this money safe for you." He counted the money again, placed it in the locker and made a note in his ledger.

That was how Pathumma left her money and with it her bundle of worries in Achari's locker. She turned up again the following Monday evening with a ten rupee note and asked Achari to add it to the earlier amount. Although his eyebrows went up and he muttered to himself, "This is going to be a big nuisance," he did not protest aloud.

From then on it became a routine. Every Monday evening Roti Pathumma would step into Achari's shop and cough softly. If Achari was not in, his eldest son Keshava or, if he too was busy, his younger son Chandranna, would collect her ten or fifteen rupees and make an entry in the ledger.

Sometimes, when there was no other customer in the shop, Achari would tell her, "Look, woman! For the past two or two and a half years now, you have been bringing in more and more money without ever asking me how your account stands. But today I have decided to give you all the details of your account. I am an old man and I may be gone tomorrow. But you should not find your money gone."

Roti Pathumma would be ready with her response. "No god will touch you until I build a house of my own. Why do you think I place the money in the holy Koran first and offer prayers for its safety before bringing it to you?"

Some time later Achari's shop was renamed "Sreenivasa & Sons." But this made no difference to Pathumma's Monday visits.

Achari's eldest son, Keshavachari, was good at his work, like his father. He was already well-known for his bangle designs using black beads. The younger son, Chandranna, however, was cleverer in his talk than with his hands. He came to work in the shop the evening his PUC examinations were over, and within a year, thanks to his gift for making conversation and his ready smile, became "Chandranna" to one and all.

By the time of the shop's next annual puja, Chandranna had given the place a new look and put up a signboard that read "Sreenivasa & Sons, Jewellers." In his father's time "Achari's Shop" had been famous for only about fifty miles around but now its fame had spread right up to Coimbatore, with the result that the elder son, Keshava, received a marriage proposal from a well-known Coimbatore goldsmith's family. On the whole, there was nothing for Sreenivasa Achari to do these days in the shop. It was more than enough if he graced the shop front for an hour or two every day, clad in his spotlessly clean clothes.

While Sreenivas Achari had agreed to serve as Pathumma's

unauthorized banker out of a desire to help a poor widow, the purely business-minded Chandranna was guided by the principle that every rupee that comes interest-free is extremely valuable. Therefore, he would welcome her as a very valued customer. Whenever she came to deposit money, he would greet her with a "Looks like you are late today. Anything the matter?" Or, "Any time you need your money, just say so. I'll calculate the amount and settle it, don't worry. It would be easier if you could give me a day's time." As he made small talk he would count the money she had brought and make the entry in her account.

Roti Pathumma on her part continued to come to the shop regularly every Monday evening, deposit her savings of the week and go home relieved. Not once did she display any interest in knowing the total amount to her credit.

Sri Ramachandra is witness that Chandranna did not insist on going to Ayodhya for the kar seva. When Ramadasa Kini invited him he declined politely, saying, "I don't have the time for such things, sir." His father was more forthright. "Look, Chandru, this is not for us businessmen. In business, we do not differentiate between one person and another and we should not. To be quite honest, it is their womenfolk who bring us a profit. If they come to know that you too are involved in this, tell me, who do you think will be the loser?"

But god had willed otherwise. A three member group had been selected from Muthupadi and just four days before they were to leave, one of them, R Sadasiva, suddenly backed out. He was a second class BCom graduate and had been working as a manager in Bhagavathi Kalyana Mantapa, managing on a salary of three hundred and fifty rupees for the past two to two and a half years. How could he reject a godsend opportunity in the form of a job offer from Muscat on a salary of eight thousand rupees?

Kasim Bava, the proprietor of Mubarak Tours and Travels, had come all the way to Muthupadi from Kasargod by taxi with the visa in original and photostat copies of official documents for the post of junior accountant in Al Mustafa Hi-tech Nursing Home of Muscat. Sadasiva had already paid him forty two thousand rupees, which seemed reasonable, but now Kasim Bava was asking for another six thousand rupees within six days, as his commission. Sadasiva would have to go to Mumbai, undergo a medical checkup and within two days after that, fly to Muscat. Otherwise, Kasim Bava could not be held responsible for the advance that had been paid. With that warning Kasim Bava had gone away.

Ramadasa Kini was on the horns of a dilemma. The list of the three members and a detailed report on them had already been despatched. It would be very embarrassing to explain now, at the last minute, why only two members were being sent instead of three, as agreed. It would be a black mark on his organizing capacity. What was to be done?

Chandranna was called once again. In the office of Bhagavathi Kalyana Mantap — the manager was away — he was cajoled till one o'clock at night. As a hot blooded youngster, it was his duty to uphold the prestige of the village in the present complicated situation. Ramadasa declared repeatedly that he would not have troubled anyone but would have sent his own sixth son on this trip if the boy had not been in the crucial second year of his PUC. Subbaraya Tantri, the priest of the local temple, was given the responsibility of securing Chandranna's father's consent. What could Chandranna say?

On the day of Chandranna's departure, his father did not utter a single word. In the evening, as Chandranna was about to leave, his sister-in-law quietly called him aside and gave him a thousand rupees. "I believe you will in any case be visiting Kashi first. Banarasi saris are very cheap there. Be sure to bring me two or three saris."

When the Muthupadi group arrived at the Mangalore railway

station, they were joined by the seven member group from Shimoga. Ramadasa Kini saw them all off and returned to Muthupadi where he was soon immersed in his textile business.

It took them six days to reach Kashi through a circuitous route with a change of trains. The next six days were spent in waiting for further orders from the headquarters in Shambhunath Panda's beautiful two storeyed "mansion" on Birla Mandir Road. There they met the Pune group which had arrived before them, and whiled away their time in manly conversation conducted in a mixture of Hindi and Kannada as they waited for instructions from above.

Faizabad was not too far from here. The journey would take only three hours by the two Matador vans assigned to them and kept parked behind the "mansion," covered against the cold. But they were not allowed to even step outside to stretch their limbs. Their only recreation was watching television. And there was the December cold to contend with.

At last they received the order. "Congratulations to one and all. Your job is done. You may leave for Delhi tomorrow itself."

Chandranna was so angry, he felt like crying. He would have created a big scene if Ramadasa Kini had been there. He was deeply distressed over the futile journey which had not even given him the chance to buy saris for his sister-in-law.

They spent two days and a night in Delhi, in Shri Rajender Singh's DDA flat at Tilaknagar, shivering in the cold, as if it were a punishment. Here, the night it was decided that they would leave for Mangalore the next morning, an incident occurred.

A member from Pune who had been observing Chandranna's impatience over the past two days took him to the terrace of the house after dinner. Chandranna was freezing in the severe cold and had to lean on his new found friend for support to reach the terrace, a hundred questions buzzing in his mind.

It was quite dark on the terrace. His friend took out a piece of stone weighing some half a kilo from the bag he was holding, and gave it to Chandranna. "Don't feel too bad. Everyone involved has discharged their respective responsibilities satisfactorily. You have also done what was expected of you. You have every reason to feel satisfied about the trip. Here is a piece of stone for you. Look upon it as a symbol of our success," he said, patting Chandranna on the shoulder. On the way down from the terrace the Pune friend whispered to him "Keep this a secret for some days. Don't tell anyone."

But Chandranna could not keep the secret. In the course of the two day return journey he revealed it to the other members of the group. He told them that the souvenir was safe in his suitcase and promised to break it into three pieces and share it with them as soon as they got home.

When they reached Mangalore, Ramadasa Kini's car was waiting for them at the station. The same night the trio was garlanded and feted in the presence of eminent citizens at a function held in their honour at Bhagavathi Kalyana Mantap.

His father seemed unconcerned. But Chandranna's sister-in-law could not help teasing him. "All right, they didn't let you go there. But what did you do in Kashi for a whole week? Sing bhajans? Couldn't you find time to buy just one sari?"

Chandranna only smiled sheepishly.

A week passed and Chandranna decided to make good his promise. He took out the piece of stone from his suitcase, broke it into four pieces and gave his two fellow travellers a piece each. He also gave a piece to Ramadasa Kini and told him how he had got it.

Ramadasa Kini had misgivings about the piece of stone. "This is rather dangerous. It would be better not to talk to anyone about this stone at least for some days. Don't tell anyone that you gave it to me. There are all kinds of reports appearing in the newspapers these days.

If someone decides to treat this as a piece of material evidence we will be done for." Chandranna could not hide his disgust. "Why did they send us if they are so easily intimidated?" he asked, without mincing words. Kini winced. "Chandru, one doesn't bang one's head against a boulder to show how strong it is," he quipped, and sidestepped the issue.

But on hearing Chandranna retort, "I am not afraid. Why should I be? I didn't even go all the way there, did I?" Kini was alarmed. "Oh, please don't say that you didn't reach the place. We have already created the impression that people from our town were there too. Now if we say, No, no, our boys had nothing to do with it, what happens to our prestige? If a time comes when we have no way out but to issue such a statement, then we can come out with the truth. What do you say?" Chandranna gave a silly laugh and walked away saying, "I don't know."

The other two who had been members of the group, like him, were also uneasy over the piece of stone although they had accepted it readily enough. They could not decide whether to talk about it or keep mum, whether to display it or hide it away. Their confusion was all too plain for Chandranna to see. "There's no fun, Chandru, in keeping mum and hiding it from everyone like an illegal pregnancy," moaned one. The other complained, "I still fail to see why we had to go so far and suffer so much in the cold as if we were undergoing punishment for some sin. It makes my head go round," he raged, "to tell some people I was there and others that I returned halfway."

To those who came to praise and congratulate him Chandranna would sometimes say, "Oh no, my friend, I am not such a daring person as you seem to think. It all just so happened. It is better not to make such a fuss about it." This ambiguous reply further increased their admiration for Chandranna. "Don't try to fool us, Chandranna. We know all about what you did out there and what you have brought from there. The whole story has reached our ears. Ha ... ha ..." they would laugh. Chandru would pretend that he was humbly accepting their compliments.

As the days rolled by, Chandranna's enthusiasm waned. In the midst of his work he would run an eye over the papers and see the statements made by the prime minister and the leaders of the Opposition and grow worried, but he would forget all about it the next moment. Meanwhile, Roti Pathumma continued her practice of turning up every Monday with fourteen to twenty six rupees, depositing the money and leaving the place without a care in the world. Whenever he saw her, Chandru wondered whether the old woman was still unaware of his kar seva trip. Poor woman. We should give her one or two hundred rupees more when we return her money, he would think and console himself.

One Monday evening, Chandranna was narrating the story of his journey to an elderly gentleman who had come to his shop. From his drawer he took out the piece of stone wrapped in a sheet of paper and was about to show it to him when he caught sight of Pathumma, who had already come up the steps. He checked himself quickly as if he had stepped on a snake. Normally he would not have been surprised to see Roti Pathumma on a Monday. But today the habitual smile was missing from her face and that unsettled him.

Usually, when she reached the steps leading to the shop she would cough softly to attract attention. But on that day she had come straight up to the shop, and he suspected that she had overheard their conversation and come to know that he had a "piece of the stone." He peered into her eyes suspiciously.

Roti Pathumma said in a dull voice, "This week I could not save any money. The roti-making board broke and had to be repaired. I came only to tell you not to wait for me today. I'll come next Monday."

With that she went away, leaving Chandranna speechless and ashamed of his suspicion.

He turned to the elderly gentleman who was eagerly waiting for the concluding part of the story of his exploits. Chandranna pretended to look in the drawer. "Oh! I quite forgot. The piece is at home. I had taken it there last week to show it to someone and haven't brought it back. I'll show it to you some other time." And shook him off.

No sooner had the old man left than Keshavachari, who had been sitting nearby, broke into loud laughter. When Chandranna realized why he was laughing, he too felt laughter bubbling up in him. The reason for their mirth was an incident that had made it impossible to keep the piece of wall at home.

The same day he had given a piece of the wall to Ramadasa Kini as an offering – it was a Sunday, a holiday – in the afternoon, unable to decide where to keep his piece, Chandranna had placed it on the agarbatti holder in the puja room, and this had led to a disaster.

That evening when Chandranna's atthige, his father's sister, entered the puja room to light agarbattis, she noticed the piece of stone lying on the holder. Alarmed, she picked it up and showed it to Keshavachari who was standing near the door. "What sort of a stone is this? Or is it a lump of loban?" she asked.

"This is a medal Chandranna got in Delhi," he told her laughing. He called out to Chandranna who was on the porch, listening to music on his tape recorder. "Chandru, Atthige wants to know the significance of your stone."

All the while, their aunt had been turning the stone around in her hands and examining it. When Chandranna came up to her she repeated her question. "What sort of a stone is this? Why was it in the puja room?"

Chandranna was taken aback for a moment, but he recovered

immediately and replied in a casual tone. "Oh, that? You remember I had gone away some time ago? I brought it from there. As a memento of the wall."

She screwed up her face in disgust as though she had unwittingly stepped on excrement. "Ayyo, Rama Rama! Would anyone in his senses keep a piece of stone from that mosque in the puja room? You must be crazy," she spat out angrily. She pressed the stone into Chandranna's hands. "Throw this dirty stone into some faraway well, have a bath and then enter the house," she ordered.

Chandranna was dismayed. The glory of his brave expedition melted away. To mollify his aunt he said, "It's not like that, Atthige. It's actually a piece of stone from an ancient temple."

His aunt's face turned white with shock. It was as though the heavens had fallen. She slapped herself on the forehead and exclaimed, "What is this Chandru saying? Does this mean that you people went with all that zeal and finally destroyed our own temple?" This new twist frightened Chandranna. He turned to his brother for help. But Keshavachari had covered his mouth and beard with his hand and was laughing.

"Ahmad Bava has come from Bahrain, it seems. Did you know that?" Keshavachari, who was polishing a bangle, was surprised to hear his brother's question. "Is that so? When did he arrive?" he asked.

"I did not get to speak to him. Last week I saw him at the bus stand getting into a ricksha," said Chandranna.

"A week ago!" exclaimed Keshavachari, unable to believe what he had heard. "Then why hasn't he turned up at the shop?"

"I was about to ask the same question. He visits our village once a year and in the past he would come to the shop the very next day to talk to us. How is it he has given us the miss this time?" Chandranna wondered. He opened his mouth to say something more but shut up.

"He must have had some urgent work that kept him away,"

murmured Keshavachari, trying to console himself.

Chandranna remained silent.

Keshavachari went on, "I hope he'll come before leaving for Bahrain."

"Somehow I don't believe he'll come to see you. If he had any such intention he would've come earlier," said Chandranna gravely, with a knowing air.

"What are you trying to say? I've known him for the past thirty years. We played and grew up together. Even the watch I am wearing is a gift from him. I didn't pay for it. I'm sure he must have been busy. That's why he could not find the time to come and look us up," Keshavachari said, looking pointedly at Chandranna.

Chandranna retorted sharply, "He must have been harbouring some doubt."

"Why should he? Would he abandon our friendship just because you went to the kar seva? He's not that sort. Nowadays you see suspicion everywhere. When someone from their community comes to the shop, you fall over yourself to please them. You reduce the labour charges by a rupee or two. Why? What has come upon you? You are tormenting yourself as though you have committed a great offence. If you had all these reservations, why did you agree to go in the first place? Now the deed is done. Why get so worked up about it? Even if what you say is true, and he did not want to come to our shop, so what? We don't stand to lose. If you have such misgivings, why do you brandish that piece of stone before all and sundry? Why don't you throw it into some well like Atthige suggested?" Keshavachari flung questions at Chandranna.

Chandranna did not attempt a reply.

For a while, both of them continued with their work in silence.

"Roti Pathumma had come to the shop this afternoon when you were away at lunch," Chandranna raised a new issue.

"Was she here today? But today is not Monday. How much did she deposit today?" Keshavachari asked anxiously.

"She came, not to give more money but to ask for her money back. She wants it by next Friday. She plans to start building her house on Friday, it seems," answered Chandranna.

"Is that so? Well, that's good news. It will also rid us of a bother," Keshavachari said.

"Do you think she is really going to start the construction on Friday?" Chandranna asked as if he doubted it.

"There you go all over again," Keshavachari said angrily. "Whether she builds a house with her money or flings it into a well, what difference does it make to you? She wants her money and that's that. All these years she has trusted us and left her money with us. Now she wants her money back. Calculate what's due to her and let her have it. That's all there is to it. Have you totalled all her deposits and worked out the amount?" he asked, looking Chandranna in the face.

"Yes. It comes to four thousand two hundred and eighty two rupees. I've asked her to come for it tomorrow evening. Tomorrow morning I will draw the amount from the bank," Chandranna replied.

"Very well. When you give her the money, add two hundred rupees from our side. Is that acceptable to you?" asked Keshavachari.

"I was about to suggest the same," said Chandranna. "If we were to calculate the interest, it would come to five or six hundred rupees."

Keshavachari went back to his work.

A while later, Chandranna returned to the subject once again. "When she comes for the money tomorrow, what if we ask her whether she is aware that I went to the kar seva?"

"Suppose she says she had known it all along, what will you do?" Keshavachari's question hit home. Chandranna had no answer.

Over dinner, when Chandranna mentioned to his father that Roti Pathumma had asked for her money back, Achari remarked, "How sad! All these years she has had such faith in our shop and kept saving money. Not once has she asked how much it has added up to," he said, appreciatively. Then, as though he had just made up his mind, "Chandru, do me a favour. Tomorrow, after settling her account, give her an extra five hundred from our account, separately. Don't talk to her about interest and so on. People of her religion are not supposed to accept any interest. Let this be our contribution to her house."

I was also thinking along those lines, he was about to tell his father but thought the better of it. Had she come to know that he had gone for the kar seva? Had that upset her and was that why she was asking for her money back? Should he put these questions to his father? He shot a troubled glance at his elder brother. Keshavachari's eyes signalled him to keep quiet.

Early the next morning, a party from Bantwal made a cash purchase from the shop of seven to eight thousand rupees and therefore there was no need to draw money from the bank.

In the afternoon, Chandranna once again took out the ledger and totalled Roti Pathumma's savings. The figure was short of the previous day's total by seventeen rupees. So he started totalling up again but halfway through the exercise he got bored and closed the book. He decided to take the previous day's total as final and took out the required amount from the safe, counted it and secured it with a rubber band. He counted out another five hundred rupees separately and bound it up with another rubber band. He put the two wads of notes together in an envelope and stretched a third rubber band around it, then sat for a while, doing nothing.

Uninterested in any work he sat staring at the road in front of the shop. Keshavachari took pity on him and said, "Appa will be coming to the shop in the evening. If he is there when that woman comes, wouldn't it be better if she were to receive the money from him?"

Chandranna nodded in agreement. He did not even bother to turn his head and look at his brother.

Half an hour passed. Keshavachari continued with his work but kept looking at his brother out of the corner of his eye. Chandranna took out the piece of stone from his drawer, put it in his trouser pocket, and stood up. "What's up now? Where are you going?" asked Keshavachari in alarm.

"I have kept the old lady's money and the extra five hundred rupees that Appa said to give her, as two separate bundles, in that envelope. In case I'm not in the shop when she comes, you give it to her. If Appa comes to the shop, all the better," he said, and left.

"Where are you going?" It was not merely a question, but also a suggestion that he should not go.

Chandranna paused for half a second undecided whether to respond or not. Then, saying "I have to settle an account with Ramadasa Kini," he ran down the steps and got on to his cycle before his brother could shoot any more questions at him.

He stopped his cycle in front of Kalpana Sari Centre. As he climbed the steps the salesman, Gopalanna, welcomed him. "He has gone home for lunch and isn't back yet. While going he mentioned that he was feeling feverish." Gopalanna was not sure if Ramadasa Kini would come to the shop again that day.

Chandranna hopped on to his cycle and rode towards Ramadasa Kini's house.

When he reached the government well near the turning to the school on the hill, he suddenly remembered his childhood days.

The school stood on the hill near the well, and during a game of cricket in the playground, if the ball were to come rolling down and fall into the well, play would be suspended for half an hour while Adram Byari fetched a bucket and rope from his house nearby and fished out the ball. For this reason, even though Adram Byari would be the first to get "out" in the game, he managed to keep a stranglehold on the captaincy. The memory made Chandranna laugh. The same Adram had jumped into the well in anger because his father had beaten him, and died. Chandranna was in the eighth standard at the time. For some days after that his friends were not to be seen around the government well in the evening. Even though everybody knew that people of Adram's caste did not become evil spirits if they committed suicide they still hesitated to go near the well. If Adram were alive today, he too would be an adult. How would he have reacted to his going to the kar seva? Would he have broken the friendship?

Chandranna stopped his cycle and rested it on the stand. It was October and the school was closed for the Dussera holidays. Chandranna walked up to the well and peered down. He could see the black water ten feet below. As a young boy he used to throw stones into the well and listen for the "plonk" as they hit the water. It was great fun. Chandranna picked up a small stone lying nearby and threw it into the well. It made a weak sound. He felt disappointed. A bigger stone would have made more noise. He looked around. Suddenly, he took the piece of stone out of his pocket and threw it into the well! The "plonk" it made gave him great pleasure. With a sense of relief, he sat down on the washing stone near the well and watched the small children playing on the slope of the school playground.

When Chandranna returned to the shop the sun had set. His brother was seated in his usual place, engrossed in work. Father was not to be seen. "Did you find Kini?" "No. I did not go there," Chandranna said shortly, as he sat down. "Was Appa here?" he asked.

"He was. That woman too had come. She collected her money. When she saw the five hundred rupees we had contributed, she burst into tears, poor thing," said Keshavachari. Chandranna was silent.

Keshavachari continued, "Did you hear about our Ahmed Bava?

It was Roti Pathumma who told us. On his previous visit he had promised to help her with her house building. But during this visit he has not been home even for a day. His sister, who was given in marriage to someone in Kasargod, was admitted to a nursing home for delivery and her condition became serious. He received a call the day he arrived here. He left for Kasargod immediately and is yet to return. The baby was stillborn and the mother's condition is serious. She has now been shifted to Mangalore, it seems."

Chandranna realized that by going into unnecessary detail Keshavachari was justifying to himself Ahmed's failure to meet him, and to avoid upsetting his brother he kept saying, "Yes," "Is that so?" and "Oh, no," finally adding, "I was mistaken about him."

"D'you know something else?" said Keshavachari and waited quietly for a little while to capture Chandranna's attention. "That old woman of yours will be coming again tomorrow evening. You have been asked not to leave the shop."

"Why? Why should she come again? Did she find something wrong in my calculation? As a matter of fact, I had added some ten or fifteen rupees more to her account," said Chandru irritably.

Keshavachari looked upset.

"If only it was to do with your calculation, Chandru. She is coming to meet you for quite another reason. If I tell you, you won't believe me." He paused and then the words came out all in one breath, "Tomorrow, Friday morning, she plans to start construction of one of the walls of her house. She wants you to give her at least a tiny bit of that piece of stone you have with you. It seems that for the last one year her ambition has been to use it in the wall of her house."

It seemed to Chandranna as though Adram Byari was guffawing in the government well. But Chandranna did not laugh.

"A Piece of Wall" was originally published in Kannada as "Ondu Tundu Gode."

The Corpses of Choolaimedu
by N S Madhavan
translated by Nita Thomas

Hope is what poor children play with.

Sitting at the garbage end of the railway station, Raghavan watched the noisy group of newspaper boys chatter and jostle their way to the edge of the platform. Suddenly, with startling spontaneity, they slipped off their trousers, jumped down to the tracks and sat in a row to defecate. Raghavan turned away. Only a few moments ago, these boys had been worldly young men concerned only with the business of earning a living. How effortlessly, the unembarrassed act of answering nature's call in the company of friends can return childhood to these boys, thought Raghavan.

Animated discussion, pursed lips, fingers tracing idle doodles in the mud, bodies rocking in an ancient rhythm of comfort. Job done, they move to the lotus pond nearby to clean up. Trousers donned, they become men again, preoccupied once more with the serious business of survival.

"Aren't you coming, man?"

Raghavan is startled out of his musings on the life and times of newspaper boys by a white sleeved arm. A fistful of pamphlets fans his nose with some strength.

"Man." A favourite word with gospel workers – making a company of instant Christians with one sweep of the tongue.

Raghavan can feel the laughter sliding up his throat. The gospel worker doesn't think he has found a soul to work on. " Man, you are growing old."

"I know."

"Can I have four annas?"

"No."

"Read *The Road to Nazareth*."

"I don't want to."

Not enough insult there to stop a true gospel worker.

"Billy Graham will lead you to the light."

"I don't think so."

A pause as preacher and prey assess each other's progress.

"Read *The Lord is my Shepherd*," exhorts the gospel worker, adding with some venom, "you are growing old. Hell is waiting for you. Hell. Hell. Hell."

Raghavan's eyes are fixed on Christ's impassive face, printed from a universally recognizable woodcut, blood stained, thorn crowned — now bobbing from a bunch of literature in the madly waving hand of the gospel worker.

"Listen to my call, man." The gospel worker knows he has lost another soul as he walks away.

Raghavan's Adam's apple feels as if it has just closed around a Golgotha, chewed and swallowed with the frustrated bile of the gospel worker.

Looking across to the far end of the platform, Raghavan spots his mother standing alone, her eyes seeking him. He walks up to her, glad to see her but not surprised.

"Amma."

Amma gives a yellow smile. False teeth flash briefly. When she had

had them made, he remembered her saying, "They feel too much."
(Or was it "They feel strange"? That's the problem with picking
random thoughts from old memories – they come out sounding like
half-truths. It's always best not to quote from the store of memories.
They are rarely reported accurately.)

"Never mind," he remembered saying to her at the time. "They'll
be fine after you've worn them for a while."

"That's not it, Kutta," Amma had insisted. "It's the taste of these
new teeth that I don't like."

Amused, Raghavan had asked, "And what do new teeth taste like?"

"Sour."

"Is your train running late?" Amma is concerned.

"No, they've just rung the first bell."

"Where will you stay in Madras?"

"I'm not sure. Probably with Kannan."

"In Choolaimedu?"

"Umm."

"I doubt you will be able to stay there very long."

"I know."

"So ...?"

"So where do you think I should stay?"

"Isn't Theresa there too?"

"Theresa? She has left me. We're separated now."

Amma gets upset. The crease on her forehead deepens with shock
and anguish. "Why didn't you tell me this before?"

Guilt chases defiance. Raghavan gets aggressive, "I don't have to
tell you everything, do I?"

Amma's voice drops a decibel. "When she first came here, you
remember, I had to teach her how to wear a half-sari ..."

Uncomfortable now, Raghavan looks away, grateful that the train
is almost in.

Like a wave pulled ashore by an unseen gravitational force, a surge of humanity first lunges towards and then heaves itself into the train.

Amma stands still, looking at Raghavan and the long snake of a train in turns. She knows she must leave now or be swept by a restless mother's instinct that tells her this is not a happy goodbye. Her eyes caress the train as if in blessing, willing it to carry her son safely. With a final glance at Raghavan, Amma leaves, as uneventfully as she had arrived.

There is a sudden lurch of the engine glad to be on its way, and the train moves out of the station. It rounds a curve and slowly gathers momentum for its unfettered run through a dark and starless Malabar night.

Raghavan looks out at the winter-bare countryside – nude trees, dim fireflies flitting about ghostly tree trunks. The compartment is warm with family. Across him sits a heavy-eyed Malayali girl with a male relative.

"Where to?" Raghavan makes the first move.

The girl eyes him, awkward at this unfamiliar presumption that she's open to small talk with strange men.

"Madras."

"From there Mary will travel to Germany." The voice holds the pride and possessiveness of family. Uppai. Mary's spokesperson.

Raghavan looks at Mary with interest. "Have you heard about the River Rhine?"

"Umm." Mary's mumble is reluctant, but Uppai's pride in Mary will not be silenced.

"She knows a lot. She always stands first in class, you know. Every month the oldest girl, Annamma, sends a thousand rupees from Germany. And now, maybe in three or four months, Mary too will, won't you?"

Mary closes her eyes. She must silence Uppai before the stranger learns everything there is to know about her. Her ears twitch as they strain to pick up the rhythm of the clacking wheels. There's a song there, muses Mary, keeping time. Rainelec ... rainelec ...

The wheels echo hollowly over the arc of a bridge. Rainelec ... rainelec ... rainelec ... A lullaby in monotone, thinks Mary, as her eyes droop.

Raghavan has been watching Uppai for some time now, giving him three dimensions in his mind. A familiar game. Raghavan is a watcher. The man could be a businessman, he thinks, seen through a Kathakali mask. And as for the girl Mary, twin images of the timid girl light his tired eyes. Here is a girl waiting for her knight. I will save you, promises Raghavan – I will be the blond German who will take you through the Black Forest.

Mary wakes up with a start. Raghavan, watching Mary through half-closed eyes, wonders if he had said the words aloud.

"Appa?"

"What?"

"I'm scared."

"Why should you be scared? Isn't Annamma going to be there with you?"

"That's not it."

"Then what is it?"

"When I close my eyes, Germany appears to me like an ashen country. Grey, colourless."

Appa's lips twitch with indulgence.

"Pray to Saint Sebastian, child. I will give you a box of candles that you can light for him."

Mary is silent for a while, conjuring up Saint Sebastian in her mind. Saint Sebastian as she has always seen him – hanging as a holy picture by the family altar back home. As Mary's breathing shallows, Raghavan looks from her to Uppai – in his mind he is now an ogre, blind to the vulnerability of his little girl as she stands at the edge of the dark and forbidding Black Forest.

I hate your half-grey head.

I hate your beetling eyebrows joined at the bridge of your nose.

I hate your varicose veined legs.

Unmoved by Raghavan's impotent dislike, Uppai reaches for a jute bag. Such an unimpressive bag, thinks Raghavan. Just like him, lacking in class. The bag, with L G Asafoetida in faded print on its side, holds Uppai's Bible – worn, like the bag. Old, wax stained, its black cover shiny with use. Uppai balances it on his knee and reaches into the bag once again. His hands root about among its dirty folds to emerge with a pair of reading glasses dangling on the end of a greasy cord.

Uppai opens his Bible with a sigh and begins to read softly, a lime stained finger tracing line after line. He reaches across to lightly tap Mary awake.

The pious and the pure, thinks Raghavan, looking at Mary, who is now huddled like a poodle against Uppai's arm.

The train clacks through the night. Green and black flashes on the windowpanes. The smell of Tamil women in the compartment wafts along the corridor. These smells, they live only in my imagination, thinks Raghavan. Just like the thoughts of my thoughts.

Madras. Omens read, signals won, the train snakes in on a tired belly. Back in Ernakulam, Raghavan had looked heavenward once and said, "I don't want omens. I want signs. A sign that will tell me what my future is." A plume of dirty smoke smudges the patch of sky above the station. A bird of paradise, perhaps? Fanciful, maybe, but prophetic, thinks Raghavan.

The beach at Thiruvanmiyur had hurt the soles of his tired feet. Looking for omens, he had wandered among the Tamils sleeping on the station platform. Looking down at the huddled groups, Raghavan had seen not men and women seeking sleep but faces of the dead. So many deaths at Choolaimedu have I walked past. So many deaths have I seen written on these walls.

The first corpse of Choolaimedu.

Raghavan is sitting outside Kannan's hut reading a book, when the first heartrending wail reaches his ears.

"Arumugam is dead." Murugan's wife from the hut next door makes the pronouncement with the bald clarity of someone beyond shock but deeply grieving.

Choolaimedu's citizens always dreamed good dreams. That they would leave their rickshas and their tangas for their children to inherit. That their children would have good lives. When children die, thought Raghavan, it is the end of the future.

On his way back to the slum from Nungambakkam station, he would usually buy a handful of boiled gram for the children. This is my rent, he would say to himself, something I owe Choolaimedu. After bhajans at the Mariamman Kovil, the children would rush out to waylay him for his treat of boiled gram. Raghavan would see in their glistening faces and foreheads smeared with scared ash, the future of Choolaimedu.

It had been a while since the children had run out to meet him.

"Food poisoning," explains Kannan, owner of one of Choolaimedu's few horsecarts and Raghavan's friend and landlord.

Raghavan looks at his fistful of moist boiled gram one last time before he flings them across the railway tracks.

Murugan's son Arumugam, Gunashekaran's seven year old daughter, two of Manoharan's children, Moodandan Raman, affectionately called Lame Raman, Imman's son born in his old age – all children who would turn up to greet Raghavan when he returned home at night. All now struck with dysentery.

The fathers of Choolaimedu reach Kannan's house when they hear that Raghavan has returned. And with them comes the doctor who usually made only one weekly visit. This is his moment. The doctor charges ten rupees per child. Choolaimedu's fathers, heads bowed at the burden of payment, wait. Raghavan removes his watch and gives it to them.

The watch fetches seventy rupees at the Gujarati seth's pawn shop.

If Theresa had been here, I would have told her that I sold "time" for only seventy rupees, thinks Raghavan. Her dimples would have flashed as if rewarding me for a funny line.

By sunset, several homes of Choolaimedu have given up their copper vessels to the Gujarati seth's shop. The doctor sells "free sample" medicines at twenty rupees a bottle to the families who can afford them.

By nightfall the children, now too tired to drag themselves outside to purge, lie where they fell, on soiled straw mats covered in excrement and flies. The bells at Mariamman Kovil begin an endless dirge trying to awaken the goddess.

Murugan's trembling hands, still smelling faintly of the arrack he has drunk to steady him through the ordeal, pours a spoonful of medicine down Arumugam's throat. But Arumugan is beyond all that now.

"Arumugam's dead," wails Murugan's wife. She cries alone.

Gunashekaran anoints his daughter Sita's forehead one last time with a wide finger of sandalwood paste from Mariamman Kovil. Gunashekaran's numb wife gently moves her daughter's lifeless body off the dirty, stained mat, her small, dark feet trailing through the filth.

Moodandan Raman is next. As Manoharan's wife's wails pierce the awful silence of Choolaimedu, Kannan runs to Old Man Imman's hut. Not a sound passes through the thin straw and tin sheet walls. As Kannan takes in the gloom, he sees that Imman has fainted in a heap in the middle of the room. His young wife sits huddled over the still warm body of her son. Imman's first wife – older, more stoic – sits aloof, her fingers combing her scalp for lice.

The postmortem takes a long time. And when it is over, the rickshawalas of Choolaimedu haul their pathetic but precious, and now sadly useless, cargo back to the parents.

There is a sudden rush of activity in the huts of Choolaimedu. The funerals will cost money. A battered aluminum lid serves as a collection plate. It passes in and out of doorways, accumulating soiled one rupee notes and small change. Raghavan's fist comes out of his pocket with all the money there is in it. All of it is theirs, he tells himself, as he places the lot on the tray. Choolaimedu is getting ready to bid farewell to its own.

Loudspeakers procured, blare old Thyagaraja songs. Coloured paper buntings and palm leaf decorations sway across the narrow lanes. The route the funeral procession will take on its way out of the slums has been freshly smeared with dung.

One by one – with a desperate slowness – the dead children are carried out and laid in a row. A short row of tiny limbs and dark, sad faces, now peaceful in their awful sleep. The women, their grief worn like a cloak, open new tins of Remy talcum powder and begin to powder the small bodies, carefully avoiding the purple sutures of the postmortem. Smoke from incense chases the flies away.

Above the muted wails, now slowing down to hiccups, another sound can be heard. Old saris being torn to form shrouds. Their children wrapped tenderly in cocoons, the mothers add one last touch of a familiar routine. Seven black dots to ward off the evil eye.

Fathers begin to return from the arrack shop where their grief has lost its acid edge. Weighed down by his helplessness, Raghavan goes in to lie down on the sagging cot. Suddenly, Kannan bursts into the hut. Outside, his tired horse stands waiting to be assigned his role in the day's rituals. Kannan walks to a corner of the dark room from where he picks up a silver rimmed conch shell and a pair of cymbals and blows the dust off them.

Outside, the strains of Thyagaraja are fading out. Women are beginning to wail with fresh vigour, the rest having restored their voices and renewed their memories. Raghavan gets up from the cot, walks out to the clothesline and pulls off a laundered net vest and shirt. Slipping them on, he moves outside to become part of this unforgettable day. The day they buried the corpses of Choolaimedu.

Cymbals, conch shells and drums come out of several Choolaimedu huts as mourners arrive to see the children one last time. Manoharan and Murugan stand below the fluttering lines of red paper buntings. Living children look at their dead friends' faces with a twinge of envy. So much attention, and all for doing nothing more than dying. Kannan sounds the first long blast on his conch shell. And in reply the cymbals take up the chords in clashing, cleansing thunder.

Manoharan bends down and lifts his two children, balancing one on each shoulder.

Murugan gathers his son to his chest. Imman, too old to bear the weight of his only child, borrows a younger shoulder.

Moodandan Lame Raman is in Fasi Kumaran's arms. Gunashekaran carries his daughter Sita. The procession starts moving forward.

Kannan's conch shell is heard once again. As familiar as Sudama's conch. Kannan's mare, startled by the sound, brays like an ass. The children smother their laughter.

"Mariamman!" a voice hails.

All of Choolaimedu says in chorus, "Guide us!"

"Mariamman!"

"Guide us!"

The procession is led by those carrying the dead.

The event has commenced. Some of Choolaimedu's young men have by then tied an old loudspeaker to a ricksha. The tinny sound of a tenor belting out a *Devadas* hit song has already been played a few times, much to the delight of the mourners.

Ulagame maayam, vazhve maayam,

Vazhve maayam

The crowd laughs and cheers and choruses,

Ulagame maayam, vazhve maayam. The world is an illusion, life is an illusion.

Occasionally, as if waking from a startled sleep, someone cries out, "Mariamman!"

And the crowd responds, "Guide us!"

The cortege reaches Choolaimedu's cremation ground in the late afternoon. A dark skinned Tamil has dug seven shallow graves. Seven sari shrouded bodies soon lie in their trenches, and the mourners move back a step. Then one more. Then they turn and return to their homes.

Back at the slum, Raghavan partakes of the funeral feast with the other men. The meal is accompanied by a 200 ml bottle of arrack. As the men finish their supper, their anguish comforted somewhat by the liquor, the women begin to trickle in. Their mourning is more ponderous and the rituals more elaborate – they bathe, weave green leaves into their braids, paint their shining foreheads with a large kumkumam dot and then – the business of mourning over – they set out, hand in hand with their men, for MGR's latest film at the nearby Golden Theatre.

Raghavan walked out of Central Station's Gents Toilet on shaking legs. Sweat beading his forehead, his stomach emptied of bile and stale food, he waited for a while, and then ran back in to vomit one more time.

Kumaran too had died in Choolaimedu. He had left for his bidi factory as he did each morning. But that night he did not return, as he always did, to curl up in a corner of the veranda that circled Old Man Imman's hut. They found his body on the railway tracks, cut in half. They found all of Kumaran except his left hand. Although two groups of young men from Choolaimedu walked a furlong along the tracks in both directions, the hand was never found. Kumaran's bidi-rolling hand, the people said with sadness. They couldn't send it with him.

The aluminium tray made the rounds once again. It circled Choolaimedu and finally reached Raghavan. This time there were fewer coins and notes on it.

Kannan and some neighbours dusted their conch shells and cymbals once again.

Kumaran was decked in flowers and taken to the cremation ground. When the mourners returned, jaggery and puffed rice was served at the rough and ready pandal that had been erected to shade Kumaran's body from the blazing sun.

In the early days, when Theresa had been living with him in Choolaimedu while he worked on his thesis, *The Ricksha Pullers of Choolaimedu*, Kumaran would bring a packet of bidis for Theresa every evening.

Raghavan wanted to call Theresa to tell her of Kumaran's tragic death.

"Do you still smoke bidis?"

"Have you destroyed the survey you wrote on the rickshawalas of Choolaimedu?"

Leaning back against a catamaran on Edward Elliot's Beach, Theresa had once asked him, "What are we doing?"

"What are we doing?" Raghavan had returned the question, not quite sure what she meant.

"Finding out more about Choolaimedu."

"What about it?" asked Raghavan into the breeze blowing in from the sea.

"You," said Theresa. "You. They are taking you for a ride for selfish reasons and you don't see it."

"Me, I am only a fellow traveller." Raghavan moved closer to Theresa. "A historian," he murmured.

"You're rubbish," exploded Theresa, getting up and walking to the waves. "What is the difference between you and the Gujarati seth? While the Gujarati gets his interest, you get a PhD."

"All right, so what? I am only a fellow traveller."

"That's right. A fellow traveller. Choolaimedu's great storyteller. Blind! So, go to hell!"

Looking for a job, coming to Madras with only a bag slung across his shoulder, he was just another Malayali.

Angered by Theresa's unusual display of temper, Raghavan had pushed her into the waves. Theresa had surfaced from the Bay of Bengal, spluttering. That night Theresa packed her bags and left Choolaimedu. And Raghavan.

Having vomited the last of the stale food inside him, Raghavan felt much better. He walked through Central Station, pretending to be on a mission. Looking purposeful but doing nothing.

Karpan's wife's death didn't make much news. The aluminium tray collected only a few coins. Karpan sold his bicycle to the Gujarati seth.

Yellamma's blood stained room was cleaned by the other women. Dressed like a bride, with a red cloth draped across her, they took her away. This time, Kannan was the only one who blew the conch shell and clanged cymbals along the way to the crematorium.

Then, suddenly, one day, old man Imman died.

After the death of his son, the Old Man of the slum had fallen into a deep silence. His two wives, like mother and daughter to him now, took care of him. When Old Man Imman died, they didn't lay him out on a straw mat. They seated him, crosslegged, anointed his forehead with sandalwood ash, garlanded him with marigolds and, finally, placed his reading glasses on his face. This death spelt Occasion.

The banners and the buntings came out. A procession began to the Gujarati seth's shop. The aluminium tray filled quickly and with some real show of mourning. The band arrived, this time wearing suits – shabby but shouting "ceremony." In the late afternoon, Imman's cortege began its slow journey to the burial ground.

The band struck up a hesitant funeral chord that quickly turned joyous as Kannan began a loud and catchy number, extolling the glory and virtue of a hearty wedding feast.

Kalyana samayal saadam
Kaay karikalum pramaadam
Anda gaurava prasaadam
Aduve yenaku pondum
Ha ha, ha ha ha ha

Imman was lowered into the grave in a sitting position. Choolaimedu did not usually bury its old people. They believed that the cold of the underground would cool and petrify the heat in their old chests and that they would return, like old memories, as ore.

The undertaker, sweaty and grim, took his payment and left with his gravediggers.

Raghavan walked away heavily and lay down in the shade of an old jackfruit tree in a corner of the cemetery.

A late mourner attempted a shaky *Kalyana samayal saadam* …

Silence – the only sign left of mourning. Murugan, alone in his grief, voiced the thought uppermost in most minds that evening – How many more funerals would Choolaimedu see before it became a ghetto of ghosts?

"For so many years," said Murugan, "have we lived here, on this tiny piece of land in the middle of Madras city. For so many generations. But now, one by one, we will be swallowed by this city."

Murugan's tears and rheumy phlegm hit the earth. Tears that would go straight through to Imman sitting there, below the grass, with his glasses on and nothing to see.

"I shall not die," cried Murugan.

"The death of poor people is like suicide," observed Raghavan. "It's as if they've given up."

As he lay on the ground looking up through the canopy of jackfruit leaves, his eyes followed a lazy trail of smoke left from a jet leaving Meenambakkam airport. Gods ascending to the heavens on ladders of string.

The ground was comfortable. It felt like he was lying with his head cradled in Amma's lap. Or Theresa's. Through half-closed eyes, reaching through the mists of drowsiness, he could touch the rolls of warm flesh on Amma's stomach. Or Theresa's. The first fold said, Sa. The second fold said, Ri ... Ga, Ma, Pa, Da, Ni, Sa.

Raghavan slept.

Looking straight ahead from one end of the platform, Raghavan could see distant red signals flashing like glowworms. The first train of the day was crawling into Central Station. They are asking me, "What are you doing, Sanjaya?"

What can I do? Except tell the story of Choolaimedu.

One afternoon, soon after Imman died, Murugan's wife Panchanayagi came running to Kannan's hut. Raghavan and Kannan were draining out the last of the rice from the thin gruel they ate unfailingly at lunch every day. Panchanayagi stood just inside the door, silent. They didn't have to ask if Murugan had died.

The aluminium tray made the rounds again. But this time, when it reached Kannan's hut, there were only three paise on it. Kannan and Raghavan looked at each other. Who would pay the undertaker? Raghavan picked up the three coins and walked to a telephone booth nearby, looking like one of the Magi carrying frankincense or myrrh. He would call Theresa and borrow fifty rupees to give Murugan a decent funeral.

The telephone booth stood like a statue at the crossroads. When he pulled the door open, out fell the body of an old man. Raghavan jumped back with a start. This was turning out to be quite a night for the Saviour. First the three coins, like the frankincense, gold and myrrh carried by the Magi from the East. Then, a Madras telephone booth opens and throws up a dead body. What next? Christ's resurrection, perhaps?

Kannan gets his horsecart ready to take Raghavan to Theresa's house. A square of light glows in the single window of the loft where she lives.

In his mind, he is still the hero of all of Theresa's dreams. Like an actor, he climbs the steps to her door and rings the bell. Dissolve.

Raghavan is taken aback by Theresa's unsurprised face at seeing him on her doorstep. Inside, the room is a film set, a still camera poised to shoot in a corner. A young man is carefully setting the needle of a gramophone. Cut.

"This is John," says Theresa.

Medium shot. Zoom in on John's face magnified – curly hair, an average Syrian Christian face.

"Hi."

"This is Raghavan." Theresa's introduction is terse.

Raghavan is watching John watch Theresa as he fusses with the gramophone needle.

Raghavan shuffles across to the sofa. The camera is directly in front of John now.

"Some tea?" asks John.

"Raghavan?" prompts Theresa.

"Umm."

The gramophone record bursts into life with an extremely loud bleat from a tuba. Theresa runs to it to reduce the volume and returns to sit across from Raghavan on the sofa. Medium shot.

Raghavan is transfixed by the surrealism of it all. Is he part of the film? Or is the film a part of his imagination? This time, the camera is intent on capturing John's languid walk to the kitchen along a narrow passage. Through the doors of the kitchen ... a part of the kitchen – the part with the shelves ... John reaches for a matchbox with the ease of familiarity. Close up.

Raghavan's eyes mirror the question on his mind – Who is this John? Medium shot.

The camera is behind Raghavan now, caressing Theresa's face. Theresa, beginning to set the rhythm of a song, asks, "What are you doing now?"

"I am a speech therapist." Medium shot.

The camera moves behind Theresa.

Theresa's face is intent on Raghavan's frown. "Stammering, stuttering ... straightening the crookedness from the spines of words. An interesting job." Medium shot.

The camera is between them now. Raghavan leans back on the sofa, secretly pleased to hear Theresa use the language of their days together.

The flapping of John's slippers breaks the mood for confidences.

He comes in rattling tea cups. Long shot. From John's point of view, Theresa and Raghavan appear like strangers transfixed in a freeze frame.

"Why have you come here?" asks Theresa after a while.

Raghavan doesn't answer, but gets up and walks out of the door.

From a distance, John's silhouette can be seen, framed in the square of light, seven storeys high.

Descending carefully, Raghavan wants to kick Theresa's carefully tended potted plants and send them rolling down the steps. One more shot. Broken pots. But there would be too much noise.

He walks across to Kannan waiting patiently outside. "Let's return to Choolaimedu."

Back in Choolaimedu, they place a string of marigolds on Murugan's stiffening corpse, roll it in a straw mat, tie it with a piece of hemp and weight it with broken bricks. When it grows dark, they load Murugan's body on to Kannan's horsecart. Kannan, ever mindful of ritual, places his conch shell and cymbals by the straw wrapped body.

"We'll take the cart down the paths that only I know about, and we'll get to Thiruvanmiyur beach," says Raghavan.

Before they set out, Kannan picks up the conch and blows it once. Loudly, strongly, almost apologetically — to Murugan's memory. Raghavan clangs the cymbals with equal gusto. Murugan, tell me the story of the stomach of the shark.

At the beach, all is dark and quiet. The sea breeze whispers through the grove of casuarina trees bordering the shore, like husk in the wind.

Raghavan is restless. "Kanna, I have to get back. I must leave for Central Station now."

Kannan is unmoved. "Can you see those lights in the distance? They are from merchant ships. They will guide the spirit on his way."

Raghavan is insistent. "Let's go to Central Station, now."

At Central Station, Raghavan paces the platform for hours on sea water wet, salt encrusted feet.

Goods trains begin their shunting. There is a juddering sound of iron cages hurting each other. Raghavan watches in familiar horror as rats jump out of rice sacks and slither and slip along the steel tracks. Raghavan had inherited his fear of mice from the women in his life. When a mouse entered their room from the corridor, Amma would jump up on the bed, hauling little Raghavan along with her. And there she would remain until the mouse went away. Little Raghavan too would stand on the lumpy mattress, clutching his mother's sari, half-afraid, half-amused as he looked up at Amma's face.

Theresa's dislike of rats was another matter. When they lived in Choolaimedu, every marauding mouse would be battered by a broom wielded with anger by Theresa. Raghavan would watch in helpless revulsion. The day before Murugan died, a small rat had tried to nibble on his toes. Raghavan recalled having lain there, paralyzed, like a lifeless lump of butter, saying to himself, I surrender.

The lights at Central Station begin to go out one by one. The cries of porters in a strange tongue begins to grow from a murmur to a chatter. Morning.

Raghavan turns and walks back to where Kannan is still dozing in his horsecart.

Kannan looks at Raghavan with sleep soaked eyes, and smiles. "He's back," he says to his drowsy, half-dead nag.

They ride back to Choolaimedu.

"Kanna, hurry," says Raghavan.

Kannan whips the tired horse.

The horse strains to hurry, foam flecking its mouth.

"Hurry, Kanna, hurry."

"Hai, hai." Kannan pulls sharply on the reins.

"Kanna ..."

"Partho," says his horseman.

"Kanna, quickly."

Kannan rises in his seat and blows the conch shell.

"Kanna."

"Partho."

Theresa's words – straightening the crookedness from the spines of words.

"Krishna."

"Partha."

Krishna. Partha. The sound of the conch.

Krishna, your Panchajanyam, and you, Partha, your Devadattam is summoning Bheemasenan's Paundram.

Kannan's shell calls out to Yudhishtran's Anantavijayam.

It blows a happy note for Nakulan and Sahadevan.

A heroic crescendo for the King of Kasi, a crashing roll for the charioteer of the gods, Shikhandi. For Drishtadhyumnan. Veeradan. Unvanquished Satyaki, Dhrupadan, Draupadi's sons, many-armed Abhimanyu. The conch shell blows from all directions.

In the distance, dawn is slowly creeping over the ash coloured expanse of Choolaimedu.

Panchajanyam (of the five lives), **Devadattam** (messenger of the gods), **Paundram** (king of conch shells), and **Anantavijayam** (eternal victory), are all names of conches.

"The Corpses of Choolaimedu" was originally published in Malyalam as "Choolemetile Savangal."

The Felicitation
by Shanta Gokhale
translated by Ranjit Hoskote

That was the first time Shekhar and I had gone to see Vatsalabai. Since then we've visited her so often, together or separately, that we've become familiar with every single tread-worn step of the staircase leading to her house. We were liberal arts students at college, Vatsalabai was a professor of biology. So the possibility of any contact between us was remote. We had heard that she was a very good teacher. But she would either go straight to the library after her lectures, or go home. Her contact with students was confined to the lecture hall.

We had also heard that when she first returned from overseas with her doctorate, she had been far more informal, sipping tea in the canteen with the students, laughing, debating animatedly, cracking jokes. That was in the late 1960s and early 1970s. The legends of that period were still legion in college. But it did not seem even remotely possible that the Vatsalabai we knew could ever have been or done anything like that.

People say that it was after the Emergency that she underwent a sudden, complete and absolute change. One of her closest friends was arrested during the Emergency. He was brutally tortured. His fingers were broken, his body hair was pulled out. Every form of fiendish savagery that men who taste power can devise to torment their fellow men was tried out on him.

When he emerged from prison, he was no longer the same. His fingers were twisted, the hair on his head had gone white, his chest was a hollow case. Vatsalabai took him into her home. She lavished her love on him but he had already been marked by death. He was, in effect, dead. All that remained was for his breath to actually stop. One day, that too came to pass and Vatsalabai snapped her ties with the world.

No one can say for certain who had relayed this story by word of mouth for twenty years, until it reached our generation. No sooner are such stories set in motion, than they begin to circulate freely on campus. They float in the air, move with the swaying grass. You stumble across them at every step. Their connection with reality has long ago been severed. They have become realities in their own right.

Vatsalabai's story doesn't end there. After her friend's death, she dressed only in white saris for a while. The stiff, starched whiteness of those saris matched her emotion-drained face. Some people say that she looked, in those days, like an archetypal Mother Goddess who had drunk all the poison in the world and survived.

Then she took to sitting and writing in the library. Like one possessed, she would cover page after page with writing every day. Gradually, her face regained its former appearance. Its severity disappeared and it grew serene. Her favourite colours began to show up in her clothes again. She threw herself into her teaching with a new enthusiasm. Her love for her subject shone once again on her face. Her eyes, however, seemed to be conducting a silent dialogue with someone beyond the students. People wondered whether she could see her students at all, so completely did her line of vision bypass them.

When Shekhar and I joined the college, Vatsalabai had only a year to go before retirement. To us, Vatsalabai was a dark complexioned, somewhat wrinkled, beautiful little idol neatly dressed in a sari. She always wore a smile, but if that smile wasn't false it wasn't wholly convincing either. She was a mystery to us.

In the last year of her tenure, a collection of her short stories was published under the title *Grains of Sand*. Because we were so curious about her as a personality, we swooped down on the book, read the stories – and were struck dumb with amazement. Just as some important insight into life was being offered to us, in these stories, it seemed to slip out of our grasp, or so we felt, and this plunged us into a state of unease. We sensed that, like her smile, Vatsalabai's stories too were poised at a frontier of some kind.

Last year, *Grains of Sand* won a state award. An occasion had presented itself at last, we felt, when we could deluge her with all the questions we wanted to ask about her literary universe, about those stories which were so fantastic and yet seemed more real than the real. We went to Principal Rao and placed before him our proposal that the college should host an official felicitation for Vatsalabai.

Principal Rao said, "Okay, let's give her an official felicitation." Vice Principal Sane interjected, "But who on earth has read her stories?" "We have," we replied. Then Mrs Kripalani said, "Why would non-Marathi students attend the felicitation? Hold it as a Marathi Association event. That should take care of it." "Her work is of considerable stature," we said. "The scale of the felicitation should be in keeping with that. We can always request Vatsalabai to deliver her address in English."

In due course, a felicitation committee was set up. At its first meeting, Professor Hazare, head of the Marathi department, said, "There's a distinct non-Marathi quality to Vatsalabai's stories. They don't seem rooted in our soil. Besides which, they're quite incomprehensible. Too difficult for the average person to understand." Shekhar spoke up, "I don't know if a college student qualifies as an average person. But we certainly understood her stories. They're not the slightest bit difficult. They're just strikingly original, that's all."

Professor Jahagirdar of the Economics department, who otherwise never spoke, said, "We must organize a felicitation for Vatsalabai. That is our duty towards culture."

"It's only natural that you should feel that way," retorted Professor Patil of the Statistics department. "She's from Nagpur, isn't she? You've travelled the world, seminaring here, there and everywhere, but your sentiments are still tied up with Nagpur."

Principal Rao rebutted this remark. "It isn't right to be parochial in all matters." Professor Patil came right back. "But there should be no objection to being pragmatic in all matters, surely." Sliding forward in his chair, he continued, "Why exactly do we wish to felicitate this lady? To express the respect, the admiration we feel for her. On such an occasion, shouldn't there be a respectable number of people who turn up to hear her speak?"

Once he had raised this point, the general secretary of the students' union, Upendra Sharma, chimed in. "Professor Patil is right. Students won't be interested in attending such a function." "Then let's organize a public felicitation for her," I said. "That way at least, her admirers beyond the walls of this college will get a chance to hear her speak."

"Where are these admirers of hers?" asked Professor Hazare, making a face. "The lady's such a recluse, such an island unto herself, that people in our literary circles begin by asking who she is in the first place!"

"Well, what's your decision then?" asked Principal Rao. "Should we abandon the idea of felicitating her?" At this, three or four voices spoke together. While it wasn't possible to ascertain who precisely was saying what, the substance of what they were saying added up to, "Certainly not. What an idea! Of course we must host the felicitation. No question about that. How can we not?"

For a long while after that, no one said anything at all.

Finally, Principal Rao broke the silence. "Right, so we go ahead with the felicitation. But we have to decide what form it will take. We have to ensure that students attend it in large numbers. Otherwise, it will seem as if we've used the pretext of honouring Vatsalabai to slap her in the face."

"Frankly, we don't think there's any need for a jam-packed hall," observed Shekhar slowly. "All the students of the Marathi department will be there. Then there will be a few students like us. There are five or six science students who are interested in literature – they'll come. That should be more than enough."

Professor Hazare pulled a long face. "We get the dregs, you know, the dregs. What possible interest can they have in the kind of stories Vatsalabai writes? I'm certainly not prepared to offer a guarantee that all the students of our department will turn up. The girls will be there, but you'll have to persuade the others."

Silence spread again over the gradually darkening room. The onset of darkness infused every individual's silence with a momentary sense of release from his or her public responsibility. Many believe that their first public responsibility, while discussing literature, is to put on a solemn face. The darkness gave all the tensed muscles in the room a chance to relax at last. In that wilting atmosphere, Sharma's voice rang out loud and clear. "What is our problem, really?" His tone bespoke the confidence of one who has taken the proceedings firmly in hand. "A group of people A wishes to host a felicitation for a lady B at a venue C. For this programme to go off successfully, we need a sizeable number of students in the audience. Now the trouble with the lady B is that her public image is zero. For which reason, she doesn't have the capacity to draw a crowd. But if the chief guest, the person invited to honour her, is a crowd puller, our problem would be solved at once. My suggestion is that we invite Rajeev Vijapure to be the chief guest."

Principal Rao's peon turned on the light at that moment, and by its illumination, the faces of all the professors in the room seemed to be glowing. Professor Patil raised his hand three times in manifest enthusiasm. "That's a good idea." Encouraged by the approving nods around the table, he went on, "After all, Rajeev Vijapure is also a credit to our college." At this, Professor Hazare asked timidly, "But didn't the college ask him to leave during his second year?"

"Rumour. Mere rumour," scoffed Professor Sane. "The truth is something else altogether. By his second year, he began to receive so many offers that it became impossible for him to attend college regularly."

"Well, that's all right then," said Professor Hazare, heaving a sigh of relief.

"And even if there was some controversy, all that was ten years ago," said Professor Patil. "The lad has done Maharashtra proud since." "Is that right?" asked Professor Jahagirdar, surprise writ large on his face. "What does this boy do? What sort of offers are you talking about?" Principal Rao scratched his chin and threw a piercing look in his direction. "Jahagirdar, do you ever lift your head from your books and look at the world around you? The next time you do so, you'll see the face of this boy on five out of every ten Hindi movie posters."

I cleared my throat. "This is not acceptable to us." Shekhar backed me. "Are the sort of people who will land up to see Rajeev likely to be interested in Vatsalabai's speech?" Principal Rao kept his eyes steadfastly on his fingernails. "We'll have to put this to vote," he said. "Raise your hands, all those opposed to the idea of inviting Rajeev Vijapure to be chief guest at Vatsalabai's felicitation."

Three hands went up. Shekhar's, Professor Jahagirdar's, and mine. The other professors simply bent their heads and looked down. Sharma, on the contrary, threw back his head and gave an imitation of a rooster crowing at daybreak. This crowing was the rage just then, having been popularized by Rajeev Vijapure in his latest film. Plainly put, the gist of the song that opened with it was – Hei girl, if the sun himself wakes up to my crowing, who says you won't?

I spoke up. "Why don't we simply cancel the felicitation instead?" "No, no, no," shouted everyone. "The felicitation must go ahead." Baleful glances were directed at us.

"Why are you so bitterly opposed to Rajeev?" roared Professor Sane. "Rajeev Vijapure may not have excelled at studies. But do you think it's an ordinary feat to succeed in the world outside, as he has done?"

"And in the world of Hindi movies, at that! He's raised the banner of Maharashtra aloft in Hindi movies, no less, not in our third-rate Marathi films," said Professor Patil. "This Ganesh Chaturthi, all of Maharashtra danced to his beat."

At this, for no particular reason, everybody burst out laughing, which produced the illusion that all the questions surrounding the felicitation had been resolved and the conversation turned to matters of organization and protocol – who would take the invitation to Rajeev Vijapure, who would escort him to the venue, who would invite Vatsalabai, who would fetch her. How to inaugurate the function? How many bouquets to get? Whose responsibility was the traditional gift of honour, the shawl and coconut, and last and most important, what snacks were to be served? This last point provoked a lively debate. Professor Jahagirdar suggested a simple menu of idli chutney and coffee. Professor Sane said, "Why is it that things like sabudana khichri and piyush are never suggested? Why do we always look to the south for inspiration when it comes to snacks?"

"Well, look to the north then. Let's have samosas," returned Professor Patil, who was famous in the college for his witty observations. When he spoke, people burst into laughter spontaneously. They did so on this occasion too. After the laughter had subsided, some suggested patties, others suggested batata wadas. Finally, the batata wadas won. "And green chilly chutney to go with them!" said Professor Patil, licking his lips in anticipation.

Since the plan seemed solidly in place, everybody got up to leave. Principal Rao asked, "Sharma will go to fetch Rajeev, but what about Vatsalabai?" "We'll fetch her," said Shekhar and I together. Then Shekhar muttered, "But we find the whole idea of Rajeev Vijapure felicitating Vatsalabai unacceptable."

Principal Rao only raised his eyebrows and looked at us through his thick glasses. But Professor Sane exploded, "You find it unacceptable? Just who do you think you are?" Professor Hazare, who was speaking after having maintained a long silence, intervened soothingly, "They're young, Mr Sane. They're idealists. As they should be, at their age." Cooling down somewhat, Professor Sane said, "But to reject the views of the majority is simply ..." Unable to find a word strong enough to convey his feelings, he settled instead for blowing his nose loudly into his handkerchief.

That was how the first opportunity to go to Vatsalabai's house came our way. With sour faces and bent heads, we walked up the worn stairs of that chawl like building to invite her to the felicitation. Climbing alongside us, on the wall on our left, were thick black heavy duty electric cables. In the long common balcony of every floor, there were children playing bat ball or killing one another with toy guns. Girls were playing hopscotch and last-letter-new-word. Every door on the way to the last single room apartment on the third floor stood wide open. And in every room, a television set shone in its place of honour. And from every television, a variety of noises, including snatches of English and Hindi dialogue, canned laughter and shrieking, assailed the ear.

The door to Vatsalabai's house was shut, though. I knocked at it. From within, a voice said, "Do come in, the door's open." On hearing this voice, we doubled up with laughter. Given our image of Vatsalabai, we had expected her voice to be deep but melodious. The voice we had just heard was like something a clown might affect to amuse his audience. I barely managed to get my laughter under control and was about to knock again, when we heard the sound of a bolt being drawn back. The door opened, and in a deep, melodious voice, Vatsalabai asked us, "Who are you looking for?"

From behind her, the earlier voice spoke again. "Do come in, the door's open." And a parrot flew out to welcome us, and perched on Vatsalabai's shoulder.

"Don't you put him in a cage?" I asked.

"No," said Vatsalabai.

"Won't he fly away?"

"He's free to, if he wishes."

"Hasn't he ever flown away?"

"Not yet, he hasn't."

"Do come in, the door's open." The parrot extended his invitation again, and laughing we stepped into the house.

Vatsalabai's room was furnished in an austere but tasteful manner. There was a harmony among the objects. The walls were a light ash grey. The curtains, tablecloth and other furnishings were red. Everywhere, there were hints of earth colours, red and moss green. One wall was covered from floor to ceiling with wide, open bookshelves. On them stood neat rows of books, systematically arranged, each book bound in an identical looking cover. The books stood in a pattern, classified according to the colours of their covers. Those colours, too, were ash grey, red, moss green, black.

"I can't see very well without my glasses," explained Vatsalabai, divining the question implicit in the manner in which we were looking at the books. "I can't read the letters, but I can make out colours easily. That's why I've bound all the books on a particular subject in covers of the same colour. And on the spine of each book, I've written the author's initials in large, bold letters. That's how I am able to stand here and read the letters on the spine of every book, even if it's on the topmost shelf." Placing tumblers of cold water before us, she continued. "And when they're your own books, you can identify them just by their shape. All you have to do is climb on the stool and take them down, your hands go unfailingly to the ones you want. What are your names?"

"This is Shekhar. I'm Neelima."

"Did you want to see me about something in particular?"

"Yes," said Shekhar. "We heard that you don't have a phone. That's why we've descended on you like this, without notice. Otherwise we would have requested you formally for an appointment."

"A phone," she muttered. "It'll arrive someday, I imagine. I applied for one years ago. Sometimes I ask myself, do I really need a phone?"

While Vatsalabai was speaking, I had been concentrating on the kitchen – which lay beyond where she sat – trying to listen for the sounds of another presence in the house. Once again, she divined the motive behind my actions. She said, "I live alone."

None of us felt like stirring to break the silence that followed. Each of us hoped that someone else would break it, sooner or later. But no one seemed about to speak – not Shekhar, not Vatsalabai, not the parrot or me. Overwhelmed by our emotions, we were reluctant to raise the matter of the felicitation, but it had to be done. And then the parrot said, "Do come in, the door's open."

We laughed. "Is that the only line he knows?" asked Shekhar.

"Oh no!" replied Vatsalabai. "Sometimes he embarrasses me. If he doesn't like a visitor, he starts saying Tata every five minutes. But he is shrewd in his judgement of people, I must admit. Well, what was it you wanted?"

"We want to host a felicitation for you at the college. To celebrate the award that your collection of short stories has won," I said. "So you're students of the college, are you? Oh no, let's not have a felicitation or anything like that." In one sense, I felt relieved at her reaction.

"Was this the reaction you expected?" she laughed. I fumbled for a reply. "Yes, no, the fact of the matter is ..." I began to mutter, when she cut through with a direct question. "Well, tell me why."

I took a deep breath and launched into the story of how the idea of the felicitation had come to us and what the felicitation committee had done with it. Vatsalabai said nothing at all. She leaned back in her chair and sat looking out of the window. So distant did she seem from our conversation that we began to wonder if she had become occupied with some other thoughts altogether. Then, suddenly, she said, "I think I ought to accept your invitation. I've virtually lost contact with the world since I retired. That simply won't do. Right, tell me when and where it is, and what it's going to be like."

The day of the felicitation dawned, and the butterflies fluttering in our stomachs began to receive support from every other part of our bodies. I lost my appetite and Shekhar's insides were in such a churn that every now and again, he would break into a sweat. We had decided to go and fetch Vatsalabai at four in the afternoon, and Sharma would go at roughly the same time to fetch Rajeev from the studios. Since Rajeev was in a hurry to get back, it had been decided that the felicitation part of the programme would take place first, and Vatsalabai's speech would come afterwards.

When we reached Vatsalabai's home, we found her ready and waiting for us. She was dressed in a dove grey sari with a crimson temple border. As was her custom, she wore no ornaments on her hands or ears. Just the spectacles on her nose, the watch on her wrist.

"I'm nervous," she said calmly. "It's true that one shouldn't break away from the world. But solitude seems so congenial these days. It's terrifying to see the emotions on people's faces." Then, smiling mischievously, she said, "That's why I've got these spectacles on. I'm going to read out my speech, so my text is all I need to be able to see. I haven't taken my glasses for distance."

In the taxi, Vatsalabai said, "What I said about the glasses is literally true, mind you. The road ahead looks like an abstract painting to me. It'll be your task to lead me to the stage and seat me in my chair."

We had tea in Principal Rao's office. Professor Patil said to Vatsalabai, "You've grown even thinner than you used to be." Professor Sane said, "But you look fresh nonetheless. Retirement suits you, doesn't it?" Mrs Wagh of the Marathi department said, "What a stunning saari! But your saris are always like that, of course."

Professor Jahagirdar said, "I've been trying to get inside your stories."

"You've been reading them?" Vatsalabai asked.

Professor Jahagirdar replied, "Some of them. I enjoyed the story about the trade in human organs, it was wonderful. Once I've read them all, I'll give you my critical appraisal."

Professors Sane, Patil, Hazare and all the other professors assembled there were tucking into their batata wadas. Their sniffling noses indicated the pleasure with which they were tackling the spicy green chilly chutney. The programme was due to start at five, but even at six o'clock, there was no sign of Rajeev Vijapure. Finally, it was decided that we would all move slowly in the direction of the hall. When Professor Patil, who was in the lead, stepped onto the stage from the side door, the hordes gathered in the hall crowed in one voice and burst into a song. "Murga bola suraj nikala, murgi bhi nikalegi, kukucch-ku!"

Professor Patil raised his hand for order and signalled, through his expression, that he was about to say something witty. "Possess your souls in patience," he said. "The rooster has yet to come. We are only chickens." The hall resounded with laughter, thunderous clapping and whistling. In the midst of this uproar Shekhar escorted Vatsalabai on to the stage and helped her into her chair. I sat on one side of her and Shekhar sat on the other.

Vatsalabai said, "One can pretend to be blind by wearing the wrong pair of spectacles. But what's to be done with the ears? How many students have gathered here?"

"The hall's packed," I said. "And how many of them, do you think, have read my stories?"

I was crestfallen. Didn't say a word. But Shekhar said, "Your admirers are sitting in the front row."

"How many are they? Describe them to me," said Vatsalabai. "Kedar Ranadive. Curly hair, blue shirt, glasses, slightly protruding teeth. Prajna Nalavade, green salwar kameez, bobbed hair, long earrings. Pheroze Keravala. Very fair, long hair tied in a ponytail, a gold earring in his right ear, black T-shirt, jeans."

"Keravala? A Parsi?" "That's right. But he's from Sholapur. Speaks excellent Marathi. And with a perfect Sholapur accent too."

"That's splendid, then. Three readers in front of me and you two on either side. It's the five of you I'll address." While we were talking, the professors on the stage had begun to get restless. Rajeev had still not turned up, and the uproar in the hall was rising to a crescendo.

Principal Rao said, "We ought to get started."

Professor Sane said, "Let's get Vatsalabai's speech over and done with. Rajeev will surely arrive by then."

Principal Rao said, "No. That will not be proper."

An idea occurred to Professor Patil. "Sir," he said to the principal, "do you recall the boy who staged a mimicry performance for the College Day celebrations? Shall I ask him to come up and entertain the kids? While he keeps them busy, I'll go and telephone Rajeev. I have his mobile number." Patil's face glowed with the pride of intimate acquaintance with so trendy an instrument as the mobile phone. Rao nodded and Professor Patil rose to his feet. The bedlam in the hall subsided somewhat. Professor Patil raised his hand. "Silence please," he shouted. The bedlam subsided further. Then Professor Patil began to speak, "I fully understand how eager you are to see Rajeev Vijapure. But what we are experiencing today is the tremendous effort that goes into his achievement of such popularity. An hour ago, Rajeev called us from the studios on his mobile, saying that he might be slightly delayed getting here, and he's apologized to you in advance."

Clapping, whistling, hooting, catcalls. "Rajeev should be here any moment. But as an appetizer to prepare us for our encounter with the real Rajeev, why don't we have an imitation Rajeev? Samir Sharangpani, alias Rajeev Junior!" Professor Patil raised his voice and shouted in his best emcee manner.

Thunderous applause. A chorus of whistles. Patting his mane into place, Samir took the stage in a single leap. Without pausing for breath, he snapped his fingers and began to dance to the tune of "Kukucch-ku." The hall responded by clapping in time with the beat. Some people clambered up on the tables and began to dance on them.

The number had entered its last stanza when, as though cued by some director's call of "Action!" Rajeev Vijapure suddenly appeared on the stage and began to dance along with Samir. What's left to say? The audience went crazy. Hardly had the dance ended than the request went up — "Dialogue! Dialogue!" Without batting an eyelid, Rajeev took off, "Son of a bitch, I will drink every drop of blood in your body. Until then I will neither eat nor sleep. Scoundrels like you have plunged my beloved motherland into filth. If young men like me don't rescue her, we should call ourselves insects, not men."

In the midst of the thunderous applause that met these lines,

Rajeev's formal presentation of the traditional shawl and coconut to Vatsalabai took place. Since Vatsalabai couldn't see a thing, Shekhar and I supported her from both sides and helped her to her feet. Rajeev gave her the shawl and coconut and touched her feet with great reverence. Then, having touched the feet of all the professors on the stage, he stood before the mike. In a voice choked with emotion, he began to speak, using the Hindi of moviedom. "The day I was thrown out of this college – that's right, I was thrown out of this college – that very day I took an oath that one day I would return, having achieved something in life. And when I was invited to be present on this auspicious occasion, I thought perhaps that moment has come, that I've reached the pinnacle I wanted to reach. Having said this, I will take my leave of you. Jai Hind! Jai Maharashtra!"

Rajeev included everyone in a comprehensive namaskar and then, tossing his locks, he quit the dais and was gone. Seeing their hero vanish before their eyes so soon and so unexpectedly, the students raised a pandemonium all over again. Those who had been waiting to ask for Rajeev's autograph at the end of the programme now began to pour out of the hall through both its exits. When both doors were substantially jammed in the ensuing stampede, a tide of students surged on to the stage and poured out through the wings. Some of the people on the dais were swept away by that tide, some swam and made it ashore, while others drowned. Shekhar and Vatsalabai were among those who drowned. First, Vatsalabai was thrown down from her chair. When Shekhar stepped forward to help her, he too was thrown to the ground. I saw all this from where I was, clinging tightly to the bars of a window on one side of the stage.

Gradually, the tide ebbed. The hall grew peaceful. I left the window and ran to Vatsalabai. My eyes were streaming with tears. Shekhar was trembling all over. That's when Professor Jahagirdar's voice came from somewhere, "Vatsalabai's all right, isn't she? Was she hurt?" He came limping through the side door on to the stage. He asked again, "Where's Vatsalabai?" To his quavering question, there came a ringing reply, "I'm right here. And I'm doing fine, thank you. I'm just slightly bruised."

Jahagirdar was followed by Ranadive, Keravala and Prajna. Prajna's kameez was completely torn down one side. Ranadive brought some water for Vatsalabai and Professor Jahagirdar. Prajna set right the overturned flower vase on the table and Keravala stood the toppled chairs on their feet again.

Professor Jahagirdar began to apologize for the contretemps that had taken place. Vatsalabai said, "Don't feel bad about it. I'm perfectly fine. Only, I've lost my glasses. Could someone look for them?" Keravala found the glasses in a corner of the dais, broken. "That's all right," muttered Vatsalabai, putting them away in her handbag. She took out another pair of glasses and put them on. Surveying the expanse of the empty hall, she said, "Now there's no harm in looking out across the distance. How nice it feels! Peaceful. Now then, shall we sit down and have a proper chat?"

"The Felicitation" was originally published in Marathi as "Satkar."

Hands

by Sharad Chhetri
translated by Prakash L Shrestha

It was a dream, a dreadful dream! Never in real life do I recall having faced such a formidable challenge. However, in the dream I felt as if a pet bird that I had lovingly nurtured had attempted to tear my eyes out.

Well, had it been real life, there was no way I would have been intimidated by the challenges of that weak generation. I am no coward! But it was a dream — no, a nightmare. A dream has an unpleasant way of rendering one helpless and abandoned, all alone, like an orphan. The challenge in this dream sounded to me like the deafening echo of a volcanic eruption.

I, a healthy man, reared in a healthy environment, how could anyone compare me with that — thing? Here was I, bred and brought up on the essence of purity, and the boy, a hybrid product of little that was natural and excessive artificiality. Any comparison between us was ridiculous. And I took such pride in my bloodline!

In the dream was my son, with the features of a veritable Goliath. I tried unsuccessfully to fetter him within the all-encompassing present. However, in the dream the present was just a small dot, an atom, while my son seemed to engulf the universe. How could the indivisible atom contend with such enormity?

The dream proved all my beliefs wrong. It began in an ordinary fashion, but I was taken aback by the tone of my normally soft spoken son. He, who had always spoken with eyes lowered to the ground, stared defiantly at me and demanded, "Give me my hands, I need those hands!"

"What are you talking about? I haven't got anybody else's hands with me," I retorted, glaring back at him angrily. He had hurt my pride and spoke without caring for the future or the consequences.

When our eyes met I expected him to turn away as usual, like someone blinded by a fierce fire. But to my surprise, his eyes appeared to be spouting fierce flames. How could a boy who had barely crossed twenty have such hatred in him?

He grimaced in hate and cried in rage, "You should be ashamed of yourself! How can you deny me my hands? You, who have so cruelly severed them and locked them away. But now I can tolerate no more injustice. I need them at once – my hands – the palms of my hands! Where are they?" His arms were covered in a large shawl and I could not see his hands.

I paused to consider his serious allegation. Strangely enough, I could not recall with certainty if he had been born with or without hands. I did not even remember if he had ever before questioned me about his hands. I had no memory at all of mutilating his arms.

So, it was in a sombre mood that I remarked, "In some past moment in history, some cruel dictator may have set the tradition of meting out punishment by chopping off a person's hands. But, recalling history is like digging up forgotten memories. They can in no way explain our present living moments. Don't forget that I am your father. Why on earth would I separate you from your tender hands?"

"My dear Pitaji! It's not correct to presume that dictatorships existed only in the ancient past. If, in the past, hands were chopped off by those who wished to stay in power, the same atrocities are being committed in the present, for similar reasons. To retain such power, overbearing fathers have been known to dismember their sons. Pitaji please, don't try to fool me, time has revealed many truths to me. Come, return those hands of mine – I have the utmost need of them. Under no circumstances will I ruin my youth by giving up my hands to you," he roared in anger.

Meanwhile his mother sat nearby, weeping. Seeing that her son was in such a belligerent mood, she implored in frightened tones. "Perhaps our choro is right. He is an adult of over twenty, and it is really unjust to deny him his hands. Why don't you give them back to him?"

What an awkward moment! Here was my son falsely claiming that he had lost his hands. Although I was not surprised that his mother was inclined to sympathize with him, my ego was somewhat hurt by the serious allegation that I had taken those hands and hidden them somewhere.

I was annoyed by all this, and said contemptuously, "How can a lad who has just barely learnt to walk, care for his own hands? He hasn't a strand of grey in his hair and yet he dares presume that he's old enough to talk of his rights!"

This appeared to wound my son's feelings and in an angry voice that seemed to fill the skies he exclaimed, "Pitaji, you should be ashamed of yourself. You are as blind as an owl in daylight and cannot perceive the radiance of my new found maturity. You should adopt a clearer and more unbiased attitude. There is a blinding brightness in my youth which I intend to use and cultivate. I wish to scoop up this light with the palms of my hands and share it with others. So, I need my hands, please give them to me."

I replied quietly, "But vatsa, I am not even sure that I have those hands with me."

He saw red when he heard my reply and roared again, "Don't try to fool me! Why devise all these schemes for some worthless power game? That sort of tyranny now is like a blunt weapon which you should cast into the progressive river of time and consider returning me my hands. It isn't necessary for you to try to lead me by my hands in the bright light of day. It's foolish of you to try to serve only your own selfish purposes. Return me those hands at once, or else ..."

Frightened by her son's increasingly ferocious threats, his mother interrupted, "Look choro, why trouble yourself at this young age with caring for those hands yourself? They are not easy to look after, let them remain with your pitaji."

"Oh Ama! I am sick and tired of your pampering. Stop trying to deceive me. I want my hands back. With those hands I will pound on some table and declare emphatically that they are hands that could take hold of the present and lift it to better things. What do those palms not hold? The lines of the sun, the head, fate, heart and life – all are in them. They even possess the precious mounds of the Moon, Mars, Venus and Saturn. They hold such promise and bear even the planets in them – there are no changes on earth that they cannot accomplish," our son continued speaking excitedly. "Therefore, I want my hands, I want change!"

Meanwhile, fearing separation from her child, his mother wept helplessly. As soon as he stopped speaking, she sorrowfully remarked, "Pyaro choro, we have endured more suffering for you than most other parents would have. We bore so many hazards in bringing you up. Why should you feel so hurt when your long suffering father decides to tend to your hands? It is for your own good. But do tell us, choro, how come this sudden interest in your limbs now?"

The boy calmed down a little and replied softly and somewhat abashedly, "I've fallen in love with a girl, Ama. I proposed to her, but she is very concerned about my hands. I want her and so ..."

Cutting him off abruptly, I mockingly inquired, "Does she have hands too?"

The tip of his nose turned red and gnashing his teeth, he burst out, "The palms of her hands are of no concern to you. What you should be concerned with are my hands. What do you think of us? Even if that girl had no hands, she would, like me, force her pitaji to surrender them to her. Then, the two of us will set out, hand in hand, to build a new world. But all this is our private concern and though our dreams may be meaningless to a domineering father, we will somehow gain your approval."

Panicstricken by our son's agitated manner, his mother implored me, "I think it's time to return his hands to him. For my sake, please give them back to him, please give them back ..."

Once again adopting a serious tone, I repeated what I had already asserted, "But I don't have his hands."

"Then where are my hands?" Enquired my son threateningly. He shrugged the cloak off his shoulders and revealed his arms, truncated at the wrists.

Seeing the stumps of his arms, his shocked mother sobbed out loudly to me, "Oh, what misfortune is this! I cannot bear to watch my choro's suffering any longer. Though severed so many years ago, the wounds on his limbs are still fresh. Please let me have the key to your secret chest."

I too was shaken by that pitiable sight, but I truly had no recollection of severing my son's hands from his arms. In a state of agitation, I handed my wife the key to my secret chest. She did not take a moment to unlock the chest. To my utter amazement, it disclosed a pair of hands. The severed ends revealed blood, still fresh, as if they had been recently cut. It seemed as if fate had decided to amputate his arms again and again, never allowing the wounds to heal.

Seeing those severed hands, my son triumphantly laid the ends of his amputated arms on them. The hands and arms were instantly rejoined and restored to their original state.

He danced and frolicked gleefully, waving his restored arms in joy. The sight drew even louder sobs from his mother, who wept in joy. I cannot explain the emotion I felt then — unbearable pangs of anguish ran through me.

It was a bewildering dream. No sooner did he have his hands restored, my son seemed to spring wings and flew off into the clouds. Other lovely hands reached out from the clouds and grabbed those of my son, pulling him away. Possibly, they were the hands of that unknown girl who was in love with him.

The two of them joined hands and danced joyfully. In what to me was still a dreadful dream, that beautiful young girl flew away with my son — taking him away from me, away from both of us — far away — far, far away.

―――――

"Hands" was originally published in Nepali as "Hatkelaharu."

The Transgression
by Pratibha Ray
translated by Amlan Dash

He suddenly remembered Sabitri as he lay on his deathbed! Sabitri was his wife, his companion in life. It was now forty years since she had passed away. He wondered if she would be waiting there for him, on the *other side*. He wondered if people really waited for each other after death. Although the husband and wife are said to be soul mates for eternity, he couldn't imagine why Sabitri should wait for a passionless person like him. Bhabanath didn't mean to blame her though.

How old would Sabitri have been had she been alive today? He could not exactly remember. However, he was certain that she would have been strong enough to look after him. And regardless of how Bhabanath might have neglected her, she would never have abandoned him to a lonely death.

Sabitri had died in childbirth, eight years after their marriage, following Shrinath's birth. Bhabanath was not the sort of person who was too fond of women – and that did not exclude his wife – but he had never imagined that she would have such a short life. Her death was followed by the death of their eldest daughter, three year old Sarala. Thanks to his stars, Shrinath escaped the jaws of death. Bhabanath was then a sprightly young man. However, he had always evaded the question of a second marriage. Now Manju, wife of the same Shrinath, had gone away to her parents' place leaving this seventy year old man to die alone! Shrinath had taken up such a strange job so far away from home that he never got leave to be with his father during his last days.

Well, why blame Shrinath's job, any job for that matter is an ordeal. You are no longer your own master, you have pledged yourself to someone else. On the one hand, you need to earn those coins – all jingling – counting each of them and, on the other, you want the freedom to visit home every month – how can both be possible? Nevertheless, time and again, Shrinath made his best efforts to visit home for a day or two, he also constantly urged his wife not to be neglectful of his father. She would go to hell if she did – everybody, including relatives and neighbours, repeatedly told her. What difference is there, by the way, between a father-in-law and a father? Wouldn't Manju have nursed her own father had he been on his deathbed?

Ever since Manju had come to this house as a bahu, she had been looking after Bhabanath as if he was a baby. She had erased thirty five years of his loneliness with her natural goodness. "She must have carried him in her womb in some previous life," everybody said, seeing her devotion towards her father-in-law. Bhabanath too believed the same. He blessed Manju from the core of his heart. He prayed to god – day in and day out – to help him sail through the ocean of life and not to torture him with impending death. As long as his death got prolonged, he believed, Manju's suffering too would get protracted. Though Manju never complained but – from her withered face, tired looks, emaciated body, sweat drops beading on her forehead when she helped him move about ... from her suppressed, sad, regretful and low sighs – Bhabanath could understand that it was more painful for her than it was for him. After all how old was she? And how much could she do all alone?

Before the illness, the old man would squat there on the veranda, hunched up and leaning against the wall – looking at her. There was nobody else at home, not even a kitten, to shift his gaze from Manju! Bhabanath had never known till then how much pleasure there was in looking at women. In his eight years of married life, he had never ever looked passionately at Sabitri – he had never, in fact, seen Sabitri's face in daylight. In a big household like theirs, it was always midnight by the time Sabitri finished her chores and entered the bedroom – the oil in the lamp would be drying up. Besides, did he ever have the desire to look at Sabitri passionately those days?

Bhabanath had a reputation in the village – he never looked at women. He had spent his youth as an ascetic in the thakurbari, studying the scriptures. In a way, he was a sanyasi. He used to come home only at the insistence of his mother. Otherwise he preferred to sleep there, spreading a mat on the veranda, surviving on prasad and talking to the balmy breeze. The thakurbari, where old people chanted incantations, belonged to their family and was adjacent to their house. The young ones gathered elsewhere. But Bhabanath was already an old man in his youth! His desire was restrained, he had none of the agitation of youth, his mind was calm and there was not a blot in his thought. He had no attachment towards the riches of life. He ate simple food and his ideas were pious too. In a nutshell, his whole heart was with god.

The villages around were filled with praise of him.

It was but natural that respectable families wanted to have Bhabanath – a young man of such lofty ideals and pure thoughts – as their son-in-law. The girl would live a happy life, so went the saying, if she had such a pious person as husband, she would become the mother of a virtuous son. What else did a woman need? Unmarried girls used to offer champa to Lord Shiva to have Bhabanath as their husband. Well, Sabitri then must have offered one lakh champas! She must have been the object of envy of girls of her age for getting Bhabanath. But, what did she actually get? Poor girl, she never knew a husband's love! She was not destined to have her husband mesmerized by her beauty and to hear words of love from him. Eight years passed by with her face concealed behind an odhani. By the grace of god, she conceived and Shrinath was born. And her life as a woman was fulfilled. The lineage was saved.

But was Sabitri's life really full? Why did she then hastily make her way to the *other side* before Shrinath was hardly five years old? What was the ailment that devoured her? Bhabanath didn't know. His parents were there to look after her and doctors to take care of the disease. Even during Sabitri's final moments, Bhabanath was not with her! How could he have sat on the bed of his young wife – so what if it was her deathbed – in the presence of everybody? There was something called decency, after all. He did experience the impulse to caress her deathly pale face, to let a drop or two of tears fall on her beautiful forehead. But, the man in him always prevailed over the lover in him. What was the use of getting attached to what was going to be dust soon? To cling to this world – knowing well that the world is useless – is a sign of attachment. Bhabanath brushed aside the attachment that made him restive.

Sabitri's lifeless body was lifted from the courtyard accompanied by the kettledrum meant for a woman not yet widowed. Strangely, no one saw Bhabanath shedding tears! Perhaps, this is what a man's self-control is all about! Those who came to console him heard consoling words from him instead, "I'm distressed at the sight of all of you feeling so sad for me. Why do you all worry? She left the world with her dharma. Why should she have been tormented in this useless world? She left as a pious woman. It's for Shrinath that I feel sorry. Anyway, he who has given him birth and he, who has made him motherless, will take care of him. Parents are mere agents."

Taken aback, they went away admiring Bhabanath rather than feeling sorry for him.

There were also reasons to envy Sabitri for her death. And why not? The few years that she had lived on this earth, she must have spent her life feeling proud of her husband. She had become the mother of a son and had never known sorrow, pain and disease. The odhani had not receded from her face as yet, the young body had not withered. She burned bright on her funeral pyre – her forehead smeared with a fistful of sindoor – a blessed woman who had not been widowed as yet. Could there be anything happier than such a life – could there be anything happier than such a death? Death certainly made her glorious!

Who can allege that Bhabanath, as a husband, was not virtuous and generous? What deficiency did he have? Was he a philanderer? An egotist? Did he ever swindle anybody, ever break the law? Did he ever abuse his wife? Which one of these flaws did he have? Both at home as well as outside, he had a calm countenance. What room did Sabitri have to complain against him? Was there any scope for her to feel that she was getting suffocated? Well, of course, she could have complained that Bhabanath had no desire for women. "Aren't you ashamed? How did you become a mother then?" Her accusation would have backfired. "Would it have been right on his part to neglect all other duties to frolic about with you day and night? There is, after all, something called the custom of the house!"

Sabitri never had the misfortune to hear such probing questions, for she had never talked ill of her husband. There was no dearth of food and clothing in the house – love and affection from her in-laws were never wanting. The house, for her, was a world in itself, complete in all respects. What was lacking then? If she ever felt anything was lacking, it must have been due to her own flaws, her own deficiencies, and such a person would never know what a full life was.

Bhabanath reminisced about Sabitri, lying on his deathbed. The things that the light of his young eyes had not seen were now becoming clear to his half-dead, cataract afflicted eyes.

Who said that it's a sin to look at women? Who said that it's lustful to love one's own wife to one's satisfaction? Who said that it's virtuous to spurn one's duty – the pursuit of wealth and desire in one's youth – for a life of asceticism and pursuit of salvation. Who, moreover, created this gulf between fame and notoriety, good and bad, between sin on the one hand and piety and self-restraint on the other?

If it is a sin to look at women, then is it a virtue to be indifferent? Where does the sin lie in calling something beautiful? We admire the beauty of Lakshmi, the mother goddess, the power of ma Durga, and the beautiful voice of ma Saraswati. Is it a sin then? And to remain above such sins, Bhabanath had allowed his youth to turn old! He had no grief for having done this, no regrets either. He had become old prematurely by devoting himself to their family deity Sri Jiu. No one had ever seen him looking at other women, ever noticed any sign of desire arousing him. He had got married only to save his lineage at the insistence of his parents. He had only fulfilled what he considered to be a mere duty. But in his thoughts and in his consciousness, he had been a brahmachari by birth. That he would have sustained his will power had Sabitri been alive – he cannot, of course, say as forcefully now.

The image of Sabitri was, to Bhabanath's failing eyesight, blurred – it was like the gust of an early spring breeze which vanishes before one can hold on to it. What was Sabitri's face like? What was her complexion? He was not sure. However, he remembered that her sharp face, behind the colourful sari partially covering it, resembled the salita, the holy wick lit in the evening to the accompaniment of conch shells ... wrapped in a sari, her fresh body resembled a bunch of tulsi leaves and flowers. Her soft feet dyed red with alta, wrists with bangles on them, palms like the petals of a lotus and her thin, long graceful fingers – all these taken together, Sabitri was like an offering for worship. In the bright sindoor on her forehead one could see the sun coming out, clearing the darkness. Where was the place for desire there? From her hair came the pure fragrance of incense, in her breath, the aroma of the smothering wick. Where was the place for sensuality there? She was only an abstraction, an idea. Sabitri was like an idol to be worshipped. That's what the relationship between Bhabanath and Sabitri was after the birth of Shrinath. With love and affection, he had transformed her into an idea. Could that be called negligence of one's wife? His incompetence as a husband? Injustice? Cruelty?

No one had ever accused him of such things. No, not even Sabitri. Today, however, he did not know why, Bhabanath was trying to justify himself.

Would god have known if Bhabanath had, after the death of Sabitri, looked at women? He, however, blindfolded himself. The eye is a receiver of beauty. And beauty, more often than not, causes desire. Hence Bhabanath had always kept himself away from beauty and that's why the world applauded his strong character and saintliness. With the blossoming of the mango tree the cuckoo starts singing, with the coming of spring, flower buds come out in bunches on their own. Passion blossoms in the body at a tender age, in one's mind there hums the cuckoo's loud note, and a current passes down the nerves. Man did not create these – they happen on their own. The way seasons change on their own. Is it a sin, then, for a flower to blossom? Is it a crime for the cuckoo to sing? Why such hostility on society's part towards what is nature's gift? Today, it seems, things have become superficial – that is, the sin is hidden inside oneself. The moon is beautiful as its other side is not visible. The other side of the heart is not noticeable and that's why there are so many sadhus and saints as well as dispassionate mahatmas.

During his young days, the teaching of vedanta, "the world is a lie and the brahma alone is the truth" had inspired Bhabanath. According to it, worldly pleasures are poisonous. The world is transitory, it is not our permanent home. To hold on to this world as "mine" would be an illusion. With the impression that brahma can be achieved only by breaking away from all the attachments and illusions of the world, Bhabanath led the life of a recluse even while living in this world. Far from achieving brahma, did he even get to behold brahma? Isn't it self-deception, then, to call this world a lie? Jagadishwara Jagannatha was the family deity of Bhabanath. If the world is false, can the lord be true?

Such questions had come to his mind again and again, but he had shaken them off, cursing himself. The world is a lie, he thought, yet god is the truth. If one brahma can get manifested in several forms in this lie that the world is, then by calling the world false, isn't the pursuit for achieving that invisible, precious brahmaloka an insult to the brahma itself? This world, this life, is the venue for attaining siddhi, which, in turn, is the way to brahmaloka. Then where is the justification for proving the world worthless? Life and death – both are subservient to the sensuality of the flesh. Yet, by forsaking all those possible achievements of life, and by pursuing the achievements of a life after death, Bhabanath was now realizing, in his old age that he had not only been deceiving himself but had also been dishonest with truth. True, he had won enough of a reputation by contemptuously regarding his wife to be the image of maya, and rejecting the rasa of love as the rasa of destruction. Why then was he not getting salvation from his miserable existence? Why couldn't he attain brahma by just collapsing from wherever he is sitting now, thus dying a painless death? If it is true that brahma is achieved in death, then why was he, lying so close to death, reminiscing time and again about Sabitri, who was maya after all? Bhishma, not Kamadeva Madana, was his idol. On accepting Bhishma as his idol he had fathered a son as a gesture of filial obligation, and had observed sexual abstinence ever since. Why then was he looking forward to a union after death with that very person whom he had neglected in this life? Was the possible tryst with Sabitri after death a reality or self-deception?

This life has slipped away, Bhabanath thought, lying on his deathbed. He had made renunciation the goal of his life, and had rejected whatever his life offered him. Then why this longing in the flesh today? He wondered whether he would ever be born as a human being again! Moreover, would there be another birth?

Why just Sabitri, Bhabanath had turned a blind eye on the entire species of women thinking that they were all maya! He had not fulfilled his fatherly duty towards his daughter. Poor girl, she left halfway through. He had never looked at his own sister after the tenderness of adolescence touched her. He had not even bothered to glance at his wife Sabitri. He could not remember if he had ever looked at his mother closely.

But he loved Manju more than one could love one's own daughter. He couldn't believe he had so much love and affection in him. He had considered himself a piece of deadwood without any emotion whatsoever. After Manju came, Shrinath did not allow him to stay at the thakurbari. He brought him home. Poor man, he had lived all his life on a fistful of prasad cooked by the old brahmin cook, which was like amrit to him. But the cook's son was not the least bit interested in the thakurbari. He somehow managed to half-boil some rice and dalma before escaping to the akhada where his main amusement was to smoke ganja and watch tamasha. Let him then, thought Shrinath, live the rest of his life eating the food cooked by his bahu, and under her care as well. Years ago, when he was young, Bhabanath had rejected his father's advice in this matter. Today, however, he could not avoid his son's suggestion. He came back to the house with bag and baggage. The thakurbari gaped like an orphan after him.

The thakurbari was not thatched regularly. Through the awning above the god's head, it was the sun and the rain that actually took care of the god. The walls were not painted. Nobody bothered to clean the well. And nobody was keen on taking the responsibility for the rituals. This is the fate of communal property – private houses will be thatched, but not god's house!

"Whatever is happening is your wish," Bhabanath said, prostrating before the god. "I had displeased my father. But I cannot disappoint my son. He has been motherless since childhood. I am but a worthless father. Poor man that I am, I do not know what love, care, and affection are. I will die seeing the happiness of my son and daughter-in-law during my last days."

As a person, Bhabanath was of strong character – religious, selfless, with no trace of deceit. When Sabitri passed away, he had not even been thirty five. There were so many proposals for remarriage. However, fearing that Shrinath might be neglected by a stepmother, he never thought of marrying again. Everything – his vision, mind and consciousness – was centred around Sri Jiu. He belonged to a Samanta Karana family, the high class kayastha landlords. To have a concubine while the wife is still alive is not against their tradition. Bhabanath's younger brother had three while his wife was still alive. Bhabanath could have taken one without marrying again, no one would have accused him of being immoral. But no, he was not a licentious person. He had a modest way of life – a tulsimala around his neck, a U shaped, long sandalwood paste mark on his nose, prayer beads in hand, a dhoti barely covering his knees, a sleeveless shirt, a kantia shawl on his shoulder during winter and a namabali – a thin cotton cloth with god's name printed on it, generally used for wrapping around the body – in summer, that's how he lived. On his tonsured head tiny threads of hair stood like paddy stumps, and a tuft of hair was tied into a small knot. He was always counting the prayer beads and chanting god's name – his passionless eyes partially closed. In terms of physical features, he was dark, healthy and had a remarkably sharp nose. Because of humble thoughts rather than age, he had a slight stoop. Narada, the greatest of all devotees, a brahmachari since birth, had the right to perpetual youth. Bhabanath, of course, could not be compared with him. In their maturity, Dhruba and Prahalad would have looked like him. While he sat on the veranda with eyes closed in devotion, people walking by on the street saluted him out of respect. In the eyes of Shrinath, Bhabanath was the image of their tutelary deity, Sri Jagannath Jiu, in flesh and blood. He had an unwavering devotion towards his father. To him, father was dharma, heaven, and salvation. Shrinath was respected in the villages around because he was Bhabanath's son. What other accomplishment did he have? On the first night of their marriage, instead of whispering words of love to Manju, he had spent the whole night praising his father. He made it clear to Manju that, for him, his father came first and then she, and any negligence in looking after his father would amount to an unforgivable crime. If his father remained happy, Shrinath would also be happy. Shrinath had always blamed his mother for deserting his father in his youth. The newly married Manju understood from the beginning that, in this house, devotion, not love was the rule.

Nobody was unaware of Manju's devotion and attention towards her father-in-law. The reason why Shrinath loved Manju dearly was not because she was beautiful or she loved him, but because she was devoted to his father.

The sight of Manju always reminded Bhabanath of the daughter who had left, betraying him. Had she been alive, she too would have cheered up somebody's house like this. Then he would have recollections of Sabitri. Had she been alive, she would have soared in happiness to have such a Lakshmi-like bahu. Poor woman, couldn't see what happiness was, couldn't know what life meant.

From morning to evening, Manju would be after the old man the way one looked after a small child. He was, to her, not a father-in-law but an elderly son. Bhabanath too would be after Manju endlessly, "Eat well … wear good clothes … be happy … take proper rest … pay attention to your health … why is your hair ruffled … why is your skin dry? Is there any scarcity of oil and turmeric in this house? … Why is your face pale? Are you missing your parents? True, your sasu is no more, but I'm here, your old bapa …"

At times, Shrinath felt jealous of his father's affection towards Manju. Never in his life had his father displayed so much love towards him, paid him attention the way he did to Manju. "You are very fortunate," Shrinath would joke. "For a nonchalant and unaffected person like Bapa to be giving you so much love and affection surprises me. I do not remember him loving me so much during my childhood. Of course, one needs to admire you as a bahu. Had you neglected Bapa, he would surely have run away to the thakurbari in fright."

Manju's innocent heart would get complacent.

Shrinath could go back to his place of work without worrying about his father. Anybody else in Manju's place would have preferred to go along with her husband. Which daughter-in-law these days likes to stay back in the village to look after the father-in-law?

Though Bhabanath was not entirely pleased with his son going to a remote place, he knew not why, he was also relieved. He felt a strange sense of happiness. Now Manju would be exclusively his. All her time would be for him. Shrinath won't be there to stake his share.

Did Bhabanath envy his son? During his stay in the village, whenever Shrinath and Manju found time to be together, Bhabanath would need her just then for all sorts of work. The old man would start getting an asthmatic fit every night when Manju finished her household chores and entered the bedroom. Both Shrinath and Manju would rush out and start attending to the old man. Even in his childhood, Bhabanath used to be tormented by a hidden jealousy – he could not bear his father's intimacy with his mother. He used to feel that his mother belonged only to him and his father's claim on her was unfair.

Bhabanath was a virtuous person, and perhaps that was the reason why he had got a bahu like Manju. Otherwise, who would have cared to stay back in the village with this old man? Me, my husband, my children – that's the definition of family in this kaliyug right from the first day of marriage. There is no place for old people. Bhabanath, therefore, was fortunate. So was Manju. Which father-in-law cares so much for his daughter-in-law as if she were his own daughter? In the absence of a mother-in-law, Bhabanath played the role of both. Shrinath's letters to Manju were like manuals of duties concerning his father. Only towards the end of the letter would there be a line for her. Manju did feel hurt at times. Then, later, she would consider it a proof of his manliness that he gave preference to his father over his wife. Not everybody gets a good human being as husband. If she didn't take care of her old father-in-law, who would? The village folk?

During the initial days, Manju would appear before her father-in-law in an odhani almost a foot long. From behind the odhani, Manju's sharp and fair visage resembled that of Sabitri. Bhabanath did not know why he was frightened of Sabitri's face now. "Don't veil yourself too much," he would tell Manju. "You are my daughter after all." Gradually, she stopped bothering if her odhani slipped, and the knot of dense hair, the round neck below the knot, and the gold necklace, Sabitri's, could be seen. In that necklace was strung the pride, memory and tradition of their family. Bhabanath couldn't remember for how many successive generations that necklace had been transferred from the mother-in-law to the daughter-in-law. From his own mother, the necklace had come to Sabitri. When Sabitri was dying, one of his relatives had snatched it from her neck and given it to him saying, "Keep it carefully. If Shrinath grows up to be considered among men, give it to his wife." Bhabanath had given it to Manju as a wedding gift. Strung in black thread and made of coral, it was indeed a beautiful necklace. In the centre, there was a small, thin golden pendant. She looked gorgeous wearing it. Bhabanath had never looked at it carefully on Sabitri's neck.

That afternoon, while Manju was taking rest, sitting at the door on the rear side of the house, a gust of unrestrained wind pulled down her odhani, exposing her neck and part of the back. One half of that glittering neck was visible from behind. Below the necklace, on Manju's white back, were two moles. Very beautiful. What was beautiful? The neck or her hair? The golden necklace or the moles on her back? Bhabanath felt as if Sabitri, hurt and sad, was sitting there with her back towards him. He couldn't remember whether there were moles on Sabitri's back. Why did Manju always appear to him as Sabitri? Just then Manju turned and seeing her father-in-law looking intensely at her exposed back, she blushed. Chi ... I'm becoming uninhibited, she told herself. How could she be so careless? She felt quite ill at ease. Her saintly father-in-law, he could have warned her. Perhaps he did not tell her anything out of nobility and decency.

Manju was more careful then onwards.

Nowadays, Bhabanath depended upon Manju for almost everything. "Manjulo ... maa Manju ... give me a glass of water ... make sandalwood paste for me ... string the flowers ... prepare a couple of paans ... pass me those prayer beads ... keep the implements ready for the puja ..." and so on – he would ask for all sorts of services. The old man felt happy if Manju hummed around him like a honeybee from morning till evening. Shrinath, during his trips home, felt happy if he heard the old man praise Manju. She too was full of adulation for her father-in-law. She had never received such love and tenderness — no, not even from her own father.

How long could Manju remain in the village looking after the old man? Shrinath was facing difficulty in the town. If the old man could be taken there, Manju proposed, they could all stay together. Shrinath too was in favour of this. However, Bhabanath got annoyed. How could he go away? Just before dying? Leaving his village, his tutelary deity and all his relatives? If Manju or Shrinath had a problem, then Manju could go with Shrinath. Bhabanath would not stop them. But he wouldn't leave his ancestral home. Shrinath in turn got infuriated with Manju for having made the proposal. Women's minds! They can ruin you! The old man thought it was Shrinath who was not able to live without Manju. "He is henpecked!" Bhabanath told himself in distaste, "Chi ... how shameful!"

"Forget about me," Shrinath told Manju. "I'm young and strong and can live without you. Besides, who else is there to look after Bapa at this age? You know that Bapa will never leave the village. As long as he is alive, don't ever talk again of staying with me. After all, I keep visiting you every now and then, don't I?"

Manju kept quiet, her guilt made her feel ashamed of herself. Really, what an ugly thing to have happened — she admonished herself. Her father-in-law must be thinking that she was getting sick of attending to him. His blessings were auspicious for both of them. She would never do any such thing in future that would hurt the feelings of her father-in-law, she promised herself. After that incident, Manju never ever uttered a word about going with Shrinath.

Bhabanath had now got into the habit of being massaged by Manju. It was on Shrinath's orders — there was nothing to feel shy about.

Who else was there in the house to do it? When Shrinath was at home, he did it. In his absence, it was Manju's job. Initially Manju felt very awkward. Slowly, however, she shed her diffidence. What's the difference between a father and a father-in-law after all?

Bhabanath enjoyed the gentle touch of Manju's soft palms. Sabitri, when she was alive, used to massage him. Manju, it seemed, had Sabitri's pair of hands. One day, during the massage, Bhabanath got up with a start as if possessed. He kept staring at Manju like a wild cat and, grabbing her tiny soft palms, clutched them firmly in his. He gasped, as if speaking in an asthmatic fit, "Your sasu too had a soft pair of hands like these. That's why I like you massaging me."

Manju disengaged her hands from his. She left the room without uttering a word. She kept thinking about the whole episode from beginning to end, sitting at the back of the house. She couldn't say what she read in the eyes of her father-in-law and what she had felt in the touch of his hands, but the house scared her now. A seed of suspicion, of an unknown fear planted itself in her mind. Her father-in-law no longer appeared like a god, but as a very ordinary human being – he appeared as the *other*. She could neither tell this to anybody, nor could she write about it to Shrinath. Who would believe her anyway? On the contrary, everybody would blame her and she would be defamed. After all, he had not said anything offensive. Why were there such unpleasant thoughts in her mind if he was only remembering his wife fondly? Because she had an evil mind, what else?

A woman, however, does not need words to understand a man's thoughts. Women's eyes are like touchstone. From the way he looks, touches and breathes, she can make out how pure his intention is and how corrupt his thoughts. Now Manju was able to see clearly through the mind of her father-in-law. As long as the gold is solid, the alloy is not detectable. Once it starts melting, one can detect the baser elements. Bhabanath no longer had control over himself – he was melting. He looked for support for everything – for sitting down, getting up, going to the toilet, taking a bath, eating and so on. Shrinath kept writing to her urging her again and again, "You must take care of Bapa. If he slips and breaks a bone at this age, it would be a disaster."

Manju found it difficult to do everything alone. If she asked for help from Dama, their farm labourer, her father-in-law got irritated. Dama was a shudra. By touching him, he would desecrate himself and could not touch the prayer beads, and if he took a bath thrice a day to cleanse his body, he would get typhoid. There were times when Bhabanath fell over Manju with the weight of his entire body. While Manju somehow managed to control herself from falling, the old man would try to control his disobedient libido. If Dama came running to his rescue, Bhabanath would snarl at him. Father-in-law falling over her not once but time and again, appeared poisonous to her. "I am not able to control Bapa any more," she wrote to Shrinath. "He is such a huge man. He needs my support for moving about. How much strength do I have? A couple of times, he has narrowly escaped from slipping. I cannot … any longer. Please come home."

"If I could get leave," came the reply, "do you think I would leave Bapa in this condition in your care and remain here? It's very difficult now to get leave even for a day. What use will it be even if I take leave for four to six days and come there? You have looked after him for so long and, now, towards the end of his life, you write such a letter? What would you do if he were your bapa? I am hurt at your reluctance to take care of a god-like person like him. Don't allow my love for you to get diminished by writing such letters again. If I take leave to come home now, how will I get leave to come there during his final moments?"

For Manju, all doors were closed now. Whom should she speak to about the misgivings of her suspicious mind? Everybody – whoever listened — would surely blame her. She would never be able to tell Shrinath, even if she were dying, that "your god-like bapa is not a god, but an ordinary human being. He is not my bapa but only my sasur." Perhaps that's why there is this custom of maintaining a distance between father-in-law and daughter-in-law ... perhaps that's why the daughter-in-law is expected to veil herself from her father-in-law. It must be a well-experimented tradition. "Your bapa is going crazy." But these words remained suppressed in her out of fear, hesitation and shame. The other day, around midnight, somebody touched her body in the dark. Manju was suddenly awakened from her sleep with a start. "Who's it ... who's it ..." she screamed in fear. "It's me ... it's me." somebody whispered. "Why are you getting scared of me?"

"What business do you have in my room at this hour, Bapa? You seem not to be able to walk without support even during daytime! How come you were able to walk all the way in the night alone without any support?"

"I got up to go to the toilet. How long will I trouble you? But, I lost my way in the dark, and entered your room. I am not able to see anything in the dark."

"Ah, what would have happened had you slipped in the dark? A broken bone, at this age." Manju spoke in distress.

"In that case, my death would have come earlier. I have no desire to live any longer and trouble others." There was boundless grief in the voice of the old man. By the time Manju lit the lamp, the old man had left the room in haste and, entering his own room, put the latch on. Didn't he say he was going to the toilet? Then why was he hiding himself in his room?

Manju was not only annoyed with her father-in-law but hated him, and also felt insecure. The aged man was, no doubt, morally weak and without any strength, but tradition granted him respect and honour taller than the Himalayas. If the time came, she wouldn't be able to raise her hands against him ... she wouldn't be able to brush him aside and, worse, she wouldn't be able to complain about him to her husband. How, and to whom, should she speak about this transgression of a sacred relationship? Who would believe her? One can forgive the overstepping of the Lakshmana rekha drawn by society in the youthful excitement of a young person, it is pardonable because the fault is that of age. However, the improper youthful excitement of an old and respected person who transgresses the Lakshmana rekha of relationships shatters the veneration, affection and reverence one feels for such a person. Manju felt feverish the whole day, the whole episode nauseated her. She had an attack of migraine. It was as if polluted air was blowing towards her. And, while praying, the beautiful statues of the deities appeared ugly to her.

"Come home soon," she wrote to Shrinath. "I no longer have the strength to control Bapa. He is going beyond control. If you delay your visit, I'll go away to my parents' place, leaving Bapa in Dama's care. Because I cannot ... any longer ..."

Shrinath, of course, could have come. But Manju's decision to go away to her parents' place leaving father in Dama's care appeared to be a vulgar threat to him. Enraged, he remained unmoved for a few days. He resolved that if Manju did that, she would never be welcome in his house again.

Manju, as a matter of habit, never latched the door to her room fearing that she might not be able to hear if Bapa called out to her. That night, she could not sleep. She felt a sharp biting sensation as if something was gnawing at her. Towards midnight she was about to doze off, when her father-in-law lost his way again and entered her room groping for her as though he was possessed by a spirit to transgress trust, relationships, customs and manners.

Manju, on her part, could not step outside the age old tradition, couldn't say to her father-in-law, "Bapa, there is something called hell. God's eyes can see even in the dark." How could she tell him this, what if her apprehension was baseless – what if her father-in-law had actually only stumbled into her room in the dark? She had screamed "Bapa" and Bhabanath hurried away, dragging himself like a frightened dog. Her own doubts scared her now, like a ghost standing before her. Just after dawn, she left for her parents' place, transgressing all the rules of duty, responsibility and patience. She took leave, touching the feet of her father-in-law, her face covered behind the odhani. She couldn't control her tears. But she turned her heart to stone and sat in the bullock cart that carried her away. They all reproached her – the villagers, one and all. Why, even the plants and the leaves were sympathetic towards the old man! The farm labourer Dama too was furious. How heartless a woman could be! She left the house because she had to look after her father-in-law! Did she not fear her dharma and her karma?

Shrinath came home when he got the news. The old man, meanwhile, hadn't eaten anything – he had been surviving on paduka, the water with which the deities feet have been washed. The corners of his closed eyes were brimming with tears. He would not allow Dama to touch him. He was absolutely quiet. His jaws had got locked. He was staring up at the roof as if looking at the ugly yamadutas waiting for him. The beautiful face of Sabitri appeared to him as the skull in the hand of goddess Kali. He had turned into a statue. Bhabanath had knowledge of god but he was not Brahma, the rishi of the gods. He was but a passionless worldly person. Had he been a rishi, he would have been forgiven all his faults. Lying on his deathbed, full of regret, he recalled the stories of rishi Sourabhi and rishi Chyabana.

Rishi Sourabhi thoughtlessly spent his youth abstaining from sex, but languished in ungratified desire in old age. He threatened King Mandhata of the Ikshu dynasty that unless he was married to the princess, he would curse the king. The king, fearing the curse, married not just one daughter but all his fifty daughters to the rishi. The rishi, with the strength of his spiritual power, regained his youth and enjoyed the wonders of sensual pleasure. Rishi Chyabana married princess Sukanya at a very late age. The Ashwinikumaras, the physicians of heaven, granted youth to the rishi, and the rishi lived happily, relishing the bliss of sensual indulgence. Bhabanath had read many such accounts of aged rishis marrying damsels in the holy shastras. King Dasharatha too had married the young Kaikeyi at a ripe age. Even kings were forgiven hundreds of crimes. But what about Bhabanath? He was called rishi-like but he was not one. He could not marry a young woman by threatening to curse somebody – he did not have such spiritual power. He was not a king either. He was a very ordinary person. All options were closed for him. Before Shrinath had got married, he had had the desire for the company of a woman. But he had flogged his desire with his conscience till it bled, and had looked for a bride for Shrinath instead. On seeing Manju, he had felt only affection. He had not harboured any forbidden thoughts about Manju. Bhabanath himself could not understand why that ugly demon manifested itself, taking advantage of a weak moment just before his death – as though the pleasure of an entire world was escaping him. Manju, to him, was a child. She was younger in age than even his daughter. She was married to his son and was his daughter-in-law. She too had seen that demon in the darkness of that night. Others may not be aware, but Bhabanath was certain that Manju knew he was not saint-like, not father-like, that he was an ugly, horrible demon. O god! The demon had slept all these years when it could have devoured so many! It had survived by consuming prasada and paduka, but it got cursed with mortified skin, nails and teeth by expressing its vain desire to devour and drink blood.

Bhabanath confessed his sin to himself. But he would not be able

to tell this to his son and his daughter-in-law, that to err is human —
that this is how it happens. This was what happened to rishi Chyabana,
to rishi Sourabhi, to king Dasharatha, and to many mahatmas. Only
if he could ask for forgiveness from Manju before dying, he would
feel better. Alas! He could never again muster the courage to look at
that child's unsoiled, pure face. Manju, he was sure, was absolutely
right in going away. One ought not to trust a monster.

He was grateful to Manju and silently wished for her wellbeing.
He was unable to look at his son. He was unable to tell him, "It is not
Manju's fault. The fault lies with this cruel and barbarous old man."
So he kept quiet.

Shrinath, seeing his father in such a pitiable condition, more than
feeling sad, became furious with Manju. "The old master was so
affectionate towards the lady," Dama said. "I have never seen him
nagging her. She nursed him for so long and then abandoned him
when he was about to die. All those years of effort gone waste. After
she left, the old master's jaws got locked. Food no longer goes down
his throat. He is very upset. The lady was more than a daughter to
him. He had given up chanting the name of lord Ram and had started
chanting her name instead."

Bhabanath felt like protesting. He felt like protecting Manju from
needless censure. He felt like whipping himself. But he was unable to
do anything. A lump in the throat blocked all his protests. Old age
had made him helpless. Manju's delicate face stared at him like the
face of the destroyer of Mahishasura. One deviant thought in his old
age had destroyed the self-restraint and piety of his entire life, the
way a slight shaking of the earth destroys a centuries old civilization.
He silently cursed those who had called him pious and encouraged
him in his indifference towards worldly enjoyment. He prayed with a
distressed heart, "God, return me my youth, give me my Sabitri ...
return me my strength and capacity. I want to taste the life of a human

being. I do not want to be a god. If I do not deserve this, then take back my salvation as a punishment for the sinful thoughts of my last days of life. I want another birth ... give me another birth ..." And the pair of lips which had chanted the name of god all its life became still while pleading for rebirth.

Manju came, on hearing the news of his death. She stood near his dead body like a culprit and wept. She could not, however, muster the courage to touch the cold, dead feet of the old man to pay her last respects. The dead body was lifted from the courtyard. She was again the target of censure.

The flow of time carries away so many mistakes of life. Shrinath and Manju lived a happy worldly life. However, Shrinath's stiff, merciless look asked her one question all her life, "Don't you consider yourself to be a culprit before god for what you did to my bapa?" Manju's eyes would then be silent out of decency and honour ... her eyes would show distress for having flouted her duty. In the experiences of Manju, an old woman now, are written the chronicle of so many transgressions of the world. Yet she felt guilty because she could not put up with that disturbance in her mind, that she had gone away abandoning her father-in-law on his deathbed. Did her father-in-law die a lonely man? Manju, with her patience and endurance, could have made his death easier and painless. She had not, however, even given a drop of water to the dying lips of her father-in-law. Every year, while offering pinda during the srarddha of her father-in-law, wrapped in cloth up to her neck and with a pure and holy heart, she knew that his soul wouldn't accept it from her. For she was the culprit. If his integrity had faltered standing at the door of death, Manju, with all her care for him, could have stopped him. Is Manju the culprit? Whom will you ask?

"The Transgression" was originally published in Oriya as "Ullanghan."

Mehndi Bazaar
by Dalbir Chetan
translated by Tripti Jain

I was a frequent visitor to Mitra's home, but his father had never been very friendly or open with me. Whenever I visited them, the entire family would gather around me, but his father would slip away from the room on some pretext or the other. I could not fathom the reason for his annoyance but his indifference always hurt my self-esteem. Every time it happened, I would decide not to go back to the house again, but then after a week or so, Mitra would bring a message from his mother, "Ma was asking about you. Please do come today." The affection his mother showered on me made me obey her summons, and I would go trudging up the mountainous road, despite my reluctance.

I had been visiting Mitra's home for over a year now. When I was first transferred to the highest airport in the world, it had seemed as if I had been exiled. Many others in the Air Force shared my feelings about the place, and friends and acquaintances had come to console me.

I knew that Leh was an extremely cold place, but for the first time I heard someone joke about its harsh, bleak winters. The jokes came like the blast of a fire in winter.

A day before I was to leave for Leh, I met a young man called Virk, whom I knew slightly. Meeting him was a godsend, for he had been just transferred back from Leh and had joined my unit only two days back.

All that I knew about Leh so far was hearsay. But here was Virk, talking from personal experience. He told me that Leh was no longer the Leh of old. There were many more people there now, many Punjabi traders had moved in. "It's a very enjoyable place now," he said, with a wicked laugh. "A bottle of rum is all that you need to sleep with a woman for a whole month. I didn't want to come back. Where else will you get women, beautiful and strong, going so cheap?" He drawled out the last phrase in a manner that made all those present burst out laughing.

It was Virk who told me about Mitra, how large hearted and well connected he was. He insisted that I should call on him and ask for any help I may need. When I left for Leh, he gave me a couple of packets of Bengali rasgullas for Mitra.

When I met Mitra, he struck me as a man whose very presence could drive away any worry and tension. A happy-go-lucky person, fond of travelling and meeting people, he was a well-known government contractor. He had a big contract at the airport. He worked all day long and when evening came, ate and drank with similar gusto.

He had a habit of elucidating his outlook on life when drunk and that too in peculiar English. It took a full bottle of whisky and a whole chicken to satisfy him. As the liquor in the bottle would go down, his use of English would increase. If a friend, tiring of his funny English, told him to shut up, he would laugh loudly and say, "Where is the fun, if you don't speak bloody English while drinking English liquor?"

He had crude, disgusting habits. He would bang his empty glass on the table. His French imperial would get dirty with grease from the chicken. Thumping the table, he would yell "Listen" in a loud voice, compelling those sitting around to pay attention, or else he would pull and push them with his dirty, greasy hands, to make them listen to him.

"Listen," he would say loudly. "A man should work like a bull and eat like a pig. Understand!"

If a new acquaintance happened to look puzzled at his behaviour, he would repeat himself, "What the hell have you understood, yaar? I say that a man should work to the hilt and guzzle like a pig. Now, do you understand?" Those who knew him well knew his habits, and those who were new came to know them soon enough.

The difference between Mitra during the day and Mitra at night was very sharp. He took many liberties when he was drunk and they were difficult to overlook, but most of his friends forgave him for the sake of what he was during the day. If something untoward happened at night, he would seek out the affected friend during the day and apologize for the incident. He would praise him for tolerating his behaviour. "I am like this yaar, but you are great ... you did not react." And the same friend to whom he apologized during the day, he would insult again at night.

I had initially made Mitra's acquaintance because of Virk, but now the acquaintance had deepened into friendship because of his mother. When I met his mother for the first time I was reminded of my mother, and gradually, because of her, I stopped missing my own mother so much. There soon came a time when it seemed to me that I did not go to meet his mother because of Mitra, but that I met Mitra because of his mother. We had nothing in common, yet I liked his company.

He was the district president of the youth wing of a political party, with which I had my differences. He would declaim about the many points programme of his party. I would pretend to listen to his raving for some time but then, when it was difficult to carry on with the pretence any longer, I would press his hand and say, "Mitra, please, that's enough for the day."

"Yaar," he would laugh, "I am really sorry."

If his ranting began during a sitting at night, one was forced to sit through the performance. If one made the mistake of interrupting him, Mitra would lose his temper, and raising his fist, would shout, "I will beat my opponents with my shoe and set them right."

He would often also get into fisticuffs with those who, he felt, did not agree with him.

"He who does not accept my politics," he would say emphatically, "is no friend of mine."

Mitra found it difficult to get along with the other members of his family except his mother. She was a wonderful person. If there was anyone in this world he could not oppose, it was his mother. If there was anything that upset him it was to see her unhappy. His love for his mother made him sentimental about all mothers in the world, and if he saw any mother unhappy his eyes would fill with tears.

He would often recall how much he had missed his mother when he left home for the first time to earn his living. During the journey, a mother had come to see her son off at the station. Standing near the window of the railway coach, she kept pressing her hand on her son's face and head, giving him instructions to write home regularly about his welfare. As the train moved, she kept walking beside the moving train and told him not to worry. But her own face mirrored the anxiety and sadness within her. Mitra had not been able to bear seeing the sadness on her face and broke down as he watched the scene before him.

Mitra had a sister, a young girl who was growing up into a pretty woman. He loved her, but most of the time she behaved like her father. Mitra did not see eye to eye with his father on anything, and he was often irritated with his sister too. Whenever his sister brought her problems to him, he felt that he should hold her hand and help her walk the road of life. But when she sought her father's approval to walk that road, he would get annoyed and would want to break off with her.

His father was a different sort of a man – silent and harsh. At one time he had been in the army, but his own strict code of conduct had made it difficult for him to march alongside the army's code of conduct, and he resigned after a few years.

His son was opposed to all that he had believed in all his life. He had never touched meat or liquor. Mitra, on the other hand, proclaimed that he had to make up for his father, and could not live without them. His father disliked politics and politicking, Mitra revelled in both. The father would be busy with incense and puja in one room, and Mitra would rave and rant against god in the next room. For the father the idea of a woman was sacred, but the son insisted that one needed more than one woman to keep oneself warm in the harsh winters of Leh.

When Mitra had been younger, his father had throttled all attempts at revolt by thrashing him. But now the son was an adult and an affluent man, and his revolt burst forth like lava pouring out from an active volcano.

The mother was the bridge between the two, tolerating her son's disobedience, as also her husband's harshness. She had deep love for both her saintly husband and her happy-go-lucky son. She liked the scent of incense and the tinkling of prayer bells, but did not dislike the laughter and the smell of liquor at Mitra's table. She would keep silent in the company of her morose husband, but blossom with the sound of her son's laughter.

But I was afraid of her husband's silence. Mitra's mother often told me that of all his friends, his father liked only me. Perhaps because I did not smoke or drink. Whenever I met him, I joined my hands in a namaskar. I bowed respectfully to the gods and goddesses in his puja room and this meant a great deal to him, for it made him happy to see a young man follow old traditions in these irreverent days. But despite all this, he kept his distance from me because of his strained relations with Mitra.

Mitra was involved in a big construction project and was also a witness to the big changes taking place all around him. This was the need of the hour, after the Chinese aggression. New buildings were rising all around, cantonments were being set up, a network of roads was being laid, electric poles were being erected and new connections were being made everywhere. At the airport new runways were being constructed.

All this meant an increase in the number of troops posted in Leh, which, in turn, meant an expansion of the amenities available.

The lives of the people in the valley were undergoing revolutionary changes. People were taking up new jobs, there had been an increase in the number of shops – from paan bidi shops to general merchants and restaurants. A new culture was developing. There was greater social interaction at all levels. People dressed differently and young girls and women had become more fashion conscious. The new environment was very attractive and appealed to one and all. Many young army feet overstepped the barbed wires of army discipline and succeeded in reaching the young beauties of the valley, and many a beautiful face found its way to the bedrooms of sahabs. Homes in the valley were flooded with gifts from army men and liquor from the cantonment. Mitra's father watched all this and became more and more morose and bitter.

When Mitra talked about the development all around to his cronies, his father thought that there was something right in what was being said. There was a distinct change in the lives of the people. They were living better and eating better. They led more comfortable lives, had better homes, their faces were brighter than before. But the price paid by them for this progress, in his opinion, was too heavy.

It may not be clear to many, yet it seemed to him that the winds of change would ultimately sweep away everything before them.

The differences between father and son deepened with time. The only link between them was the mother. She tried her utmost to keep the family together. The father and son hardly spoke to each other. If there was anything that was important or necessary to be communicated or asked, Mitra's mother was the channel of communication. And if this led to acrimony then it was her presence that kept tempers in control. His mother's scolding was enough to silence Mitra.

That day, when I reached his house, the air was heavy with tension. Something unpleasant had obviously occurred. The mother as usual welcomed me with a smile, but she was not her normal self either. The father greeted me but his face was drawn in harsh and rigid lines. Mitra was already at his table, much before his usual time.

What had happened was that the father had tried to erect more barriers around the family, and Mitra had opposed this. The father had accepted the revolt of the son, but when he saw the same signs in his growing daughter he could not take it. Every small thing she did was criticized. Every step the young girl took outside her home was watched. The way she dressed, the physical changes her growing body was undergoing, were all regarded with suspicion. This was unacceptable to Mitra.

The father felt that not just his daughter but every young girl in the valley was on the road to hell. The people of the valley were still traditional, but no such considerations of respect or shame restrained the people of the cantonment.

He still remembered the time he had spent in the army. He had kept himself strictly within limits. Despite all his preoccupations he had stuck to his regimen of daily prayers. He had not touched liquor either then or at any other time in his life. If there was loose talk about women he would leave that company.

An incident had taken place when he was posted at Hyderabad. He heard a great deal of talk about a newly arrived young and innocent girl in Mehndi Bazaar, and all that talk impelled him to visit the bazaar. He went there with a great deal of trepidation. The friend who had taken him tried to keep his courage up, but he felt as if his feet had turned to lead. He kept his head down as if he was carrying a heavy load. His friend had left him with the girl. He felt lost and wanted to ask the young and delicate girl, how she could survive in that place where it had been difficult for him to walk even a few steps. But he could not say anything and felt as if his lips were sealed. Finally, in an attempt to make conversation, he had ended up by blurting out that very question. She burst out laughing.

"This is the one place where I and those like me can walk with our heads held high."

Her laughter had shamed him. He sat with his head down, blinking his eyes. Then, getting up hurriedly, he said, "I came only to say that you should leave this place immediately."

"But where can I go?" The girl was still laughing.

"Anywhere," was his reply, as he got up to leave.

"But I have come here from a similar place." The girl was still laughing, but now she also seemed to be crying. Later, she had told the friend who had accompanied him, "Don't bring such preachers here. It spoils my trade."

He had been there for only a short time but he remembered the girl's face, her hazel eyes and mannerisms very clearly. Even now when he saw a girl laughing and happy, his thoughts would go back to that lovely face and he would feel that he was back in Mehndi Bazaar.

It seemed to him that the whole valley had become a Mehndi Baazar. He was aware of the fact that wherever there was a cantonment, such a bazaar sprang up alongside. This bazaar may be a very small part of the whole town, occupying only a lane or even a half. But it seemed to him as if the whole valley had turned into a Mehndi Bazaar, and every laughing girl appeared to be waiting for customers. The laughter of his own young daughter reminded him of the laughter of that girl, and he tried to raise walls of restraint and control around her. Sometimes he would think, if a person like him, abstemious by nature, could have flouted the bonds of restraint and control, then why wouldn't those who were not so inclined? The very idea drove him to the edge of despair. He did not know what he should do to save the valley from the fire raging all around. He wanted to put up a barricade that enclosed the whole valley, which even the wind from outside would not be able to breach. Ultimately, he realized that the valley apart, if he could at least save his own family from this hell, it would be enough for him.

The situation that was developing in his family challenged him. What he had hated in others during his days in the army, his own son enjoyed. He abhorred the brazenness that characterized the behaviour of people around him and wanted to spit on their faces whenever anything indecent or obscene was said or done. He was not willing to accept the fact that his own daughter was about to attend an army party with her brother and had not even sought his permission.

This had led to a clash between father and son. Whatever affection existed between them seemed to have been destroyed and thrown into the deep of the valley. The son had always praised the development and progress that was taking place all over the valley and the lifestyle generated by this development. He believed that the valley had become more beautiful, while the father averred that the virgin valley had been violated and soiled. The recriminations led to tension and heat at home. Both tried to overcome this tension in their own ways – the father, by turning to prayer, and the son, to drink.

An almost empty bottle on the table showed that Mitra had been at it for quite some time now. It was futile to talk to him at present. The father sat in the next room reading a religious book, with an electric heater beside him. I thought it better to sit with the mother in her room and talk about inconsequential things.

A constant murmur could be heard from Mitra's room, but we ignored it. It was his habit to mutter to himself, especially when he was drinking alone. But suddenly the murmur turned into a boom. "Remember, all the comforts you enjoy are due to modern developments. If you like all these comforts then you must accept the defects that accompany them. It's a package, understand!"

There was a loud thud, the sound of the empty glass being banged on the table.

It was embarrassing to be there. I was afraid there would be bitter recriminations from the puja room now, and that would make my situation even more embarrassing. Mitra's mother caught hold of my hand and took me to her husband's room. Perhaps it was her way of stopping her husband from retorting. And of letting him know that I was there.

Mitra's outburst had been heard by his father, and he was hitting his forehead with his hand. She stood before him with folded hands and implored, "For god's sake, don't say anything. Things will sort themselves out." Ignoring her, he made me sit beside him and in a normal voice said, "It seems you are very proud of the changes taking place and the new culture spawned by them. But I ask you, what has all this given us? All this that you see around here," pointing to his son's room, he continued, "you must realize that we are paying a very heavy price."

He placed the book in his hands on a small stool in front of the idols and went on, "Let me tell you about our time. If a girl did not come home at night, then the parents thought she was with a girlfriend." His tone betrayed his agitation. "But now the situation is different. This new culture of yours has turned the whole valley into a brothel and you pride yourself on this progress!" His voice was rising, adding to the mother's agitation. She opened the door softly and went into Mitra's room.

I knew she would plead with her son not to say anything, and say that things would sort themselves out. And this would soften him and avert the clash between the two for some time.

However, this time, it seemed that Mitra was in no mood for a compromise. His drunken raving had become serious, "Look Ma, I am a businessman, and I love markets. Whenever there is a change there are bound to be problems. But you cannot stop change." Holding her folded hands in his own, he asked her, "Ma, tell me, what walls will you raise against the sun? Do you know that the rays of the rising sun are accompanied by many dangerous and poisonous rays?"

His mother knew no such thing. But she knew and remembered very well how, when she was young, not in any Mehndi Bazaar but in this, her own valley, the mehndi even on her feet had turned scorchingly hot.

"Mehndi Bazaar" was originally published in Punjabi (India) as "Mehndi Bazaar."

Cracks in the Heart
by Farkhanda Lodhi
translated by Bhushan Arora

With the crack of the bullet, the dove would flutter to the ground and never draw another breath. This trauma had been inflicted on her by her own kind. The kites and the crows — may their tribe be wiped out — who were birds like her, had done this out of some kind of spite. These birds which sailed the swift breezes of the deep blue skies had eyed her nest from the day she had laid her first egg ... while she sat hatching her eggs oblivious of the whole world and of all that was happening around her.

She had made her nest in the arjun tree at the advice of her mate. The arjun, also known as the sukhchain. She knew she would be safe in the thick grid-like branches of the sukhchain because no kite or crow would be able to spy her nest through its dense foliage. She would see her chicks emerge from the eggs without any evil eye falling on them ... they would fill her nest with the primeval song of their cheeping. And when they grow up and start cooing and huq-hoing, how thrilled she would be that this immortal song was being sung by her — or another dove's — offspring! In fact, all doves sing the same message to the same tune, a song of basic truth ... a song of love, and peace, and coexistence, huq-ho, huq-ho.

She had taken all possible precautions to protect herself and her offspring and had chosen to build her nest near the end of a thin branch to put it out of the reach of prowling cats. Human children, on their way back from school, played in the shade of the sukhchain and raised quite a racket. The dove would watch happily while the children played their many boisterous games, and showered them with blessings from the core of her heart. The children too felt happy as they watched the dove flit in and out of her nest. They had known this dove and her mate for a long time. They would watch the two birds as they flew rapidly against the blue sky, and in the evenings when the doves settled on the thin top branches of a eucalyptus tree to swing away the day's tensions, they would gleefully watch the birds and point them out to each other. So impressed were they by the birds' antics that one day a delicate young girl burst out, "Oh, oh! How I wish I were a dove!"

"No, child! God has given you life among the noblest of his creatures ... give thanks." The girl's father had gently chided his daughter for her blasphemous outburst.

Just then the noise of a burst of Kalashnikov fire opened up from the college building across the street. Father and daughter ran into their house, and the dove and her mate flew off into the sky ... The burst of bullets was not aimed at them ... The bullets were flying from right to left and left to right and the raining continued for a long time. The birds began to get tired of being continuously on the wing. It was getting dark, and the time to rest and relax was approaching but peace was not returning to earth. What were they to do? The pair of doves got distressed. Which branch of which tree would they be able to roost on tonight? It was then that they espied the sukhchain tree and one after the other came down to hide in its thick foliage.

The male dove addressed his mate, "Bhaagwaané! Build the nest in this tree. It's nice and green, the branches are crisscrossed closely, and it has many thick clumps of leaves to hide in."

"All right!" she answered. "But go to sleep now, it's quite late."

"Bhaliya loké," the male dove replied, "there is no sleep in my eyes ... my heart is heavy ... who knows what is going to happen ... These bullets don't seem to stop ... have these people lost their reason? Both sides seem to be firing nonstop."

"Does it matter to us? Let them go to hell." The female dove's only concern was sleep at that time. She was feeling very drowsy.

After some time, there was a loud explosion, vrroooooom ... of a huge bomb somewhere. The birds resting in the trees flew out in all directions, screeching in alarm and floundering and crashing into each other in the dark in search of refuge ... Everything seemed to be shaking and trembling. Was that an earthquake or was it the end of the world? People had come out of their houses and were making such a noise! This was soon followed by vehicles rushing on the roads with their sirens blaring. Vooh ... hooh ... hooh ... hooh. There was noise everywhere, utter bedlam! What with the whoosh of the vehicles and the shouting of the people, the birds could not get even a wink of sleep the whole night through. After the blast, they settled wherever they could find room. The dove could not see her mate anywhere nearabout. Tired and apprehensive, she waited for him anxiously, shivering and dozing, and waking, through the night. The cataclysmic moment passed but it left wails and screams behind ... fear settled in every heart.

At last dawn appeared on leaden feet. The muezzin called as the first streaks of silver appeared in the eastern sky and the rays of the newly risen sun slowly devoured the darkness. As the insects and birds started their early morning chorus, the dove took wing and flew here and there in search of her mate. She noticed that a crowd of people, young and old, had gathered under her sukhchain tree, and a child was saying, "Abba, this dove's heart must have failed. It seems to have died from the shock of the blast."

"Forget it, beté! Don't talk so big," his father told him as he nudged the body of the dove's dead mate with his foot ... The boy immediately moved his father's foot aside and picked up the little body. "I am telling you Abba, it's heart must have failed, because last night there was no storm or rain ... and it was neither too hot or cold ..." The boy was no less a detective than 007. The father cut him short. "So, the poor bird died of shock ... what else? Its days were done, throw it away somewhere," he said carelessly pointing toward a clump of grass and weeds.

"No. I want to bury it in a grave."

"Why?"

"Because ... because ..." the boy could not clearly articulate his reasons.

Meanwhile his mother came and joined them, her head uncovered, in a state of agitation. She was carrying the day's newspaper and reading from it as she walked. "See how many people died from the bomb blast last night," she said as she came to stand beside her husband. But the boy, intent on his own concern, was pulling his father and saying, "Come Abba, let's dig the dove's grave. Otherwise the cat will tear it to bits ... the ants will eat it."

"Let, them, yaar!"

The father and son dug a small hole a little distance away. The boy laid the carcass of the dove's mate in the hole, covered it with sukhchain leaves, made a small heap of earth on top and sprinkling water on it said, "I'll put a plant above it, a narcissus. The narcissus has an eye, that's why."

"Children should not be too clever," said the father with some impatience. By now the whole family had gathered around the newspaper.

"The fire which was raging outside has been brought in," the father roared angrily. "We are playing with fire."

"Unheard of, illogical problems are coming up," the mother, quite distraught, continued agitatedly, "and people are dying unnecessarily."

"But those people say these dead are martyrs," the elder daughter interjected.

"Which people?" the mother asked.

Ignoring her mother's question, she turned to her father, "In which account will these deaths be entered?"

The father, fully absorbed in the newspaper now, replied, "These are poor, oppressed, helpless people."

"Are poor, oppressed, helpless people of no account?"

"To lay down the status of the dead is the job of the Maulvis. I am just a small time teacher."

"Hai, Hai, may these tyrants lose their all," the boy's mother was wailing as she looked at the pictures in the newspaper. The boy had only one thought in his mind. What would happen to the dove that was left behind?

Many days passed. The dove rearranged the bits of sticks and straw in her nest all by herself and when it was done to her satisfaction, she laid her eggs and sat down to hatch them. One morning when she returned from her flight in search of food, she was assailed by the popping sounds of bullets. Today, they were coming from all directions. The boys and girls of the college as well as the pedestrians on the street were running helter-skelter in search of safety. The dove, too, flew away from her nest. When the hail of bullets stopped, she saw that hordes of kites and crows were flying around her sukhchain tree. Alarmed about the safety of her eggs, she plummeted in their midst like a rock. Many of them chased after her, and as one of them pierced her wing, she fell down, wounded. The crows hovered around her, and she found refuge under a bamboo fence where the crows, kites, and cats, could not get at her. The bullets kept flying throughout the day. She remained where she was till evening, waiting for the crows and kites to return to their roosts for the night.

Suddenly, calm descended all around as the sun set. The muezzin called, Allah ho Akbar ... Allah ho Akbar. It was not easy for her to come out through the bamboo slats of the fence as the feathers of her wounded wing were drooping like a fan and needles of pain shot through her chest as she tried to stumble out. The little boy had somehow seen her and he now came running out of the house. "Abba! ... Abba! The other dove is dying too."

"No ... No, son! Don't go out ... there are bullets flying all around," a voice called out to stop him.

The child picked up the dove, and kissed it gently.

"I won't let it die ... won't let it die," he crooned.

The little boy's sister quickly brought some water and poured it down the dove's throat. Then they arranged the feathers of the wounded wing, applied a poultice of mustard oil and turmeric, and secured it with a bandage. They placed her under a basket turned upside down in a warm corner of their room for the night. They left a sprinkling of broken rice and a small bowl of water beside her. For half the night, the little boy kept getting up to look at the dove by torchlight. The dove opened her eyes each time he lit the torch and the boy was reassured that all was well with her.

The dove was fine in the morning. When the boy was leaving for school, he put her in the empty chicken run of the lawn, so that she could move about freely and the warm rays of the sun could comfort her aching wing. When he returned from school, however, the run was empty. Tears of alarm clouded his eyes. Where had she gone? Who undid the latch, he wondered, as he walked all round the chicken run. Finding it secure on all sides, he called out psst! ... psst! ... near the bamboo lattice, and the dove came tottering out. This time blood was oozing out of her other wing and she looked quite unwell. The boy picked her up in his palms again and called out to his sister who came running.

The dove's wing had a lacerated wound this time. The boy ran his eyes over the enclosure wondering who could have hurt her, or how she could have got hurt. He then realized what he had not noticed in the morning in his hurry to go to school – the wire mesh was somewhat wider in one spot. It was evident from the soft feathers which had got caught in the wire there that the dove had hurt herself trying to escape through that opening.

"Free birds cannot remain in captivity, Veer," his sister told him as she dressed the wing with the mustard oil poultice. "A dove least of all."

"Why?"

"Because Liberty is its other name, child!"

"Is that so?" he asked in surprise. "Then Baji, after she gets well, I'll set Liberty free."

"Is that a promise?"

"Yes," the boy replied, looking up at his sister.

"Sure?" She was shocked to see tears in her little brother's eyes.

"Yes. Sure!" the boy replied with complete sincerity as he put the dove under the basket for the night. A deep depression boiled within him and assailed him without.

The boy slept more soundly than usual that night. Maybe because he had had a disturbed sleep the night before, or perhaps because he was sad the dove had got hurt again. As soon as he woke the next morning, he rushed to the basket and lifted it. The dove lay dead ... since ... who knew when? "Baji! Liberty is dead ... Liberty is dead!" the boy shrieked as he clung to his sister, "Liberty is dead, Baji!"

The boy's mournful cries echoed through the house and the high ceilings of British vintage resonated loudly with his screams of "Liberty is dead ... Liberty is dead." Their parents came running agitatedly enquiring, "What has happened? What ..." The hysterical screams of the boy had inflicted countless cracks on the placid, mirror-like morning ambience of the household.

Today they haven't sent their son to school. Not because the dove has died and the little boy is sad, but because there is a rain of fire outside ... all previous records of shooting are being broken. Bullets are flying constantly, from right to left and left to right ... from left to right ... and right to left ...

"Cracks in the Heart" was originally published in Punjabi (Pakistan) as "Hirdey Wich Tararein."

A Desire to see the Sky
by Motilal Jotwani
translated by Nandita Bhavnani

Today, in the coal mine, Kalu seemed to be in complete despair. He had not been able to sleep at all the previous night. He had spent the entire night tossing and turning in bed. This morning, when he left for work, his wife Mohina hadn't been at home to give him his lunch – a few rotis and a whole onion, wrapped in paper.

It hadn't been very long since Kalu got married to Mohina. Before his marriage the sun and its light had not been very different for him from the harsh bulb-light in the coal mine. Whether inside the mine or outside it, it had hardly made any difference to him. This morning he again felt that the world outside was also a giant coal mine, in which people wearing bright clean clothes go about doing black deeds.

This morning on his way to the mine from home, Kalu had confided in his close friend, Karmu, about how Mohina had left his life. He had also told him how he had had sunlight in his life for just a short while. During those days, he would get up from bed full of life, and Mohina would bring him a cup of tea. He would look out at the gentle sunlight through the window and inside he would gaze at the gentle smile on Mohina's face. The sunlight and the smile – how similar they are! But no – just then he realized that, apart from those few days, he had spent all his life in the mine in a dark black room, with no window and the door of which was always shut.

Now, in the coal mine, seeing Kalu totally immersed in thought, Karmu asked him, "Why Kalu, don't you think that Mohina will come back to you? Your heart shines like a diamond – she will never be able to stay with this babu of the coal mining company ..."

A deep sigh escaped Kalu. He retorted, "If she saves herself and comes back, then Karmu, my future will be bright. She should come back safe and sound. But ..."

His "but" expressed the uncertainty of the situation. Along with the "but" his thoughts took flight again. He was lost in himself, thinking all kinds of things ... Mohina and he, along with their fellow workers, work together in this mine in Ranikhet. He mines coal and also helps in transporting it up, and she loads the transported coal on to the rail wagons together with the other women workers. Thanks to this coal, trains run on steam, hearths are lit in homes, and clothes get ironed. And the babus of the mining company dress up in these ironed clothes and ensnare these women workers in their traps.

Thinking this, his eyes shone like embers. But soon these embers were covered over with the ashes of his helplessness and vulnerability. After all, what could he do? Even if the babu, wearing ironed clothes, had done something wrong in making Mohina come to him, what was right about what Mohina herself had done? Last night, when he was returning to the workers' colony with the other workers, he had seen the faint light of the coal company's bulbs in the lanes, and the even fainter light of bulbs in the houses. Bright bulbs shine only in the mine or, outside it, in the colony where the mine officials and babus live. The houses in the workers' colony are lit only by love ... but if that too is not there, what then?

Last night, while returning home, he had wanted to quicken his pace. But since he was with the other workers, he had to walk slowly. They were all tired out. But he wasn't tired, he was worried. And in this worry lay his hurry. As a last warning, he had told Mohina that she should stop working in the mine and keep away from that babu. She could get work elsewhere, there are many mines in Ranikhet ...

But she had gone away instead and darkness had descended all around him.

Now, working listlessly in the mine, Kalu felt that having spent the whole day here, he too had turned into a piece of coal. Karmu had said that his heart shines like a diamond. But until he could bathe himself with soap and wash off the coal-black, until then who could glance inside his heart to see the shine of the diamond? Mohina had not been able to wait. Did she know that coal and diamond are true brothers, both born in the same mine?

Now, who was there for him in this world? For whom was he to stay alive? A desire to die unfolded itself within Kalu's heart. Couldn't an accident happen here like the accident in the Chashnala mines? Some time back, due to a sudden flooding of the Chashnala mines, around four hundred workers had drowned. If such an accident were to take place here too, he would be able to free himself from this life of despair, a life in which nobody belongs to anybody. But how could this happen? As in every other mine, in this mine too, the owners have made all provisions for the safety of the workers. And this was for the benefit of the owners, that the workers would not fall prey to accidents, but would continue to make more and more money for them.

A moment is enough for everything to change. Suddenly an uproar went up in the mine. From all directions the workers began running to climb a slope at the other end of the mine. The level above the one at which they were mining coal had become water logged after the coal had been fully mined. This water had then burst forth and gushed down to the lower level. That level of the mine too was soon flooded with water. Perhaps this was the moment Kalu had been waiting for. He stood immobile.

But how long could he stand immobile? Running to save themselves, his fellow workers coming up from behind began pushing to go further and further up the slope. And in this melee, stumbling and tripping, Kalu too reached the top. When he turned around, he saw some of his fellow workers were being carried away by the water and were shouting "Help! help!" He hurried down the slope. But by the time he reached the water to try and help them, these coworkers had drowned in the water that flooded the mine. Who were they? Unlike him, they had not wanted to die and escape this unhappy world! They had been caught by surprise and engulfed by the first onslaught of the rushing water. But now the desire to live had Kalu in its grip. Now he didn't want to unnecessarily endanger his life. He thought of those men, drowning in the water and trying to survive by flailing their arms and legs. Retracing his steps, he slowly began to climb up the slope again, and lost himself in the chaotic crowd of the survivors. He saw that they were all safe together. They all half-breathed a sigh of relief. Worried about what would happen next, the other half-breath remained stifled in their chests. He looked into everyone's faces. Coal-black faces! They were like pieces of coal themselves — small and big, thin and fat. There was space in their faces only for their eyes, eyes in which feelings of hope and despair showed up distinctly.

The overseer hurried a short way down the slope to reach the telephone and conveyed to the mine office upstairs the news of the accident — that due to a sudden flood, the workers were stuck on this slope in the mine. After this, the telephone began to ring feverishly at short intervals. Kalu thought, the people upstairs are worried about those of us down here ... which means that they have not forgotten us helpless and defenceless people.

Out of habit, the overseer looked for his attendance register. But it had been carried away by the water. He began to call out everyone's name from memory. A worker's name was called out, and in response that worker said, "Yes." A name ... "Yes," a name ... "Yes."

But the call for Diplo was not answered by a "yes." There was another call for him. No response. Had young and strong Diplo left this world? Had he been immersed in the water, had he taken jalsamadhi? A sharp intake of breath escaped everyone's lips. But the gasp remained stifled in Kalu's chest.

A name ... "Yes," a name ... "Yes."

No response to the call for Karmu. Another call was made for him. There was still no response. Had the saint-like Karmu also said farewell to this world? Another sharp and sorrowful intake of breath filled the mine, but the same confusion continued in Kalu's chest. Karmu's image rose before his eyes. How much faith he had had, that Mohina would return ...

And through all this the calling out of names continued. A name ... "Yes," a name ... and in response, "Yes." But after the absence of Karmu's answer, Kalu withdrew into himself like a deaf-mute.

Suffocated, choked on the half-breath, Kalu kept thinking about god knows what. He was no longer aware that the overseer was continuing to register the attendance of the surviving workers in the mine. Among the names to which there was no answering "yes," and at which sharp intakes of breath were audible, was his own name!

The telephone kept ringing feverishly and the overseer kept talking on the telephone. Then, as the workers' colony received the news, other workers and their families joined in the phone calls, back and forth. In such a large world, who did Kalu have to talk to? Whom did he have to inform of his survival? He stood, like a statue, in a corner.

The overseer had a big problem. There were fifty five people there, but every time, the attendance recorded only fifty four people. The people in the office upstairs kept asking him, "Have you counted yourself? If you have, then who is this fifty fifth person? There were a total of sixty one people in the mine ... So what happened to the remaining six? Have they ...?"

At night, it became colder in the mine. Darkness is in any case cold. On top of this, death was in the air. Death too is cold. As is inertia. Darkness, death and inertia – because of the cold, many workers in the mine fell ill.

Three worlds had come into existence by now. The netherworld, where the workers were. The earth, from where they hoped to get help. And the heavens, to which the people on earth look for succour in times of trouble. The people of the netherworld, keeping the map of their world in mind, informed the people on earth where exactly they were stuck.

In a few hours, by the next morning, an eight inch wide tunnel was dug through the roof of the mine through which food, clean water and medicines were sent down to the people stuck in the mine. In fact, three years earlier, engineers had had a two inch boring done above this mine as an experiment in order to find out whether mining could be started from the other end of the mine or not. They had not been able to start at the other end of the mine but at this time of crisis they increased the two inch boring to eight inches to send down necessities.

The thought gradually filtered through to Kalu's consciousness that the people on earth were like angels of mercy to those in trouble below. He felt that people are not always self-absorbed, they do look after each other.

Just then the overseer, in a loud voice, announced to all of them that the mine officials would make a twenty four inch bore into which they would put a steel casing, so that the tunnel would be surrounded by a steel wall. They would then lower a capsule, seventeen inches round and six and a half feet tall – taller than a man – inside this steel casing. "One by one, we will all go up in this capsule."

Kalu stood there sadly. Smiles appeared on everyone else's face. The overseer had given them really good news.

The telephone rang again and the overseer left halfway to answer it. Returning quickly, he stared hard into each worker's face. Coming close to Kalu, he said, "You have really given us trouble. You are the fifty fifth person. Now hurry up, go and talk to your wife Mohina on the telephone."

"Mohina? ... Has she come back?" Kalu asked, shouting.

"Yes, hurry up. She can't wait to talk to you. She said again and again to inform you that she has come back to you, safe and sound ..."

Now the fifty fifth person, Kalu, suddenly felt safe together with the other fifty four survivors, and finally breathed the suppressed half-sigh of relief. A desire was born in him, to see the sky.

"A Desire to See the Sky" was originally published in Sindhi (India) as "Akash Disan Ji Chahna."

The Bird
by Amar Jalil
translated by Mohan H Keswani

Mmy mother roused me in the middle of the night and whispered, "There is a dangerous bird sitting on a branch of the neem tree in the compound outside."

Turning over, I said, "It must be an owl, Amma, go back to sleep."

"It is not an owl," she insisted.

"If it's not an owl, it must be one of its relatives."

Since I had been fast asleep when she woke me, I could barely keep my eyes open. I mumbled, "Let me sleep, Amma."

She shook me violently, and shot back, "How can I let you sleep when there is a dangerous bird sitting on the neem tree outside?"

For the first time in my life, after many big recommendations, I had recently secured an officer's post in the department of population planning, the original and generic name of the department of family planning. To celebrate my newly acquired status, I had bought myself a large tin of Romeo and Juliet luxury talcum powder. I would dust my body liberally with it before retiring for the night and drop off to sleep fantasizing about a beautiful and charming lady health visitor. When Amma woke me up in the middle of that night to tell me about the fearsome bird sitting on a branch of the neem tree in our front compound, I had been dreaming of a beautiful lady health visitor called Gazal gadding about with an executive officer, while I played a folk tune on my flute. Amma shattered this dream and I was really upset. It fleetingly crossed my mind to upbraid her and tell her clearly how wrong it was to wake up a Sindhi officer from his sleep, even if he happened to be her son, because this post had come after so many recommendations. I did not voice my thoughts, however, and composed myself to go back to sleep again. Seeing this, Amma caught me by the arm and shouted, "You are a strange fellow! I have just told you there is a dangerous bird sitting on a branch of the neem tree outside, and even after hearing this, you turn over and try to go to sleep!"

"Oh! For heaven's sake, Amma! You're troubling me for nothing," I said, feeling very annoyed. "It must be an owl, or a bat, or some such bird or the soul of Khalifa Haroon-ul-Rashid, disguised as one."

"No, no," she insisted, "It is neither an owl nor a bat – it is a very dangerous bird."

"Is it standing on one leg?" I asked, hoping to divert her.

"No."

"Is it talking?"

"No."

"Then, Mother dear, be assured that the bird sitting on the branch of the neem tree outside is definitely not dangerous," I said, thinking I had set her mind at rest. "Please calm down and go back to sleep."

Amma, however, was wide awake. She went to the window and stood staring fixedly at the neem tree in the compound. I suggested that we should turn off the light in the compound, explaining, "The compound will be dark then, and you will neither see the tree nor the branch on which you have seen that dangerous bird."

Khalifa Haroon-ul-Rashid: A legendary Caliph who used to travel through his realm incognito by night to personally observe how his subjects were faring.

"I have already seen the dangerous bird and even in the dark, I will feel its presence," she replied, coming back from the window.

"You are imagining things," I told her, and got up. "What do you want me to do about this dangerous bird?"

She stood facing me quietly for several moments – just staring at me unblinkingly, saying nothing. I found this very unnerving and experienced an eerie sensation as though wax was boiling and melting under my skin and trickling thickly through its layers. Hiding my unease, I asked her, "So, what do you want me to do about this dangerous bird?"

She was silent.

Suddenly I felt that I was face to face with an unknown woman, a stranger. In the stillness and dark of the night she looked like an apparition. I felt a peculiar, unidentifiable fear enter my being. Then I heard Amma's voice, "Kill the bird."

"What? Kill the bird?" I gaped at her.

"Yes," she said. "This is the bird that has thwarted you at every step in the past, and this is your very last chance. Kill the bird sitting on the tree."

"Listen to me, Amma," I said, trying to break out of the unhealthy miasmal spell. "I neither believe in these old wives' tales nor in ghosts and phantoms."

Amma's face contorted in anger and her eyes narrowed. Without batting an eyelid she said, "Silly boy, this is not mere folklore. It is history, as real as hard cash of the past and gold of the future."

"But what does history have to do with this bird?"

"The same it has to do with you and me."

"I don't understand a word of what you're saying. I am going to sleep," I said.

"Whenever that bird has been seen, you have been asleep," she said, adding, "this is the last confrontation and you have to kill the bird, or it will kill you."

Her words made me wonder if she was talking to herself incoherently ... because she was eighty years old and had finally gone senile.

"You must kill the bird," she repeated. Going to the cupboard, she took out the double barrelled gun, loaded it, and handing it to me, said again, "Go kill the bird."

I took the gun and looking at her, asked, "If I kill the bird, will my job not be in danger? You know that I have got this job after many recommendations!"

Amma became livid. She snatched the gun from me with shaking hands and spat out in a withering tone, "In the past, you were never the inattentive idiot and fool you seem to have become now, and although I know you are my son, your strange behaviour is making me doubt even that."

Sleep had deserted me by this time and all I could do was to stare at her uncomprehendingly! Amma proceeded towards the compound and said, "I am going to kill the bird myself and I think from now on, you should wear the bangles."

She marched out of the room and took position in the middle of the compound. I ran out after her and stood behind her. She had raised the gun to her shoulder and was in the process of taking aim at the branch on which she had seen the dangerous bird. I too caught sight of it then, and was shocked to see that the bird my mother had declared dangerous was just a brown dove! Grabbing the gun barrel, I told her, "Amma, the bird sitting on the neem branch is a dove, a bird which represents peace."

"That is the bird that is most dangerous to us, it is the enemy of our very existence," she said, roughly brushing my hand aside. "I have to kill it."

But before she could pull the trigger, I reached out and turned off the light. The compound was plunged in darkness.

"Oh, what have you done, you fool?" Amma yelled.

I heard the whirr of the bird's wings as it flew away.

I turned the light on. Amma wailed, in a voice filled with pain, anger and sorrow, "What did you do? ... Oh, what did you do?"

In an attempt to pacify her I said, "Amma, this is a cantonment area. The noise of the gunshot would have woken up the army personnel and I might have lost my job. After all, I have become an officer after many recommendations!"

Removing the cartridges from the gun, she threw them aside and handing the empty gun to me said, "Son, I am not putting a curse on you, but I fear that after some time you will lose the use of your arms and legs and become a cripple. You can then use this gun for support in place of a walking stick."

I looked at the branch of the neem tree and felt happy that the bird had flown away unharmed and unhurt.

"The Bird" was originally published in Sindhi (Pakistan) as "Pakhi."

The Wild Buffalo
by Piyaseeli Wijemanne
translated by Chiranthi Rajapakse

Hell ...! Hell! ... ah ... Doctor, Good morning!"

"...?"

"Yes, yes, ha ha! Am I bothering you? You visit your ward at this time, don't you?"

"...?"

"No, no ... but since you have told me to phone you if I have a problem ..."

"...?"

"I feel bad about troubling you. I'm very sorry ..."

"...?"

"Sure. Thank you. I ... I ... I don't know whether I should take this seriously, but I don't feel well. I have a heavy head. I have no appetite. I can't sleep ... Doctor, you aren't busy are you? I hope I'm not troubling you. Samawenna Doctor."

"...?"

"Thank you. Before she went to work today even my wife suggested that I should consult you."

"...?"

"From a phone booth. My wife gave me her card. She of course holds all the cards. Phone card, SET card, PET card. I too had a wallet stuffed with cards before I lost my job. Finally I was left with only my identity card. Now I've lost that too."

"...?"

"Yes, it's lost. I don't know how or where I lost it. An identity card is like no other card, Doctor. Wherever I go they ask me for my ID. When I tell them who I am, they pretend not to hear me. They ask me for my ID again. I'm sure this is someone's trick to paralyze me. I suspect it's my wife's, but she says I'm responsible for my lost identity."

"...?"

"My sickness? Am I being a nuisance?"

"...?"

"Are you sure? Thank you. Mm ... mm ..."

"...?"

"It's not really a sickness, Doctor. I can't sleep. After tossing and turning for hours I finally drift off to sleep. And then you know what happens? I have terrible dreams, nightmares. I jerk back into consciousness. Doctor, I have the same dream most of the time."

"...?"

"Mm ... I really don't know whether I should. You'll think I'm crazy."

"...?"

"Sure? Nooo ... I always dream that I am being chased by a wild buffalo. Sometimes I see it glaring at me from a distance, a huge black beast about to charge. Even though I'm carrying something like a gun, I have no chance of saving myself. By the time I take aim, he is upon me. He has already mauled me into a mangled heap. It's terrible, Doctor."

"...?"

"Why not? I've seen wild buffaloes at Yala. I've also seen them in films."

"...?"

"Yes, yes, I dream of wild buffaloes almost every other night. I'm telling you, Doctor, one night a wild buffalo was glaring at me menacingly and I looked around trying to see which way I could escape. When I looked back, the buffalo was nowhere to be seen. In his place stood a woman!"

"...?"

"Ha, ha ... hee, hee ... ho, ho, ho. What a joke! Ané, my sides are splitting with laughter. A she-buffalo, you say? Ha, ha ... Jokes apart, Doctor, do you know who that woman was?"

"...?"

"Ha, ha, hee, hee, ho ho ... It was my wife standing there. Hee ... hee ... hello! Hello ... hello ... Doctor?"

"..."

"..."

"..."

"Yes. Of course. Why not? Why!"

"..."

"..."

"..."

"Chi chi ... no, no, I've not misunderstood my wife. Listen."

"..."

"True, true."

"..."

"..."

"..."

"Absolutely true. I agree with what you say. Yes, but how can my wife be more important than I am? I agree with you, Doctor. Yes, yes. She's a bank officer and a graduate. But if I had my job what would my position have been? I would have drawn my pay cheque, bought the groceries, met all my son's demands for money and for this and that, bought season tickets for all three of us and told my wife, Bank your money. Household expenses are my province. In the market vendors would have called out, Sir, sir, come and buy. Excellent beans. Take five hundred grams. And I wouldn't have haggled about the price. But now … my son goes to her for money. Even the tricksters who come with contribution lists call out for Madam. Madam, my foot!"

"…"

"There's no peace at home. Fights every day. Do you know, Doctor, one day she called me Pin gona and Donkey in the presence of her friends who had come visiting? I barged into their conversation and asked her how dare she insult me by calling me that. She denied my charges completely. She replied that she had only said that Kingsley who works at the bank had gone to Singapore. Rubbish."

"…"

"Why do you think she sat for the degree examination in spite of all the problems we were having? She wanted to spite me, to show the world that she was superior to me. Balderdash … and that too an external degree. Who cares for external degrees?"

"…?"

"Imagination? Doctor, do you really believe I am imagining these things? My wife uses the same word. I wonder where she picked it from. Doctor, I know that woman. In my hearing she must have told at least a hundred people that she paid for our son's boarding fees. She says I'm a parasite living on her earnings. She says that some men are worse than women these days."

"…?"

"No, I've not actually heard her say that, but …"

"…"

"Though she's a Staff Officer, can she speak five words of English? When my son comes home for the holidays she speaks to him in English. Oh my goodness, you should listen to her! Our son can teach her a few things. You know, I've never been able to carry on an intellectual conversation with her."

"...?"

"Yes, I too studied in the Sinhala medium, but my English ... not bad, no?"

"..."

"I've given up!"

"...?"

"My friends? Yes, yes, some of my friends understand my position. Last weekend I had a long chat with my neighbour Dougie. We discussed a lot of things. Dougie didn't disagree with anything I said. In fact, he was very impressed. He said that my views on the unemployment problem were very advanced. Doctor, do you know what Dougie said after listening to my discourse on inflation?"

"...?"

"Dougie said that if they could send me to Parliament somehow or the other, most of the urgent problems in the country would be settled quickly. That's what he said. Honestly! I haven't changed a word of his. You can ask Dougie yourself. My friends know my real worth. I'm a very modest man. In a way, when a man with my capabilities decides to shun publicity and hide his talents under a bushel, it is a great loss to the country. Don't you think so, Doctor?"

"...?"

"There you are! Thank you. Thank you. Dougie is very impressed. He loves to listen to me. So I didn't feel like going away. After all it is very rude to cut short an important discussion midstream, isn't it, Doctor? It's very unfair. That day I had lunch with Dougie and at about three in the afternoon I started speaking about the political situation in Sri Lanka. I'm a good speaker, you know. I was Vice President of our union. Dougie was fascinated by me, but I was dragged back home."

"...?"

"The madam from the bank."

"...?"

"The madam from the bank? My wife, of course. My wife!"

"...?"

"That's Dougie's wife at work. She didn't understand a word I said. It was all Greek to her. I saw her poking her head out now and then. Later I saw her near the wall, standing on her toes and peeping into our house. Oh women ... women ...

"This morning I was inspired by thoughts of Sri Lankan family life in the twenty first century. I saw Dougie leaving for work, so I went to my other neighbour Ekanayake's house. I rang the bell, I knocked on the door, but there was no response. I'm quite sure Ekanayake was at home. Eka, that baldie, sorry Doctor, forgive my language. We call our friend Ekanayake Eka, that one, and it suits him.

"While standing in his garden I suddenly remembered that Ekanayake is a journalist. My word! If I spoke to him, he would write in the papers, passing off my ideas as his own. I was saved in the nick of time. Do you know what happened to me during the strike, Doctor? My ideas are very advanced. I'm at least fifteen years ahead of these nincompoops. Employers don't like that kind of person. They fear them, so they knock them out totally, so that it is impossible to make a comeback. That's what happened to me."

"...?"

"A morning walk? Yes, I tried that too, but I'm sick of walking."

"...?"

"When I'm out walking who do I meet on the road? All these people who are rushing off to work. They have no time to say even a hello to me. Doctor, do you know what I did one day? I got dressed in my office clothes, rummaged in the storeroom, found my old briefcase and dusted it carefully. Then I stepped out and hurried along like all the others. I ran to the Nugegoda junction, like I used to. I didn't look right or left. A route number 138 bus was pulling out. I ran behind it and scrambled in. I went up to Kirulapone. I realized I had no money when the conductor asked for my fare. I scrambled back to the exit and jumped off the bus. I walked back home. Yes I did. I had to walk back home, I had to!"

"...?"

"Hobbies? Mm ... let me see."

"...?"

"Reading? Ah yes, yes. Dougie often lends me the newspapers in the evening. He sometimes brings them over himself. Sometimes he sends them through someone. But I don't like it, Doctor. It's demeaning."

"...?"

"I don't need their sympathy or their dirty tattered newspapers. Huh! During the last few days I've been going to the library to read the newspapers. My ... the things you get to read in the papers these days! Recently there was a news item about the discovery of an unidentified dead body on the beach. When the body is found days after the death you can't even get fingerprints. So how can you trace the murderer? I mean, if he at least had his identity card in his pocket he could have avoided the ignominy of being called an Unknown man."

"...?"

"Poor devil. Then I remember reading in *Reader's Digest* about a wife who introduced a dangerous drug into her husband's coffee every morning."

"...?"

"No, no. What I mean to say is that last night my wife gave me a pill because I was not able to fall asleep. She said it was Diazepam, which she had bought on one of your former prescriptions. I didn't take it."

"...?"

"Me? You want me to come for a checkup? Where?"

"...?"

"To your ward?"

"...?"

"Please, Doctor. Don't ask me to come to your ward for a checkup. Your ward is a loony bin. They will say I am mad too if I come there."

"...?"

"My wife phoned you? When?"

"...?"

"She phoned you on Thursday and came to your clinic on Friday? Why did she do that?"

"...?"

"Prescription? She wanted to know whether to continue with the same drugs? For *me*? What's wrong with me? You devil, what are you two up to? Do you think I don't know? I knew it all along. You and that bitch. Are you trying to fool me? Both of you are trying to drug me and send me to the loony bin so that you are free to carry on your dirty business. Imagination! Imagination, indeed. Now I know who puts words into that bitch's mouth. I'm not good enough for her now. She's hunting for bigger prey. Do you think I didn't see her coming in your car that day? I saw you dropping her off near our gate. I knew you from those elephant ears of yours. I didn't make a fuss that day because I wanted to catch you both redhanded. And when I do that I'll ... I'll twist your ... Hello! Hello! You filthy dog, you put down the receiver, didn't you? He must be thinking he can get away from me easily. I'll ... I'll ... I'll dial again! Where's that number? The number ... now where is it? Where's the bloody number? I'll dash this thing on the floor! Ah? ... What are these? They look like wild buffaloes! Why are you devils glaring at me? Get out ... Get out of my sight. Leave me ... let me go! ... don't, don't touch me ... Leave me alone ...! I'm ... Jayamanne. Tissa Jayamanne. I've lost my identity. Let go off me!

"The Wild Buffalo" was originally published in Sinhala as "Kulumeema."

Bhuvana and Planet Guru
by R Chudamani
translated by Ramiah Kumar

So that the tears of the widow
May be wiped away,
She was sent to a temple.
There —
The goddess bedecked
In flowers and new robes,
Stood united to her consort.

Muran

On a sudden impulse I offered him a lift.

I had stopped at the Mount Road petrol pump to fill the car. Having collected the bill, I was waiting for my turn behind a line of cars when I spotted him at the bus stop.

Would he be fifty, I wondered. His veshti and shirt were gradually changing colour due to sweat. The forehead, broadened by a receding hairline, glistened in the sun. His slippered feet shifted frequently, taking the weight on each by turns. From time to time he wiped his face and adjusted the black leather bag that was tucked under his arm. He was looking fixedly in the direction of approaching buses. I got the feeling that he had been waiting for a bus for a long time.

There was no one else at the bus stop. He was all by himself in that scorching heat, like an orphan.

When the two cars in front moved away, I filled my Ambassador with petrol. I drove out of the petrol pump and slowly drew up beside him. Leaning out of the window I said, "Excuse me, saar. Where do you need to go?"

He was visibly taken aback, confused at such a query from a total stranger. The result was a slight, inexplicable agitation. Instinctively his body moved backwards, as if in anticipation of a blow from a raised hand.

"You ... I don't think I know you."

"I don't know you either. From the petrol pump across the road, I saw you standing at the bus stop. If we are both going in the same direction I thought I could offer you a lift. That's all."

He looked puzzled. Maybe he thought I was some kind of a nut! Observing him from closer quarters, I gauged that his face was not that of a fifty year old. The premature balding and the weary emaciated appearance were certainly not the effects of age.

"My name is Rajasekhar. S T Rajasekhar. Accounts Manager with Saravana Exports." Putting my hand into my shirt pocket, I pulled out my wallet, took out my business card and extended it to him.

"Oh no! That's not necessary."

"I have to establish my credentials, don't I? What if you think I am an abductor?"

He laughed aloud, displaying sparkling white teeth. "What can you gain by abducting me? I am neither a millionaire, nor a political heavyweight nor a young woman. Just an insignificant guy who lives from day to day."

His laughter caused me some discomfort.

"You've been waiting for a bus a long time, haven't you?"

"I'm quite used to that."

"Where do you have to go?"

"T Nagar. Thirumalai Street."

"Get in," I said, as I opened the front door of the car.

"Don't bother, saar. You may be going in a different direction ..." His eyes moved away from me.

"I am going to Bazullah Road which is nearby. I can drop you and then carry on."

"Too much trouble for you."

"Not at all. You will keep me company too. How long will you stand suffering in the sun?"

"I forgot my umbrella. That's the mistake." He turned away again to look down the road. There was no sign of a bus.

"No use waiting for a bus. There may even be a lightning strike by the bus staff. Don't hesitate."

"Are you really going to Bazullah Road?"

"Come on, just get in saar. We can do all our talking in the car."

He was still hesitant. But his feet, tired with the long wait, had already taken the decision for him.

He paused before getting in. "My name is Mahalingam. I am a clerk in a private company," he said, as if it was his turn to establish his credentials. He then climbed into the seat beside mine. I closed the door for him, got back to the driver's seat and started the car.

He stretched out his tired legs for comfort, closed his eyes and let out a deep sigh. But the grip on the leather bag remained as tight as ever.

"It seems to be a very important bag," I said by way of conversation.

"Yes," he said, and tightened his grip on it.

"May I ask what it is that you have in it?"

"A horoscope. My daughter's horoscope," he burst into laughter. "For an average lower middle class person, can there be anything more important than this?"

In spite of the breeze created by the moving car, drops of sweat still glistened on his face. Every drop seemed to proclaim the burden of his responsibility as a father who had to arrange for his daughter's wedding.

My thoughts came to a halt. I was also a father to a daughter. But I was not sweating from standing in the sun. Instead of the odour of sweat, there was the smell of my aftershave lotion. In the place of his handloom veshti were my terene trousers. And in the place of those slippers which slipped off his feet slightly as he stretched his legs, were my polished black shoes.

"I too have a daughter. Her name is Niranjani. What is your daughter's name?"

"Bhuvaneshwari. We call her Bhuvana."

I refrained from telling him that we call Niranjani Nikki-Tikki.

"I am going to a house in Thirumalai Street to give them her horoscope," he continued.

"Are they known to you?"

"No, they were referred to me by someone in my office. I was told that they may not expect too much. So I thought I would give them Bhuvana's horoscope to consider. God willing, the marriage will take place."

"Do you know the house number?"

"Mm ..." Unzipping the bag, he took out a few papers and examined them. There was a horoscope with the traditional turmeric yellow marks on the four corners. Other papers too – perhaps the address to which he had to go. A letter of introduction from his friend, maybe. Or papers regarding other matters.

I looked straight ahead as I drove the car. When I stopped at a red light, he offered to show me something. As I turned towards him, he took out a passportsize photograph from a small envelope and showed it to me.

"This is Bhuvana."

Though not a raving beauty, there was an innocent charm to that face. Big eyes. Jet black hair that was plaited tight, almost as if it was plastered to her head with gum. Small ear studs with a single stone embedded in each. The stones appeared dark in the black and white photograph – possibly rubies, certainly not diamonds. The pottu on her forehead looked rather large for a face so young. A little make-up would have made the face look more beautiful. Nevertheless, the large eyes, blossoming with expectation as they beheld the world, were radiant with a brightness that is unique to youth.

"This is Bhuvana," he repeated with a bright smile, as he turned to look at me.

"Very good looking! How old is she?"

"Last December she completed nineteen years."

"Just nineteen! What's the hurry to get her married?" As I said this, I recalled my daughter Nikki who has turned twenty, saying, "After completing my MBA, I would like to do a course in Computers and then get a degree from abroad. Right, Dad?"

"What do you mean by saying I'm in a hurry? Do marriages happen as soon as we start looking around for prospective alliances? Once Bhuvana turned eighteen, I set out with her horoscope. No success so far," he remarked, as he returned the photograph to its envelope and placed it inside his leather bag.

"Eighteen! At eighteen, a girl is still a child, swami!"

"That depends on the kind of family the girl is born into."

I felt as if someone had hit me hard on the head. I did not venture to speak further. The traffic signal turned green. We started moving once again and went past the statue of Kalaivanar.

"With my limited means I have managed to educate her up to the plus two stage. I have another daughter and a son after her. My wife does some tailoring at home and earns a little. Even then, is it easy to organize a daughter's wedding? Sons-in-law come at exorbitant prices. I don't know how I'll manage. But that doesn't mean that I can keep my daughter unmarried."

As he kept speaking, a weariness seemed to envelop him once again, weariness in spite of the comfort of travelling in a car.

He got off a couple of houses ahead of his destination. "I don't want them to see me arriving in a car. They may take me to be a rich man and scale up their demands. See you then. Thanks for the lift. It appears destiny had ordained a car ride for me today." His hand lingered on the door of the car, as he once again bid goodbye.

He pressed his hands together in a gesture of leave taking. I responded in the same way. His slippered feet proceeded to move quickly down the street.

I turned my Ambassador in the direction of Mylapore. I had to see an industrialist friend. Apart from praying to the almighty, I also needed to sound out such people, in case I should need their help for the fulfilment of my daughter's goals.

I did not have any work at Bazullah Road.

God's grace was completely with us. Nikki-Tikki completed her MBA with flying colours. She got a diploma in Computers from my friend's institute, went to America on a student visa, studied Computer Science there, got a degree and worked for a year before returning to India. Today she is an officer with a big firm in Bangalore. Her husband is an engineer who, like her, has a foreign degree. A son-in-law I acquired for four lakhs. In accordance with the current family planning mores, they have only one child. The only object of her parents' wealth and doting, Nikki Junior studies in a convent and is at ease with English.

God hasn't let me down either. By dint of capability, I rose to become GM first, a company director next, and received recognition as a financial expert. After retiring at the age of fifty eight, I launched my own business called "Nikki Finance" and am rolling in wealth today.

As for my wife, even in the hottest of summers, she has worn nothing less than silk. What she likes most are Chinese jade ornaments and Blue Jaguar diamonds cut in Amsterdam. We live in Mumbai and come to Chennai once in three years. We have relatives here. We enjoy our sense of belonging in a place where Tamil is spoken. We long to see Marina Beach. Diabetes has enforced restrictions on my diet and my grey hair needs to be concealed by Godrej hair dye – who can escape the delusion of returning to youth? Having to buy silk saris from Kanchipuram for my wife is another reason for coming to Chennai.

Today, once again, wafting over me is the breeze of Chennai.

Waiting to fill petrol, I sit inside my car at the petrol pump. The Ambassador gave way to a Maruti and is now a Contessa. I bought this car just last week, here in Chennai. It will have to be sent to Bombay later. Wishing to undertake the first long distance journey to a place of worship, I will be driving down with my wife, my daughter and her family tomorrow morning to Maangadu. So I need to fill the car with petrol.

It seems it will take some time. I get out of the car and look at the road. In terms of the increase in population, noise, number of vehicles and high rise buildings, Chennai seems to be catching up with other progressive cities. Wherever you look, there are dish antennae on top of houses. Day and night you hear the deafening sounds of cable television. Don't all cities wear the same look? But then you hear a car driver screaming at a careless pedestrian, "Have you bid your final goodbye to your family? Making arrangements for a funeral, eh? Move off, you piece of dirt!" – a typical local idiom, a pleasant enough pointer that you are in Chennai!

In the midst of the screaming and screeching of buses, taxis, autorickshas and cars darting to and fro, there is a moment's respite and what I see in that moment strikes a deep chord in my consciousness.

It is him.

In the heat of the month of Chittirai, there he is, veshti and shirt discoloured by sweat. A leather bag tucked under his arm. Standing at the bus stop. His hands shielding his eyes from the sun, his eyes searching the distance, surely looking for the bus which he has to board.

Hurriedly I remove my dark glasses and look at him intently. My eyes, removed of the cataract growth and implanted with contact lenses, can still see well. It is him, unmistakably. What is his name? Chokkalingam? Ramalingam? He wears glasses now, his head is almost completely bald. But the features are still recognizable.

My head spins momentarily. Was some naughty little fellow deliberately turning back the hands of the clock? I, on this side of the road, at the petrol pump. On the other side, he, waiting for the bus. The same sight ... How many years back was that? 1970 ... yes, almost fifteen years ago. Fifteen years!

Fifteen times calendars have been replaced. An entire twelve year period has elapsed. The country has seen six prime ministers. In the world arena, a superpower has disappeared. After twenty eight years of imprisonment, a freedom fighter has obtained release. America's *Voyager* has leapt many million kilometres into space towards Jupiter, the planet Guru.

He is still standing in the same place.

I shake my head. I bring myself back to the present. After filling the car, I drive straight up to him and stop. I get out, press the palms of my hands together in greeting and ask pleasantly how he is and whether he recognizes me.

His reaction is exactly like before. His eyebrows rise in a display of bewildered confusion. There is a grey strand among them. Apart from the balding, there are lots of lines on his face.

"I am Rajasekhar. S T Rajasekhar. Fifteen years ago I gave you a lift from a bus stand. Do you remember?"

The blank expression tells me that he cannot recall at once. The hands tighten their hold on the leather bag. That act helps to refresh my memory and I say, "Your name is Mahalingam, isn't it?"

"Yes."

"Last time you had to take your daughter's horoscope to Thirumalai Street and I took you there. This time too, let me take you where you have to go."

"I am beginning to remember faintly ... Didn't you say you were going to Bazullah Road?"

"Yes."

"Did you go?"

I burst into laughter. "You got me there! Come, get into the car. Let's talk as we go." I open the front door for him.

"What did you say your name is?"

"S T Rajasekhar. Get in."

"I don't want to bother you ..."

"Not at all."

"I have to go to an address in Chintadripet."

"I have to go in the same direction."

He laughs as I speak these words. But his teeth do not sparkle as before. They too appear to have lost their gleam with age.

"You have a kind heart, saar. However, my bus should be arriving now."

"Let it come. Assume that you are giving company to a friend whom you have met after a long time."

His tired face longs to accept my invitation. However, manners make him look in the direction of the bus. A bus, which is not going towards his destination, arrives, stops and then leaves.

"Forget about the bus, Mr Mahalingam. I tell you, just get into the car. The car can't wait here. If a policeman notices, he will give me a ticket."

"Thanks," he says, as he climbs into the front seat. Removing his glasses, he wipes them and his face too with the edge of his shirt. "Going out in this heat, I should have brought the umbrella," he remarks.

After closing the door for him, I walk around to the driver's seat and ask, "Where do you have to go?"

"Turning in to Periyar Road, over the bridge and further."

I start the car. The air conditioning within the darkened glasses is very comfortable. Neither of us speaks for some time.

Just as I am beginning to wonder whether he has dozed off, he says, "I am a retired man now."

"Not surprising. It's been fifteen years now."

"My wife died three years ago."

"Oh! I'm very sorry."

"She was destined to go then ... In a way, she was fortunate ... After retirement I am now working as a clerk to a school correspondent. The headmaster is known to me. I owe the job to him."

I do not say anything. I experience the neem-like bitterness of his misery. The air conditioned coolness offers little comfort.

He opens the leather bag and takes out the contents including a brown paper bag containing something, reorganizes them and puts them back.

"Today is Saturday, you see. So the school is closed."

"Why didn't you just relax at home then? You look quite tired."

"How can I? There's work to be done. But as soon as I return home, I'll have a cool glass of buttermilk and rest."

There is silence once again. The car is moving past people, houses, streets, shops, cinema posters and cutouts of politicians. We reach Periyar Road.

"Where are you living now?" he asks.

"Mumbai."

"Do you come to Chennai once in a while?"

"Once in three years."

"Chennai must seem quite drab in comparison to Mumbai."

"But it is my native place after all."

"True. Your car looks new. It is very good with its air conditioning and all."

"Thanks," I say, as I negotiate a turn in the road. "My daughter, son-in-law and granddaughter from Bangalore are also here. We plan to go together to Maangadu temple tomorrow morning."

"That's a good thing. While you are there, also make an appeal to Goddess Karumariamman that my Bhuvana should get married."

I turn to look at him with shock. I almost lose sight of the taxi in front and come very close to a collision. "Look where you're going, saar. You appear to be an educated person. Still ..." the words of the taxi driver trail behind me.

"For Bhuvana? Bhuvaneshwari?"

"Yes. Guru has still not bestowed his favour on her. Even now I am on my way to an address at Chintadripet to give her horoscope for their consideration."

I cannot bring myself to speak. I feel a burning sensation all over me. I feel disoriented. It is a surprise how I manage to reach him to the street he mentioned without an accident.

"The car cannot enter this narrow lane. Drop me here and I shall go by foot."

Mechanically I stop the car, get out and open the door for him. He gets out.

"Thanks a lot. I'll take leave, then."

In his hurry to get out, the brown paper packet falls down from his bag. He had probably forgotten to zip the bag.

I bend down. The packet had opened slightly on account of the fall, momentarily revealing the object inside. Without drawing his attention, I close it once again and hand it to him.

"Thanks, saar. It's something that Bhuvana had asked for. If I had lost it, I would have had to go to the market once again."

He places the packet in his bag and zips it up.

"I shall take leave, saar. I've put you to a lot of trouble. Sorry. Goodbye."

His slippered feet slowly drag themselves into the lane.

I get back to the driver's seat. My eyes look vacantly at my expensive Gucci shoes. My head slumps on the steering wheel.

That packet had in it a bottle of Godrej Hair Dye.

"Bhuvana and Planet Guru" was originally published in Tamil (India) as "Bhuvanavum Vyazhagrahamum."

The Homecoming
by M A Al Asumath
translated by Uma Balu

It was all a coincidence ...

At last, after fifteen years, the Sirimavo-Shastri agreement had accepted me as a citizen, and at last, after nine years, thanks to my wife, I could make a trip to Mathalai – my hometown.

Was it, really?

My tongue never said so, but my heart did. Sounds contradictory? Well, there wasn't much to feel so proud of ... neither for me nor for Mathalai.

My colleagues are quite different. Proud of their homelands ... Obsessed with their memories. Each trip is a revival – an enriching experience – for them. It all seemed very queer to me. What else would I, who had left the countryside to live in the city, feel like?

Perhaps Mathalai really had nothing so special. My parents didn't belong to that place, nor did the earlier generations. Even the birth certificates of my brothers and sisters didn't bear its name. Not a piece of land to call my own ... no vote ... not even an in-law.

So, I belong to the whole world!

The cemetery assures me of "the land I need." But Mathalai's estate checkroll wasn't that generous – it didn't offer me a millimetre!

Officially, I was born in Mathalai. But what right does that give me? MGR, they say, was born in Kandy – so what?

Digiria Estate and its store shed ... my first soil. Soon after I was born, my parents took to working as estate labourers. In fact, my father toiled in every estate of Mathalai. So I was a pukka estate labourer, right from birth!

It often confuses me – how people change their hometowns casually, to some Kolluppatti or Kurunthuvathai ... as if life at Colombo requires it ...Well, I couldn't do so myself.

Those seventeen years I spent in the warmth of my parents' love and support were the only link between Mathalai and myself. Armed with ten years of schooling and the hope of a prosperous future, I bid goodbye.

The link loosened ...

Since the sixties till now, there have been occasional revivals – when my father and a younger brother died, a few anniversaries, when brothers found wives and sisters found husbands, when someone in the family managed to turn seventy or eighty ... Some twenty times or so ...

What big future is there in store for an estate labourer, after all? I suffered the same fate and in the mid-seventies, entered city life.

After 1983, the link was broken.

Amma used to pay frequent visits, as if on business. Perhaps she didn't want me to go there or maybe, I was satisfied with that.

A place I can neither forget nor call my own ... Mathalai intrigues me.

Suduganthai estate. Shed No 2, Room No 2. Amma's address is still the same. Kattayan's wife and three children, the three children whom Kuttappan left behind after his death ... all live with her. Kattayan is employed in Jeddah.

Yet, Suduganthai or Mathalai seem no dearer to me ...

Amma is worldly wise and practical. London or Paris would have highlighted her worth, but perhaps she chose Mathalai just for our sake. Her responsibilities never let her leave Suduganthai, or else she would have been a prized possession – for my elder brothers or me ...

She wants to be buried alongside Appa and Kuttappan. That's another reason for her to remain there. After all, who are we, however modern, to interfere with her wonderful sentiments?

Well, Suduganthai is innocent of such delicate emotions. To those people, we are just citybred sons, neglecting their poor mother ... But Amma knows better.

Two months back, there was a letter from Amma regarding the sale of a portion of Digiria's estate. She had also written to Kattayan asking him to purchase some ten units or so.

The reason was clear. She knew very well that Kattayan was more capable of such things – more dependable too – than all her "citybred" sons! Why, that's the truth.

But Kattayan had a choice – to be a "countrybred" owner of an estate in Mathalai or a "citybred" pauper like myself! God knows, but aren't we children of the same pauper?

It was all a coincidence ...

At last, after fifteen years, the Sirimavo-Shastri agreement had accepted me as a citizen, and at last, after nine years, thanks to my wife, I could make a trip to Mathalai – my "so called" hometown ...

The luggage was ready. Saris and other such things for the mother-in-law, (my savings had served her wonderfully well!) In her excitement, she even grew a bit impatient ...

But I felt somewhat guilty. My youthful years had gone by without any sense of duty ... now it was just the opposite!

Well, it wasn't too late. I could at least share the benefits of my newly acquired citizenship. For my part, I added a few more items to the lot ...

My heart felt much lighter now.

Carrying me, my younger son and of course, the luggage, my C-90 stirred. My wife waved bye, warning of possible rain, but the sky was clear ...

Three hours passed, with no sign of rain. We reached the outskirts of Mathalai.

A whiff of a cool breeze welcomed us.

I felt a strange sensation within. Perhaps because I was visiting Mathalai after a fairly long gap, or because of the change in weather ... I can still recollect those childhood days when I used to gape in wonder at the vehicles speeding along the road. Today, I was driving my own vehicle down that very same road! Possibly, it was that excitement ... but definitely not that "feverish attachment" to one's hometown.

Well, habits don't die that easily ...

Mathalai was new to my son. Of course, he had been there once – when he was three years old. Did he too experience a similar feeling? I wasn't sure. Well, I was no different from him.

That "sense of belonging" was still missing ...

Mathalai looked much changed now. Those old buildings seemed to sport a friendly smile. To the new ones, I was a total stranger. Faces familiar from my childhood still existed, revealing signs of age. Kombilivalai's streams were filled with fresh Mahavali waters ... like a made-up old face from Saudi.

The government hospital (which never stocked medicines!), mounds (or playgrounds?), meadows and parks (our open air theatres!) and cemetery (does one have to die to go there? Not in my case!) ... I circled the whole place driven by excitement to introduce those childhood haunts to my son. The Pillaiar temple, where we used to compete for pieces of smashed coconut, and the school, my alma mater, were also on the way.

As an old student, I was left with hardly anything to boast of. Maybe earth weighs more than education. The school building was in ruins, its founder and his ambitions, mere memories.

A sigh escaped my heavy heart.

Our journey continued – St Thomas, the banyan tree, Mariamman temple, Azhagar hills, the old Sadananda Bidi factory, Gunasena's residence, Madandawale junction, Rathodai pathway, the triangular cemetery, Thokku Thuvan's piece of land ... the Kaludavalai slope was the last stop.

Hidden beyond the meadow on the left lay my birthplace, as if ashamed to face me.

I was moved.

"Look, that's the place." I blankly pointed out to the spot, which included the land Kattayan was to purchase. (Will he?)

My son didn't seem interested. Was I acting like a fool? Well, he had hardly any sentiments for his own birthplace either.

As we neared the estate, everything looked different. Louis' coconut grove was now a thriving place for new "businesses." The potters' huts had turned into secret hiding places, Paravathai division sported a bus stand, in place of Kattandi's shop, stood a grove ...

The Suduganthai river's ripples were not new to me.

I crossed the bridge.

Suduganthai — my eight year old hometown!

I felt a pang within.

The burial spots of my father and brother couldn't be traced. Fighting back my tears, I pointed out blankly to my son.

The rubber and cocoa trees had vanished. The once owned lands reminded me of grandfather and grandmother. They now seemed to belong to the pre-British period. Everything had changed hands.

The tar road took a turn. The rough pathway reminded me of childhood pranks, quarrels, movie chats and teashops along the hill track.

The vehicle staggered along, the stones and dents juggling my thoughts.

I wasn't sure about the way ahead and there were no familiar faces around to guide me.

The path took an upward turn towards the Kali temple, leaving tyre marks behind. I forced the vehicle forward – it seemed to groan beneath me in constant warning.

The change was drastic. Once, this path used to be the centre of a six hundred acre estate! Now both the estate and its activities had vanished – a wild patch of land was all that remained after the estate had been partitioned. The small estate community had scattered far and wide, retaining just enough space to live.

The economic status of the partners of the estate was quite evident from its present state. I remember Amma resentfully telling me about this.

But I was now concerned about my vehicle's condition.

I suggested, "Why don't we park it near the Kali temple?" The priest was Kattayan's father-in-law.

My son refused, "Let's drive a little further. The temple doesn't seem a safe place."

I was trying to convince him, when I had a flash – a face ... a beaming face ... a poor mother's ... proudly watching her son and grandson arrive at her doorstep on a motorcycle ...

My mother was no exception.

It used to be a short walk, about a quarter of a mile. Crossing the ridge beyond the Kali temple and taking a turn, you would reach the shed. Now there stood a fence near the ridge, blocking the way ... that meant a half-mile walk along the riverbank and going across the narrow steps of a ridge adjacent to the white cedar tree. Some twenty times up and down the ridge used to be exciting in those days. Now, the very thought made me gasp for breath. On my vehicle, it definitely meant a three mile drive.

The surroundings were quite familiar and I felt confident. As we drove along the curve, I spotted a figure walking slowly towards us. That face ... with all the grey and wrinkles of eighty, was still strikingly recognizable. Appa's fellow cutter Jayasekhara Basunne! Yes, it was him ...

His appearance made me remember my father. Would he have looked like this if he were alive? Oh no, even at sixty five, his hair used to be black. Why, Amma is sixty five too, but without a single grey streak, and I, at fifty! Hmm ...

Basunne was now approaching us.

I stopped the vehicle and called out to him, smiling, "Basunne!"

He paused. He reminded me of so many people. Meanwhile he was making desperate attempts to recognize me. I was thrilled, but checked myself, wasn't that cruel?

I took off my helmet.

He bent closer ... the next moment he straightened up and ... "Ha ha ha!" he exclaimed. He was beaming.

"It is our Ponnaia's elder son!"

He began chiding himself for being so forgetful. His enthusiasm burst forth in a shower of enquiries, "How are you? You've come after such a long time! Are you still in Colombo? Who is this boy?"

"My second son," I answered.

"Oh, you have such a grown up son!" He expressed surprise and in all innocence, asked me to ward off his "evil eye" at the earliest.

I wondered what he would say if he saw my elder one – with beard and moustache!

Basunne's topics were endless – my family, income, expenses, business, house, property – he wanted to know everything ... then and there.

The typical rural "interview" was a welcome change for me.

For about half an hour, I stood as if mesmerized – while my son, bored and exhausted, seated himself on a rock. He was a total stranger to such sentiments and memories.

By this time, a small crowd had gathered around with their own

load of questions. They seemed to be very familiar with our family ...
possibly Amma's friends. So I responded patiently. They recalled my
past while I shared with them my present.

I didn't want to disappoint them, but I couldn't afford to wait
either. I pushed on.

"Park your vehicle by the cedar tree and cross the ridge on foot.
But take care to leave someone with the vehicle," the deaf Thirumalai
advised. (Well, he knew little of my wife!)

"Our bungalow sahab rides on a similar vehicle and he crosses it
at least five or six times a day!" Muthuvel Ocharayya tried to encourage
me.

"Well, the road isn't that bad ... a little slippery, but you can drive
slowly." Basunne added.

"Go to Padamathi junction. Take the bungalow road and drive on
till you reach the crossroads to the shed. It leads straight to your
house. Shall I show you the local tracks?" Velanna drew a verbal map.

Armed with these bits of information, I started moving.

My mind was tingling fresh.

The trouble began after I crossed the cedar tree. The road was
deeper than I expected. Only the bungalow sahab's bike could travel
on this!

Those people were not to be blamed. Perhaps these were minor
difficulties compared to their hardships in life.

My son hopped down. I followed, for I was fully aware of the
tube's condition. I pushed the vehicle along, accelerating slightly.

The one and a half mile journey via Padamathi was really exhausting
for both of us. The road took a left turn, to lead to the bungalow. It
was uphill now – for about three quarters of a mile ... and that wasn't
all. The path to the shed was then downhill – each step forward
required extreme care and caution.

What was once a cart road was now overgrown with bushes. My

son waded through, his trousers getting torn in the process.

He pushed from the back as I inched forward ... it was very steep. With great difficulty, we reached the outskirts of the shed.

But our troubles were not yet over.

The shed lay up there, on the right. The crossroad leading to it was about fifteen feet long, ascending all the way. The path we had taken so far now ran downwards, to the Kaliamman temple.

Our uphill journey continued ...

My C-90 seemed to have grown much heavier. Those fifteen feet were really challenging. By the time we reached the shed, we felt as if we had performed a great feat!

The last room was in a dilapidated condition. We stood there, gasping for breath.

A face peeped out.

It was Kamakshi. She looked as if she had come on parole from the Middle East.

"Is that Sarasu's brother? Please come in!" she welcomed us and rushed to inform Amma.

Her squeaky voice reminded me of Jaya – as loud as that of the deaf Kankani.

Jaya came running from the middle of the shed. She called out to Kattayan's son, "Radha, your uncle has arrived with a boy. Come and help them with the vehicle!"

Kattayan's wife Sarojini was equally excited. She corrected Jaya, "It is our machan's, our brother-in-law's second son!"

The shed soon buzzed with activity.

I was bombarded with all sorts of queries from the young and old alike.

"Is this your son?"

"Didn't Akka (my wife) come with you?"

"Radha, hold on to the front!"

"Sarasu's mother has been expecting a guest right from the morning — she said she heard the crow calling!"

The whole shed watched in amazement as my C-90 went round and round — in all its majesty.

Amma was silent, but delighted.

Her daughter-in-law had showered her with gifts, her elder son and grandson relished her cooking, the relatives forgot their misunderstandings and gathered for a family chat.

By dusk, she was preoccupied with preparations to ward off the "evil eye."

Now her worries were all over.

Amma was content with such simple things. As long as she was there, my links with Mathalai would exist ... though we don't belong to one another. For, a mother means a lot more than just dishes and delicacies.

As we took leave the next day, Amma, after a deep, meaningful silence, asked, "When will you come again?"

"The Homecoming" was originally published in Tamil (Sri Lanka) as "Virakthi."

Mirage
by Allam Seshagiri Rao
translated by S Krishnamoorthy and N S Murty

The scorching summer was at its height!

The blazing sun spat fire. The streams, springs and rills in the forest — all had gone dry. Wild fires were raging on the hilltops, sun stricken birds were dropping dead like dry leaves in autumn.

Thirst! Thirst! Thirst! Thirst all around!

Tigers, wolves, deer, birds and sundry creatures were on the run — migrating to safer pastures by day and by night, with just one desire — to quench their wrenching thirst.

"If only I could kill a large deer, I wouldn't ask for more. That would fetch four hundred. With good luck, if I stumble upon a wild boar that would mean two to three hundred. If it is a deer or a buck, it would fetch a reasonable hundred bucks. That'd be quits to Soorayya's debt." Continuous drought for the last three years had compelled Byri to mortgage his meagre holding of dry land. The principal and interest together compounded to three hundred. If he failed to release the mortgage this year too, Soorayya would, for sure, grab the land forever. Byri knew how Soorayya, the moneylender, had turned a millionaire ruthlessly appropriating the lands of the poor. He was, therefore, all the more determined to retrieve the land from Soorayya's clutches.

Byri took out his country rifle and dusted it. He pulled out a pouch of gunpowder he had concealed under the roof of his hut, poured out a little and test fired the rifle. Like the desire of a poor man, it burned instantly. Satisfied that the powder hadn't lost its strength, he stuffed it in the barrel, took out a bag of old nails, screws and iron trimmings and filled them in place of buckshots. He then wadded the barrel with waste paper and cotton rags. Byri pulled the bamboo door shut and marched into the woods holding the rifle in his hand, the bag of ammunition slung from his shoulder.

Byri was sixty. The wrinkles on his face made it look like dry, parched, broken land. Emaciated by age and the endless struggle for existence, his body resembled a skeleton wrapped in skin. His streaked eyes, however, shone like embers. They hadn't yet lost the tenacity and resolve to fight.

It was well past noon. The sun was still blazing. The parrots in the bamboo grove chattered and fluttered away in fright as the dry leaves rustled under his feet. A set of crows, disturbed by Byri's intrusion into their domain, hovered over him in circles and followed him a long way.

In order to reach a water source before sunset, Byri walked briskly taking shortcuts across copses, bushes, thickets, hillocks and rocky ridges. Puffing and fuming, by sunset he reached the spot he was seeking, having crossed two mountain ranges.

In the midst of the dense forest, beside a dried-up stream in the shade of a thicket, the ground was still wet. There was just a small puddle with water slowly oozing out. As Byri approached the puddle, mosquitoes swarming on the water rose. That was the only place in the forest where all the animals could come to quench their thirst. Byri carefully scrutinized the surroundings of the puddle. The footprints of animals were clearly visible on the wet ground about the pool. Wild boars had dug a large number of pits in the sand in search of springs.

The sun setting behind the trees provided a panoramic backdrop. The wind blowing down the sunburnt rocks was still stingingly hot. Byri pulled out a hatchet from his bag, trimmed a bamboo bush twenty yards from the pool and made himself a comfortable hideout. He camouflaged the hideout with trimmings from nearby bushes and made room for the barrel of the gun, so as to be able to shoot from within the hideout. He patted himself upon the perfect workmanship. He carefully crept in, took up his position and started looking out keenly from the crevices of the hideout for signs of animals approaching the puddle, keeping the gun in readiness. His ears were sensitive to every little sound. Byri was a seasoned hunter.

Cluck, Cluck, Cluck!

Peacocks somewhere nearby. Various small birds were also coming down to the pool, drinking water and flying away. A couple of peacocks came running over the dry leaves to the pool and looked around. They stretched out their necks and gulped the water. His thirst quenched, a peacock jumped around in joy spanning his plumage. His spread out tail reflected the iridescent colours of the twilight. He and his mate danced for a while and flew away. As the evening spread its wings, a large number of wild fowl and birds came to the puddle, quenched their thirst and left.

Gradually darkness descended on the forest. The chirping of birds grew thinner and thinner as they flew nestward. Now it was time for the animals to arrive.

Having sat still for hours, Byri's back had started aching. As the darkness deepened, the creaking of insects increased. A muntjac barked somewhere on the hilltop. A bright star was reflected in the water in the pit. Even in pitch darkness, Byri was able to see the well-laid out sand carpet of the stream.

The hours passed. A cool wind blew over the fluttering dry leaves, comforting Byri's sweat soaked body.

"Faunk, faunk." Suddenly the forest reverberated with the barks of a large deer. The animal ran past Byri so quickly that he could make it out only from the sound of its hooves. The crickets fell silent. Silence reigned. Byri shivered in the hideout. His body was trembling. Unconsciously, his hand leapt up to the trigger of the gun. He wondered what was making him shiver. He was confused.

Byri sensed a dark figure moving in the thicket adjacent to the bed of the stream. His eyes pierced through the darkness in an attempt to identify the figure. Lifting the rifle, he took aim at the moving creature. The figure trod heavily up to the water and lowering itself on all fours, started slurping. A sudden gush of wind filled his nostrils and sent waves of fear down his spine. Byri's heart missed a few beats. It was a tiger! And Byri was holding a country rifle with just one shot in it! Should his aim miss, he would be finished. Even if his aim were perfect and hit the target, he couldn't carry the animal out of the forest, nor could he sell it away from the watchful eyes of the forest guards. He would then land himself in deeper trouble. Let alone clearing Soorayya's loan, he would get a minimum of six months in jail. Byri quietly brought down his rifle and sat still like another bush among the bushes, haplessly looking at the tiger.

The tiger quenched his thirst, stood up leisurely, whipped the sand bed two, three times with his long tail and strode into the forest leisurely. A monkey atop a tree, perhaps having spotted the tiger, sent "Hoop, hoop" warning signals to his tribe. The forest was agog with the twitter-twatter of monkeys all of a sudden. The noise subsided gradually as the tiger proceeded into the interior of the forest. Silence reigned once again.

Byri was disappointed. Smelling the tiger, no other animal would dare come near the water. He sighed in despair that all his efforts would come to nought.

When Soorayya flashed across his mind, the moneylender appeared more ruthless, cruel and dreadful than the tiger. He would gobble up Byri's piece of land – his lone resource in life.

Past midnight, the wind picked up speed and occasional lightning streaked across the far off skies. Byri looked up to find dark encircling clouds.

Hell! It's going to rain! He thought. He sat disgruntled, cursing his luck. More clouds engulfed the sky. The moist wind blew more vigorously, causing the bamboo bushes to sway wildly. Dry leaves rolled in whirls. The dust raked up by the wind formed a veil of mist in the darkness.

"Damn it! Which bloody animal would come out in this stormy weather! Wretched luck and wretched weather!" Byri rued bitterly. Adding to his woes, the sound of rain lashing the hills was clearly audible. Soon it started drizzling. There was a creeping sound on the dry leaves. Byri thought it was the gale at first, but as the sound grew louder and came nearer, Byri realized it was the sound of hooves over dry leaves, of a band of animals on the run – perhaps in search of water.

In a sudden flash of lightning Byri saw bucks running towards the pool. Then darkness fell again.

The bucks were pushing one another to have the first gulp of water. The sounds of their horns locking in the melee were clearly audible. In a flash Byri pulled out his rifle and took aim, going by the sound. He could see some moving figures in the darkness but could not make out any clearly enough to take perfect aim. But if he dithered any longer, the herd would be off in a jiffy. Aiming at the middle of the pack, he pulled the trigger. The silent forest reverberated with the "thoom" of the country rifle.

The bucks ran helter-skelter. The wafting smoke bore the cruel smell of gunpowder. Byri came out of his hiding. Wading through the smoke, he frenziedly searched for his game. About two yards from the pool, in a bush, he spotted an animal struggling for its life. He ran in that direction.

A high horned buck! Byri looked at it in wonder and satisfaction, holding his bleeding shoulder by his hand. It'll fetch two hundred at the least and I can clear half of Soorayya's debt, he thought. Plucking at some herbs in the dark and chewing them to a paste, he spat the mixture into his palm and hurriedly applied the salivated mixture to his wound. The wound burnt acutely. Wriggling in pain and fanning the wound with his mouth, he sat there till the burning subsided.

A fat male buck! Very heavy! Byri was worried about how he would carry it home. It would be next to impossible to lug it and scale two mountains. There was a short cut of course but it was full of thorny brushes, thickets and dried-up streams. He would have to walk along narrow paths and at times even crawl under creepers. But he had no choice.

He tried to lift the buck but failed. Then, holding his breath and summoning all his strength, he heaved it up with a jerk and put it over his shoulder. He was staggering under its weight. He took the rifle he had left at the hiding for support and started homeward taking the shorter route. He was up against the blowing wind. It had also started drizzling. In the hope of clearing Soorayya's loan, he forgot all his pain. In the dead of night, he walked through thorny and rocky footpaths in the forest. The blood and spittle oozing from the animal's mouth formed a sort of glue and rolled down his body. The bamboo and the thorny brushes made umpteen scratches on his body. Whenever he had to bend low to pass through narrow openings, he squeaked in pain and felt his back would break. He pondered if he should put his weight down and rest for a while but decided against it for fear of not being able to lift it back onto his shoulder. He trudged along.

Suddenly Byri heard some whistle-like sounds from a distance. Gradually the sounds came closer. Initially he mistook them for chattering of birds, but he soon recognized – seasoned gamester that he was, having been born and brought up in the woods – that they were bays of wild dogs. Smelling their prey, they would surround their victim from all sides and attack. They would eat their prey alive. A howl followed another as if they were orchestrating.

Byri's heart thumped faster. The baying and the clattering of feet was drawing nearer and nearer. The hounds must have smelt the buck's blood and were running towards it, he thought. Although he was sure that they did not harm a man normally, he wasn't so sure with the buck. They might attack finding him all alone in the pitch darkness amidst a dense forest. That thought unnerved him a bit. Soon he collected himself. He thought of concealing the animal under a bush initially but realized the futility of such an exercise. He knew the wild dogs can smell the animal from a long distance and once they get it they would leave nothing but the bones. He looked around for a secure place. There was a banyan tree nearby. He hurried upto it, reached out for a branch at proper height and safely lodged the animal taking enough care that it did not slip down. Bucking his loincloth, he climbed up the tree just in time before the wild dogs encircled it. They found the buck on the branch and out of their reach. They were howling at it, moving impatiently. In their attempt to climb up the tree some of them were scratching the trunk peeling off the bark here and there. "Hoot, hoot," Byri tried to scare the wild dogs away with his hooting. They did not care a hoot. Instead, they were waiting for the buck to drop down, vying with one another for licking the drops of blood dripping from the buck's body.

Byri was exhausted trying to hoot them away. He despaired that they might not leave him. Firing a shot at them came to his mind but the realization of forgetting the ammunition bag at the hiding made him curse himself. To his great good fortune at that very moment he heard the "Barr ... barr" sound, as if coming out of a bronze pipe, of a roebuck. Instantly the wild dogs were on their feet sticking out their ears. The hair on their back stood erect. Wagging their tails they contemplated in silence for a while and in a flash, as if they were unchained, they ran in the direction of the sound in search of a new prey.

Byri thanked his Elements for the turn of events. But, before he could even climb down and resume his journey, what was until then a drizzle suddenly intensified into a heavy rain and soon into a storm as the wind picked up speed. Thunder and lightning were splitting the skies. Branches were felled by the gales. As if it were doomsday, it started raining cats and dogs. Byri was drenched to the bones. As the winds shook the tree the buck dropped down with a thud. Pouring thus for about two hours, the rain relented.

Byri got down and with great effort pulled the animal on to his back. The butt of the rifle was no longer giving him the required support as it was sinking into the rain-soaked ground. The rain washed buck was slipping from his shoulder. Yet he persevered through dirt, slime and slush and through thorny paths and uneven terrain summoning all his reserves with just one resolve – he should reclaim his land from Soorayya.

It must have been about two in the morning. The rain cleansed sky was now looking clear. There was a liberal splash of waxing luminescent moonlight too. The raindrops suspended on the edges of leaves sparkled like pearls. The forest was filled with the croaking of frogs and creaking of crickets. The determined Byri had covered quite a distance. Just a stream and a mile separated him from his hut.

As he drew near the stream the croaking of frogs intensified. A surprise greeted him. The stream which had been totally dry and sand heaped until a few hours back, was now in full spate, its waters curling, swirling, whirling and stretching to its banks.

Byri had no choice but to cross it. Otherwise, he would have to walk four times the distance he had already covered, besides having to trek across a few hills. He knew that though the stream was in full flow, it wasn't very deep. At best the water would come up to his chest. It was hardly ten yards wide at the widest point. For an ace swimmer like him this was not a matter of concern. With confidence he embarked upon crossing the stream. He realized it would not be easy to cross it with a buck on his shoulder and the rifle in his hand. He put down the buck on the ground and rubbed his aching feet and neck with both hands. Taking the rifle in his hand, he swung it round and round and threw it with great force on to the opposite bank. It fell in the slime abutting the opposite bank. He complimented himself for his strength and skill even at this age.

Byri slowly stepped into the water. Frogs leaped into the water at one go. The soil was slimy and slippery. Ensuring a firm foothold, he pulled the buck on to his shoulder. Taking its whole weight on his neck, he held the four suspended legs of the animal in his hands. The soil beneath his feet was giving way under the weight. Measuring each step carefully, he advanced towards the opposite bank. The stream resembled a crawling snake under the moonlight. As the water came kneehigh, the undercurrents pulled him by his legs. Felled branches of trees and logs were floating downstream at full speed. The earth on the banks was caving in. The water was now up to his loins. The speeding column of water was exerting greater force on his knees and legs. Balancing himself with the load on his shoulder, he moved forward step by step. Suddenly his foot landed in a ditch. That was it. He fell flat into the water and the buck was thrown some distance away. The next moment he realized he was being swept away. He was sinking and surfaced with effort. Though his feet touched the ground, the strong current did not allow him to get a foothold. As he was being swept away, he watched his buck, floating ahead of him. Even at that hour of crisis it was Soorayya's loan that came to his mind. Sinking and floating by turn, Byri summoned up all his energies, swam fast and caught hold of the buck.

The stream was racing faster as it was narrower here. Rolling along with his catch, Byri tried to swim upstream. Logs, branches and reptiles sped past him. Managing to float along for about two furlongs, he found a wider and shallow part of the stream. He caught hold of a tree branch swinging down the water. Careful not to let the buck slip, with the help of the branch he pulled himself on to the bank. Fortunately, it was the bank he wanted to reach. Having rested for a full hour but yet unable to summon enough strength to carry the buck on his back, he dragged it along the bank up to where he had thrown his rifle and recovered it.

The twilight in the east indicated the ensuing daybreak. The forest was already awake with the calls of birds. The wild hen was clucking. Bitten by the stinging cold breeze, Byri was shivering like a leaf but determined to reach his hut before dawn, he pulled the buck over his shoulder once more. Puffing and heaving, he reached his hut long after daybreak. The bovines in the village were already mooing and lowing.

Putting the buck down and leaning the rifle against the door, he squatted in front of his hut, gasping for breath. Every inch of his body ached. There were scratches all over him and some of the wounds were fresh with bleeding. A hard lump had formed on his neck where the load had grated him throughout. The hoof-indented shoulder was inflamed and was all needles and pricks. Capping it all was the wolf raging in his stomach. Sapped of all energy, he leaned against the wall.

Well ... it's worth the effort, he closed his eyes and tried to console himself. Soorayya's loan will be cleared and I can retrieve my land.

Just then, he sensed a moving figure in front. He slowly opened his eyes. With a jerk he was on to his feet trembling like a frog taken unawares by a sudden snake.

Spilling venomous looks at him, the forest guard enquired, "Is this all or are there more? You son of a bitch, you must have hidden them somewhere in the forest."

Taken aback and dumbfounded, Byri stood with folded arms.

"Do you have a licence for this rifle?" The forest guard shot another question. Byri fell at the guard's feet.

"Speak up, you bastard!" roared the forest guard.

"Sir, please sir, I am a poor man. I'll never do it again." He prostrated before the guard.

The guard pulled him up by his hair. "Do you think the forest is your grandfather's property that you bastards can poach at will? I heard the shots from your gun last night itself and I've been searching around. Now I've got you, bastard!"

"Please sir, I won't do it again. Promise. This was the first time. If you see me at it again, hit me with your slipper." Byri's voice went hoarse.

"Come. Take this game on your back and follow me to the town. I'll book you. Six months for poaching and another six for the unlicenced gun. Your itch will be cured serving that sentence. Son of a ...! Unless you people are put behind bars, you'll never learn. Come on. Proceed. What are you staring at me for? I'll kick you on your chest."

People going to the forest to gather firewood flocked to Byri's hut overhearing the shouting of the forest guard.

Byri was pleading with the guard for mercy.

God knows when he sneaked into the crowd. Soorayya made his way to the front and asked the guard, "What is the matter, sir?"

"Look at these sons of bitches. They are poaching every single animal in the forest. They treat it like their legacy. He has no licence to enter the forest or for his gun. They take themselves to be lords of the government!" the guard said pointing to the buck and the gun.

Soorayya looked at Byri and said, "This is why you don't get even a square meal. Even god turns a blind eye. You are an old man. Your kith and kin are dead and you are all alone. You too are about to die any time. Why do you need to poach at all? Why do you hanker after money?"

"Come on, move! Do you hear me?" the forest guard ordered Byri with all the authority at his command.

Soorayya intervened. "Look here, sir, forgive my interference. But what will become of him if you don't show mercy? He's a poor fellow. Who else can save him but you?"

"What do you mean? You want me to let him off? What a suggestion!"

"Please sir, please, wait a minute." Soorayya turned to Byri and commanded, "Look here, Byri! Pick up that buck and walk to my house. Let us sort it out there."

Turning to the crowd, he shouted at them, "What are you looking at? Useless folk! Haven't you any work? Is there a bioscope or group dance going on here?"

Byri walked in front with the buck on his back.

Walking behind, Soorayya was negotiating with the forest guard.

They reached Soorayya's house. Soorayya took them inside and shutting the door, he turned to Byri and said, "Listen Byri! Is it legal to poach in a government forest without a licence? Think of god almighty and answer me. Speak up. Don't you agree, it is illegal? Then is it not fair that you should be punished? But the guard is young and considerate. Upon my word he has agreed to let you go. Pay him a hundred. Don't say another word. Agreed?"

"Leave it, Soorayya. I had better book him," said the guard.

"No, no, no sir, don't be harsh upon him. He will die." Turning to Byri he lashed out, "You fellow, what are you waiting for? Pay him. Quick!"

"Where is the money? ... I'll leave the buck."

"What did you say? You'll leave the buck, will you? Bastard! Who are you to leave it for him? It's his anyway. Did you rear it that you can now give it to him? It is government property and rightfully belongs to the government officer. What do you say? If you dilly-dally, the guard will change his mind. If he books a case against you, you will get six months in prison on each count and you will never see your village again. You will die in the jail itself. Understand?"

Byri felt as if they were digging his grave, to bury him alive. "You know it. I don't have any money," he said.

Soorayya pretended to contemplate for a while and then, casting a look at Byri that smacked of mercy, annoyance and concern, he said, "Well, it looks as if everything is my headache!" He went inside and quickly returned with a blank piece of paper.

"It is up to me to mediate and sort out every silly issue! Come here and put your thumb impression on this paper ... Okay, now you had better leave. We'll meet later. If the guard sees you here any longer, he might change his mind. So get out, fast!" Soorayya pushed Byri out after getting his thumb on the blank paper. Relieved of whatever attachment he had to his small holding, Byri walked out with downcast eyes. Offering prayers to Lakshmi, the goddess of wealth, Soorayya secured the paper in a chest and locked it.

"Listen to me, Soorayya! Send the animal to the forest ranger's house. Tomorrow is his daughter's wedding. He needs it. Give him as much as you can, the fellow is never satisfied and is always looking for more!" The forest guard shook hands with Soorayya and left fingering the hundred rupee note in his pocket.

Sitting alone in his hut, Byri wept his heart out. Without his knowledge, he dropped into a deep slumber. In his sleep ...

The scorching summer was at its height!

The blazing sun spat fire. The streams, springs and rills in the forest – all had gone dry. Wild fires were raging on the hilltops, sun stricken birds were dropping dead like dry leaves in autumn ...

Thirst! Thirst! Thirst! Thirst all around!

Tigers, wolves, deer, birds and sundry creatures were on the run – migrating to safer pastures by day and by night, with just one desire – to quench their wrenching thirst!

Among them was Soorayya, the forest guard and himself. Running ... racing ... thirst ... thirst all around!

Byri woke up from his dream with a start. It was nightfall. He was delirious. His scratched and inflamed body was aching and the fever was running high. He came out. It was dark all around. The forest too looked gloomy, like his own life. He was spitting fire from his eyes and through his mouth. He was boiling with fever, spite and vengeance.

He took his rifle, this time not for game.

He walked like a blazing sun into that darkness.

Tigers were roaring, wolves were chasing, like a fine edged arrow that would cut them to pieces, in single minded pursuit, he walked deeper and deeper into the woods. Through shrubs, bushes and rivulets he marched.

Byri, who thus marched into the woods with his gun, never returned.

"Mirage" was originally published in Telugu as "Mrugtrushna."

Doves

by Joginder Paul

translated by Bhushan Arora

Yahan khariyat hai, aap ki khariyat nek matloob.

As Lobh Singh began his letter to his old friend Fazal Deen conveying his well being and wished his friend the same, he recalled that even in those days, when they had both been teachers in the primary school at Chaunda in Pakistani Punjab, Fazal Deen used to correct him whenever he wrote khariyat instead of khairiyat. "You are an Urdu teacher, Lobhé! Don't you know even this much – khariyat is to do with khar, an ass?"

"Don't pretend to be an Ilm Deen, Mister Know-all Fazal Deené! The fewer dots there are, the simpler and neater is the writing."

"But ..."

"Forget the but vut. You teach English, don't you? Tell me, why is it that your English is so easy that Englishmen's children speak it fluently and why do our Punjabi children not speak Urdu with the same ease?"

"Why are you talking to me in Urdu, Lobhé? Do you think I am one of your pupils?"

"Because you are answering me in Urdu."

"Ha! Ha! ..."

When Pakistan was created, Lobh Singh left his Chaunda to come to Delhi. There, he gave up teaching and became a taxi driver. "Friends!" he took to saying, "ever since I lost my home, even when I am sitting still, I feel that I am running away somewhere."

After he had been living in Delhi for several years, one day he received an envelope with a Pakistani stamp on it – from Maulvi Fazal Deen, Headmaster, Chaunda. Reading the letter he felt he was holding his old friend Fazal Deen in a close embrace. "Oi Fazlé, you haramkhor, you eater of evil gains, you are a big maulvi there, and I didn't even know! You headmaster of your father!" He wept as these imprecations ran through his mind and tears, as copious as the five rivers of the Punjab, flowed though his beard. His grown-up son Jaswant Singh asked, "Why, Bhapa, has somebody died?"

From that day on, Lobh Singh made it a habit to give up everything and sit down to write to his friend Fazal Deen once every month ...

Yahan khariyat hai, aap ki khariyat nek matloob ... Aap ki!

He laughed involuntarily as he used aap, the deferential plural, for that black faced maulvi ... even his wife used to call him tu as she pushed him out of their house.

"Did you get a beating again today, Fazal Deené?"

"No, Lobhaya, today is payday, remember!"

"Yaar, my poor Dharam Kaur is laid up with fever even on payday." Lobh Singh's wife used to suffer from intermittent fever.

"Come, I'll take you to my mama today. He's a big hakim."

"I am hale and hearty, you silly fellow. It's your bhabhi who is ill!"

But, in fact, how well could he be? Worry about his wife's illness was slowly eating him inside. In the conflagration that followed the Partition in 1947, they had to flee from their home and come to Delhi. If they had not had to leave Chaunda, one way or another, Dharam Kaur may still have been alive ... but they had been in Delhi less than a year when he had to surrender his Dharam Kaur to Wahé Guru's care.

"O King of Kings, Saché Padshah, till I too finish my time here to come into your service, please keep my Dharam Kaur safe ..."

But my time is done now, so what am I still doing here? Lobh Singh asked himself, and then distractedly stroking his white beard, mused that he too would set out without hesitation but then how would he find Wahé Guru? Dharam Kaur must have become old and decrepit like him by now ... but how pretty she had looked in the heat of the fever just before she died! He had sat on her bed for hours, holding her hand as if to say that no matter what happened, he wouldn't let her go.

"Don't worry Jassa's bhapé, I won't go," she would console him. "Have no fear, I'm not going because I know that if I go, you'll die!"

And that is what happened after Dharam Kaur went. Worse still, even though he had died, Lobh Singh did not know how long he would have to keep on breathing. Nothing in the world had changed. He still drove his taxi all over the place and talked and laughed with people, but without his Dharam Kaur, he just wasn't alive. When she was dying and he knew her time had come, he had held her hand even more firmly than before, but it soon lay limp in his hands and she went away into the Unknown.

In days of yore, the furthest she had ever gone from Chaunda was to her parents' home in Kotli Loharan. And while she was there, he would write to her every other day.

Post Office Kotli Loharan
Tehsil Wazirabad, District Gujranwala
For Sardarni Dharam Kaur
C/o Sardar Ranjit Singh Ghodewalé

Where could he write to her now? This letter he is writing is to his friend Fazal Deen ... Aap ki khariat nek matloob ... The aap amused him again — what is this formal aap vap when you are writing to such an intimate friend? Like he was sitting as a respectful pupil in Class Four of his own primary school. In Punjabi, you can lovingly mock abuse your friends as much as you like, but when you write a letter, always address the person you are writing to as Aap. He then thought of the people in Delhi who, even when they shower the choicest abuses relating to the recipients' incestuous designs on their mothers and sisters, never fail to address them as Aap! And he burst out in a loud chuckle.

Jaswant Singh left his wife and came running to see what had happened to Bhapa. Since he stopped driving the taxi himself, he had taken to sometimes laughing and at other times crying without apparent reason. Jaswant had suggested to his father that he should go along with the driver if he did not want to go around the bend sitting idle, doing nothing. Lobh Singh then told his son, as always, "If you are so concerned about me, why don't you give me a grandson to keep me occupied?"

"You've really gone mad, Bhapé!" he said. "Are grandsons sold in the bazaar, that I should hop into the taxi and bring you one? One has to work hard for grandsons!"

"Work hard then, puttar! Work hard!"

Jaswant's wife tittered coyly in the adjoining room, and Jaswant went away smiling and shaking his head.

Lobh Singh recalled one of Fazal Deen's letters in which he told him that he has fifteen grandsons, and five granddaughters. In other words, my lion of a headmaster has grown from one to twenty, he reflected. If he had been somewhere close by, I would have surely brought one or two of them home as soon as they were born. I would have lovingly bathed and dressed them with my own hands. My Fazal Deen would never have said no to me. And even if he had, I would have brought them anyway ...

If they are yours Fazal Deené, aren't they mine as well? Read your book carefully, you headmaster, you! It clearly lays down that you should share everything with your friends and companions. The karah parshad is for the entire congregation. May his Allah keep him well and happy, and may my Waḥé Guru look after me, why would Fazal Deen refuse me my wish?

Driven by this desire and yearning, Lobh Singh had parked his taxi in front of Fazal Deen's house. Honking his horn vigorously, he had collected all his grandchildren and brought them to Delhi ... and was showing them the sights.

Look! That is the Qutub Minar, and that is the Viceroy's House, and now we are at the Red Fort! Yes, yes, bhai, give them all a kulfi each. Eat, children! The kulfi here is very good. It'll clean your throats. Hei, Shabbo! Where are you going? Come back here. We'll now go to Chandni Chowk on foot ... Come, come ... careful now! Watch your step! Panting from his exertions, he was back in his room, tired but happy from the outing with the children.

Yahan khariyat hai. Of course, all is well here, Hee ... hee ... hee ... ha ... ha ... He heard the muffled sounds of his son and daughter-in-law laughing softly in their room. They sounded like they were grappling with each other. With a contented sigh, he asked himself, "What else does one call khariyat?" I had opened my letter to Fazal Deen with the same words even when my elder son Jaswinder was killed in an accident with the taxi seven or eight years ago and my world had collapsed around me. That had truly displaced me and I had become so unsettled that I could not find a place to live even in my own head or heart. But if I could not send good news to my dear friend sitting so far away, I couldn't send him distressing news either. And, of course, if bad news has to be given, the basket of woe should be opened so slowly that only the tail of the black cobra comes into view at first.

Is Jaswinder Singh your son's name?

Yes. Why?

Did he take the taxi to Agra yesterday?

Why? What happened?

His taxi was involved in a collision with a motorcycle, and the motorcyclist died on the spot.

It couldn't have been my son's fault. He is a very responsible driver.

Yes. Meanwhile a speeding truck rammed into the taxi from behind and ... the cobra had spread its hood, but Lobh Singh had had the time to prepare himself for its strike.

Jaswinder was to be married a week after the day of the accident. Lobh Singh had invited every member of the local branch of the taxi drivers' union to the wedding. The commissioner of transport had risen from his chair to shake him by the hand and assured him that he would attend. It was to be the first marriage in his family and he was determined to celebrate it with great pomp and rejoicing. He had even decided that he would indulge in a drink or two on the occasion although when he had given up alcohol, he had vowed it would never touch his lips again. Wahé Guru would surely forgive him this small transgression. After all, if one cannot commit such a small sin to celebrate such a happy event, what is the fun of living! He would perhaps even ask Wahé Guru to share a drop with him to celebrate his Jassa's wedding ... For my sake, my Padshah!

Lobh Singh could hear the band playing and following the band, Jaswinder, looking handsome in his turban, adorned with fragrant rose and jasmine garlands, riding the mare. A few steps ahead of him, dressed in his heavy silk shalwar kameez and a saffron coloured striped turban on his head, he himself was doing bhangra, turning around every few steps to sprinkle keora water on all the members of the marriage party. The faces of the baraatis were glowing, and everyone, band and all, had begun to rise upward into the sky. Only Lobh Singh and his younger son Jaswant were left on the ground and they were yelling hysterically, Veerji ... Jaswinder! ... Vindré! ... Wait, ... And then he was helplessly wringing his hands. His turban had come undone and fallen to his shoulders and he was telling passersby – He is a very dutiful son ji, my Jaswinder. He has gone up to get his dead mother's blessings ...

Lobh Singh started sobbing softly.

"What happened, Bhapé?" Jaswant called out from his room.

"Nothing."

Lobh Singh got up to wet his towel to wipe his face and then came back to sit on the bed. Yahan khariyat hai ...Where is all well? But one has to accept Wahé Guru's will as khariyat.

"It's all right, puttar," he called out loudly this time to set his son's mind at rest.

"Relax!"

He then picked up the letter to resume writing.

Time hangs heavy on my hands. I spend the entire day and night lying quietly in my bed. The only time considered well-spent are the few moments when I drop off to sleep and find myself back in Chaunda.

Lobh Singh heard his mother call out to him from across the space of fifty five, sixty years, "Lobhaya! ... Lobhaya ..."

"Yes Bébé?" the old man turned boy called out involuntarily.

"Answer the door, puttar. Fazla is calling you."

What a life that was! It took care of everything. All one had to do was to live on, and keep growing.

Lobh Singh sighed deeply and went back to writing.

Could you not possibly fill your pockets with the soil of Chaunda and come to meet me here? If you can't get a visa, come surreptitiously. What do we have to do with the fights of big people? We small people want to meet only to embrace each other. How can anyone object to that? You come secretly, and my son Jaswant Singh will take care of everything else.

The sound of his son and daughter-in-law's playful whispering in their room felt like music to his ears. Lobh Singh smiled and began playing with his giggling grandson ... O, Bhai Kesar Singha! ... O, Gulab Singha ... O, your mother's Mo'atbar Singha ... and the mother's Mo'atbar Singh also shrieked in glee every time his name was called ... But where is he? Heavy hearted, Lobh Singh picked up the letter again.

In fact, I feel very lonely now. A few months ago, as soon as I completed sixty five, Jaswant Singh told me not to drive the taxi any more. My first reaction was to give him a slap and refuse. I thought I would tell him, the taxi is mine, I am mine, so who are you to decide whether I should drive the taxi or sit at home? But to tell you the truth, driving the taxi is beyond me now. I can now only race imaginary horses. Had it been a case of being a headmaster, like you (here he wrote the familiar tumhari tarah, then crossed it out and replaced it with the deferential aap ki tarah), I too could have given the wrong age and dragged on for another ten years or so. But enough! You too should apply for your pension now, and start holding classes with your grandchildren. After you retire, if you go around teaching outside your house, you will be put in a mental asylum within five or six months. Ha ... ha ... ha!

Lobh Singh stopped writing.

One day a well dressed, mad old man had climbed into his taxi and told him gravely, "Let's move, chalo!"

"Where?"

"Back."

Unable to suppress a smile, Lobh Singh had said, "The taxi can only go forward."

"But I have to go backwards!"

"Then sir, why do you need to ride in a taxi? Just get down and go walking back in your mind." And today, it was as if he had landed in his own taxi.

"Where?"

"Chaundé."

Chaundé? He laughed at his own madness. There is only one way to go there ... across the skies. So, turn into a dove and fly away, Sardara!

But why? Why, Bhai Waryam Singh used to ask him. The late Waryam Singh had been his Dharam Kaur's brother as well as his bosom pal. He would ask, "You were chased out of Chaunda with nothing. Why do you want to go back there?" And Lobh Singh would answer simply, "Because Chaunda is my haven, bhai." Every time he became restless for Chaunda, he would head for Saharanpur to spend time with Bhai Waryam Singh, who had settled there following his displacement after Partition.

"So, you've come to go back to Chaunda, Lobhaya," Waryam Singh would say as soon as he saw him.

"Open the bottle, bhai. We'll talk after we reach Chaunda."

And if, for any reason, Lobh Singh was unable to go to Bhai Waryam Singh, he would settle down to write a long letter.

Bhai Waryam Singh, Sat Siri Akal, Yahan khariyat hai. Aap ki khariyat matloob. I am writing to ask you to open the bottle quickly. We have to go to Chaunda without delay ...

Even these days, Lobh Singh sometimes had an irresistible urge to write to Waryam Singh, but where does one address a letter to the dead? Had he been alive, Lobh Singh would not have hesitated to walk all the way to Kucha Dilbaran in Saharanpur to deliver his letter at the door of the fourth house on the right, but who knows at which address Wahé Guru places people after their death! Even so, one day his desire got the better of him and he wrote a letter to his dead brother-in-law, but the letter came back. Or should one say it came to the right address, because when we speak to the dead we have to be the listeners as well. After all, they are dead and it is we the living who keep them alive.

Lobh Singh was dozing now, and wandering about in a dream. He had got lost and had eventually walked out of the dream to find himself here. Ah! This is the primary school at Chaunda and this dirt track opposite, it goes straight to his house ... and there, at the threshold, Dharam Kaur is waiting for him. Even when she is ill, this is how she waits every day for him to come back ... He stops in his tracks to admire her. My wife is radiating a golden aura like the yellow mustard flowers, he thinks. But then he jumps and rushes forward with a start. Here I am lecherously fantasizing about her while she is burning with fever ... and when he is still only halfway to her, and even as she is smiling at him, she suddenly collapses in a heap ... Dharmo! ... Jaswant! ... Jassi!

Jaswant came running out of his room.

"What happened, Bhapé?"

"Nothing."

Lobh Singh was trying to quell the turmoil in his heart.

"Go to sleep Bhapé," Jaswant told his father and noticing the half-complete letter asked idly, "Are you writing a letter?"

"Yes, to your chacha at Chaunda."

Jaswant looked indulgently at his father and said, "You have truly become senile, Bhapé." And reminded him that Fazal Deen Chacha of Chaunda has been dead and gone these many years.

"Doves" was originally published in Urdu (India) as "Fakhtein."

Ghost
by Saleem Agha Qazil Bash
translated by Subhash Chandra Malik

The sound of the heavy stick hitting the ground, the loud call of "Jaagté raho," the barking of stray dogs, the rising and falling howls of jackals from a distance – would all be audible. As the night progressed the stars would show themselves more and more shamelessly, and the tone of the chowkidar's "Jaagté raho" would become more and more serious. He would go around the village seven times, like a saint drawing seven circles around a condemned person to save him from bad spirits. After every round of the village he would come straight to the chaupal, the village square. In winter, he would warm his shoes, made of thick, hard leather, over the embers of the fire that had been lit in the chaupal in the evening by holding his shoes upside down as if to gather the heat and store it inside them. He would puff hard at the dying hukka, trying to revive it. The hukka would gurgle for a while, but would die out again. The chowkidar would then get up, mumbling to himself, wrap the blanket tightly around, and set off to complete his next round, hitting the ground again and again with his stick. In summer, he would wear just a loincloth around his lower body, no other clothes, but he would always have a thick amulet tied around his left arm, given to him by a saint with the words, "Go child, and always remain happy." And then, when the chowkidar heard the weak "cockarako" tearing the breast of darkness, he would look up at the sky, trying to judge the time by studying the sleep heavy, blinking eyelids of the stars. He would then spit out the night's bitterness on the awakening morning. During the day he would work, along with his three sons, on the small piece of land allotted to him by the government. He would cut fodder for his pair of bullocks, take the cattle to the canal to drink water and in the evening, when waves of parrots settle down on the banyan tree for the night, fighting noisily over the selection of branches, the chowkidar would drive the cattle home and enter his house patting the neck of his favourite ox. He would tie up the cattle and shout for his wife whom the villagers called the Old Chowkidarni. She was older than the chowkidar by a year, and as such had been known as the old chowkidarni ever since she got married. Now she had really grown old, having been knocking at the door of old age with her husband for the last many years. The chowkidar would then ask his wife, "Lado's amma, where is the utensil for milk?" Lado was the chowkidar's youngest daughter who had got married the year before last and lived happily with her in-laws. Every evening, before milking the brown buffalo, he would address his wife as "Lado's mother," happy to remember his daughter this way. He would keep the bucket full of milk near the hearth, untie and retie his turban properly, prepare the hukka and walk towards the chaupal, carrying his stick under his arm.

The chowkidar was very fond of talking. Nobody had ever seen him sit quietly in one place. He would either be narrating stories of his younger days to some young man, or sharing mutual memories with people of his own generation, or discussing harvesting procedures with some farmer. Sometimes he would be seen advising some lady about the treatment of her ailing child, or giving the benefit of his experiences to someone whose cattle were sick. Apart from this, he had a characteristic sweetness in his voice and the villagers would usually ask him before dispersing from the chaupal in the evening, to sing a few stanzas from Waaris Shah's "Heer," and warm their souls. He also had a repertoire of hundreds of stories, jokes, anecdotes and poems. So groups of children would regularly surround him and demand to be told an interesting story, particularly the one about the Black Thief who was famous for his brave dacoities in the surrounding villages, and who tried to break into the Chaudhri's house. Although this story was known to everyone in the village, the way the chowkidar narrated it was something else. At the request of the children, he would first laughingly hurl a few light abuses at them and then sit cross-legged in the middle of the street with the children around him in a circle. He would take a few pulls on his hukka, clear his throat and start off – "That night when I was going around the village, I saw …"

This was the chowkidar's daily routine. He just could not sit idle – always talking and working. Everyone was aware of his unlimited energy, his stamina. It appeared that the strength of hundreds of persons was concentrated in him. The whole night he was on guard duty and the whole day he worked in the fields. Looking after visitors to the village and government officials was also a task entrusted to him, just as he was responsible for entertaining people in the chaupal. He had always been a guard for the village, but another relation linking him with the happy and sad moments of the villagers existed in the form of the Marriages, Births and Deaths Register, which he had to maintain, being the official chowkidar. As such, he would be present on every happy and sad occasion, and in no time all the arrangements would automatically be in his hands. Whenever sickness struck any house in the village, he would be the first one to reach there and start looking after the patient. He was as restless as mercury and as untiring as the wind. He could be on his feet all day and all night. People used to say that he was not a chowkidar but a ghost, for whom rest and sleep meant nothing. But the strange fact was that he did all this not to please others, but to satisfy some inner urge within himself, which did not let him sit idle.

One day, however, an obstruction suddenly arose in the fast pace of his life. His younger brother, who was very dear to him, wanted to leave the village because of his wife's nagging. The chowkidar tried to persuade him not to leave saying that women's altercations do not mean anything and that this should not result in the severance of blood relations, but his brother remained adamant, dumped all his belongings on to a bullock cart, and left. For the first time in his life, the chowkidar did not feel like doing anything. He kept lying on a cot near the chaupal with his eyes shut. He did not eat the whole day, nor did he talk to anyone. In the evening when the parrots started shouting, four men carried the cot to the village on their shoulders. That day, the chowkidar was walking not on his own feet but on the feet of these four persons. A man was sent to the neighbourhood village to call the doctor. The entire village turned up at the chowkidar's house on hearing about his condition, and the men and women kept asking each other what had happened. Ultimately the doctor arrived and was taken inside the house. After some time it was learnt that though the attack of paralysis had left the chowkidar alive, it had taken away his power of speech and ability to walk forever. The villagers were stunned. After some time the people started going back to their houses with bowed heads. That night was very painful for the chowkidar, each minute passed with difficulty. The night was dark and silent. Only once or twice an owl hooted from a clump of trees. Around midnight a dog growled near the well, on hearing which the jackals howled for a moment, and then there was complete silence. This was the first night the chowkidar had spent on his cot without moving at all, as if a sorcerer in a story had turned the body of a prince into stone. Sounds from the village well announced the arrival of the morning, and life, which had been lying as if paralyzed, woke up with a shrug. But the chowkidar, who was now like a past moment, lay motionless, while life carried on with all its moments.

People had been saying that his days were numbered for the last ten years. Although he lay there like a corpse, the restlessness in his eyes constantly accused him of being alive. But he should have died the day a piece of very sad news hit him like an explosion. The horse rider had gone away after giving him the news. The chowkidar kept thinking till late as to why these horse riders always go away immediately after giving such news. The news was about his Lado who had died after giving birth to a stillborn child.

This was the first funeral in front of his eyes.

When they were taking her away, the chowkidar called out in his heart to his daughter not to go, but perhaps for the first time in his life Lado did not reply. Death stood next to him with its red tongue hanging out and its hair in disarray, and kept staring at him. What kind of revenge was this that death wanted from him, or was it he taking some kind of revenge on death? There was a long wait on both sides. Then another piece of news hit him. His elder daughter's husband had died of tuberculosis.

This was the second funeral in front of his eyes, and he remained a mute witness.

Like last year, this year too the chowkidar was constantly feverish. His condition had been deteriorating ever since the cold had set in, and everybody thought he would not be able to survive the winter. At least one member from every family would come to his house every day to enquire about his health, with the hope that he may be the fortunate one to see the chowkidar alive for the last time and be able to tell the others proudly that the chowkidar had breathed his last in front of him. But all hopes proved fruitless. The chowkidar kept breathing, but his elder son died of cancer in the hospital.

This was the third funeral in front of his eyes, and he continued to watch with empty eyes.

Perhaps this was the compensation for being alive, which he had to pay by way of the deaths of his dear ones. What was the harm if, in addition to losing speech, he became deaf and blind? But he was being forced to see all this. Death was slowly sucking away his life, but he was refusing to die. Then his remaining two sons started fighting over the distribution of land and became sworn enemies. On the day the news of Dhaka's downfall was broadcast over the radio, a dispute arose between the brothers that gradually got worse and abuses started getting exchanged. The chowkidar could neither speak nor move, but he could see everything, and so kept watching. After some time, the blows of an axe and a chopper made blood spill all around, and in front of his eyes one of his sons was killed by the other.

This was the fourth funeral, and he watched without blinking his eyes.

After a while the police arrived, and took away the other son in handcuffs. He was tried for murder and sentenced to death by hanging. One morning his dead body arrived in the courtyard of their house.

This was the fifth funeral in front of his eyes, but there was not even the moisture of tears in the eyes of the chowkidar.

A strange scene was enacting itself in front of the villagers. They watched that skeleton of a man propped against a dirty pillow on a cot under the banyan tree, his legs paralyzed and tongue silent. One after the other dead bodies came out of his house and disappeared in front of his eyes, but his face was clean as a slate and bereft of any emotion whatsoever. But in the two holes in the slate of his face his pupils constantly moved. It seemed as though all the strength of his legs and tongue had travelled to his pupils, and that they were trying to look for something all around but were unable to locate it. He looked like a ghost that had been nailed to the cot. It could neither move nor speak nor walk. It could only watch and watch. The chowkidar would lie the whole day under the banyan tree watching its branches and counting the birds that sat on those branches. He would pray that the next morning should not arrive, but the morning would always yawn and get up as soon as it heard the sound of the tap being opened by the chowkidarni. The chowkidarni would then start coughing while lighting the fire, ask her daughters and daughters-in-law to get up, urge her grandchildren to go and have a wash, and herself start cooking for them.

One day, early in the morning, the chowkidar's eldest grandson came and told them that their old ox was lying unconscious and was breathing with difficulty. When they learnt that there was no hope of its survival, they called the village butcher. In front of the chowkidar's eyes, a knife was applied to the neck of his favourite ox. Thick red blood started flowing on the ground. The body of the ox was hacked to pieces. The chowkidar kept watching quietly, feeling as if not the ox but his own whole life was being cut into pieces. The sound of the chopper ended after a long time. The butcher wiped his hands clean on his loincloth, lifted the severed head of the ox in one hand, put the skin on his shoulder, took the blood soaked chopper in the other hand, and left, looking meaningfully at the chowkidar. The chowkidar kept watching the severed head of his ox being carried away. In the afternoon, when five pieces of meat dipped in gravy were placed in front of the chowkidar, his fingers touched one piece and jerked away. He felt as if his whole body had been cut up into pieces and the whole family was busy eating those pieces with relish. The chowkidar then, under the influence of some deep emotion, picked up one piece with trembling hands and started chewing on it. For the first time tears broke the dam of his eyes and started streaming down his face, making the meat more and more salty. He started crying uncontrollably and went on chewing the meat, but could not bring himself to swallow ...

"Ghost" was originally published in Urdu (Pakistan) as "Aaseb."

ASOMIYA

Arupa Patangia Kalita writes short stories, novellas and novels for adults as well as for children. She has won a number of awards including the Katha Award for Creative Fiction, the Sarlesh Chandra Dasgupta Sahitya Setu Award and the Bharatiya Bhasha Parishad Award. Besides writing features for Asomiya journals, she also edits a little magazine called *Damal*. She teaches English Literature at Tangla College, Darrang, Assam.

Bonita Baruah is a journalist with *The Times of India*, New Delhi and has written several articles. She translates short stories from Asomiya to English.

BANGLA (Bangladesh)

Akhtaruzzaman Elias wrote novels as well as short stories. Some of his notable works include *Chilekothar Sepai* and *Khoabnama*. He has many awards to his credit, including the Bangla Academy Award, Alaol Literary Award, Ananda Award, Sadat Ali Akand Award and Kari Mahbulullah Gold Medal. He died in 1997.

Amar Kumar Majumdar retired as a geologist from the Geological Survey of India in 1995. He has a keen interest in Bangla and English literature and has a few short stories, scientific papers and articles besides some translations to his credit.

BANGLA (India)

Gautam Sengupta is a writer with a Bangla film magazine after a career in sales with Hindustan Lever Limited. He has written a few stories, all of which have been published in well-known Bangla magazines. *Sahaj Path* is his published anthology of stories. He is the recipient of the Katha Award for Creative Fiction.

Jayati Dasgupta lives in Chennai and actively pursues her interests in vedanta philosophy and scientific literature. She has taught Physics in a school for almost a decade. She writes proficiently in both English and Bangla.

GUJARATI

Suvarna has several short stories, articles on various issues and a novel to her credit. A freelance journalist and social activist, she is proficient in several languages and has a keen interest in the fine arts.

Kamal Sanyal is fluent in Gujarati, Marathi and Bangla and has a number of published translations to her credit. She has won the Katha awards in both the Gujarati and Marathi sections of the Second All India Katha Translation Contest.

HINDI

Usha Mahajan has several short story collections for adults and children to her credit. She has extensively translated Khushwant Singh's works to Hindi, as well as authored his biographical profile. She received the Delhi Hindi Academy Award for Children's Literature and the K K Birla Foundation Fellowship.

Pamela Manasi writes short stories as well as poems, besides translating from Hindi to English and writing scripts for documentaries. She has two anthologies of short fiction to her credit. A reader at the Department of English, S P Mukherjee College, University of Delhi, she is also a regular voice at All India Radio kavi goshthies.

KANNADA

Bolwar Mahamad Kunhi, a bank officer by profession, is a prolific writer. His writings have been included in many prestigious anthologies of Bharatiya Jnanpith, Bharatiya Bhasha Sansthana and the State Sahitya Akademi. He is the recipient of the Katha Award for Creative Fiction, the Karnataka Sahitya Akademi Award, twice, the Bharatiya Bhasha Sansthana Award, and Life Time Achievement Award by Karnataka Sahitya Akademi, among others.

K A Parthasarthy is a freelance translator and translates from Russian to English and vice versa. He has worked as an engineer with Indian and Russian companies.

MALAYALAM

N S Madhavan has three short story collections to his credit. He has won the Katha Award for Creative Fiction thrice and is also the recipient of the Kerala Sahitya Akademi Award. He is a civil servant currently posted in Bihar.

Nita Thomas is a children's writer, broadcaster and journalist. She has scripted several short films and documentaries for FTII, Pune, EMRC, Poona University and Mumbai Doordarshan.

MARATHI

Shanta Gokhale has to her credit several short stories, a novel and a play besides scripts for many award-winning documentary films and a feature film. Her novel *Rita Welingkar* won the V S Khandekar Award for the best novel. Her latest book, *Playwright at the Centre* has been much acclaimed. She has translated poetry, fiction and drama from Marathi into English, including her own play and award winning novel. A theatre critic and cultural columnist, she has also been the Arts Editor of *The Times of India* and the sub editor of *Femina*.

Ranjit Hoskote is a poet, art theorist and independent curator and has six books, three poetry collections and one translation to his credit. He received the Sanskriti Award for Literature, and the First Prize in the British Council, Poetry Society All-India Poetry Competition.

NEPALI

Sharad Chhetri is a short story writer, poet and novelist, with around twenty one books to his credit. He has received many prizes, including the Sahitya Akademi Award, the Bhanu Bhakta Puraskar, and the Ratna Shree Suvarna Padak. He also contributes articles to various journals.

Prakash L Shrestha is a lecturer in English at Ace Institute of Management, Kathmandu and also works as the editor of South Asia Partnership-Nepal (SAP-NEPAL), a Kathmandu-based publishing house.

ORIYA

Pratibha Ray has eighteen novels, twenty short story collections, seven travelogues, along with a number of books for children and neo-literates to her credit. Several of her short stories and novels have been adapted for radio plays, television serials and films. Her works have been translated into English and other Indian languages. She has received the Katha Award for Creative Fiction, twice, the Moorti Devi Award by the Bharatiya Jnanpith, the Orissa Sahitya Akademi Award, the Sahitya Akademi Award, and the Rajiv Gandhi Sadbhavna Puruskar.

Amlan Dash works with NABARD in Bhubaneshwar and translates from Oriya into English.

PUNJABI (India)

Dalbir Chetan, a retired excise officer, has several short story collections to his credit. Some of his stories have been translated into English and other Indian languages. Three of his books are part of the syllabi in Delhi University and Punjab University. His story, "Baj Bharawan" has been serialized by Jalandhar Doordarshan. He is the co-editor of the monthly magazine *Shillalekh*.

Tripti Jain has authored several books and is now a freelance translator. She has translated for the Sahitya Akademi, Delhi and the National Book Trust. She was a lecturer in Political Science in a government college for over thirty years and now heads a senior secondary school in Ajmer.

PUNJABI (Pakistan)

Farkhanda Lodhi has six short story collections, two novels, and one novella to her credit. A librarian by profession, she writes in Urdu and Punjabi. She has also translated folktales from Norway, China, Turkey, South Africa and the South Asia.

Bhushan Arora, a retired tea planter, worked as a freelance editor and translator in Delhi. He was interested in languages and fluently spoke English, Hindi, Urdu, Punjabi, Nepali, Bengali and Assamese and a bit of Spanish and French. He won the Katha Award for Translation. He passed away in 1999.

SINDHI (India)

Motilal Jotwani writes proficiently in Sindhi as well as in Hindi and has around fifty four books to his credit. He has a doctorate in Sindhi and has been a visiting scholar at Harvard. He is a Reader at Deshbandhu College, New Delhi where he teaches Indian literature. He is the recipient of the Katha Award for Creative Fiction and the Padma Shri. He has also received six prizes from the Ministry of Education for his works in Hindi and Sindhi.

Nandita Bhavnani is currently working on Sindhi cultural history and the long-term effects of Partition on the Sindhi community. She is also associated with the Centre for the Study of Developing Societies' project on Partition memories and violence.

SINDHI (Pakistan)

Amar Jalil has written ten short story collections and a novel besides several research papers, articles and scripts for a number of plays and television serials. He writes in English, Sindhi and Urdu. He is the former Station Director, Radio Pakistan and Vice Chancellor, Allama Iqbal Open University. He is the recipient of the Pride of Performance Award for literature, Shah Latif Award for Mystic Literature, Pakistan Writers Guild Award (twice) and Best Playwright of the Decade Award, PTV, Islamabad.

Mohan H Keswani works as a part time consultant after retiring as a senior tea garden manager in 1986. He loves reading and writing.

SINHALA

Piyaseeli Wijemanne has seven short story collections, one novel and more than thirty research papers to her credit. She has also translated two books into Sinhala and edited two collections of research papers. Several of her short stories have been translated into English. She has received three State Literary Awards for short stories. She is an Associate Professor of Sinhala at the University of Peradeniya, Sri Lanka.

Chiranthi Rajapakse, a student of Dentistry at the University of Peradeniya, usually writes in English. Some of her short stories have appeared in *Channels*, a magazine published by the English Writers Co-operative of Sri Lanka. One of her stories has been the regional winner for Asia at the short story competition organized by the Commonwealth Broadcasting Association.

TAMIL (India)

R Chudamani has thirty seven books in Tamil to her credit which include novels, plays, novellas and short stories. Her stories have been translated into English and other Indian languages and are included in anthologies. She received the Tamil Nadu Government Award, twice, and the Lily Devashikhamani Prize for her short story collection.

Ramiah Kumar is interested in classical Tamil poetry. He retired as an engineer in 2001 and now lives in Delhi.

TAMIL (Sri Lanka)

M A Al Asumath has authored several collections of verses and won prizes for his short stories. For his literary achievements, he was awarded with the title "Najmus Shuaara" (Poetic Star) by the Ministry for Muslim Religious and Cultural Affairs, Sri Lanka.

Uma Balu has written a lot of articles for magazines and has translated quite a few stories. She teaches Japanese at Indo-Japan Centre, Chennai and is currently engaged in translating Cicero's *De Senectute* from Latin to Tamil and is working on her book *Parellel Proverbs in Tamil and Japanese: A Study of 100 Commonly Used Proverbs*.

TELUGU

Allam Seshagiri Rao has two short story anthologies, *Manchi Mutyalu* and *Aranya Ghosha,* to his credit. He was the recipient of the Andhra Pradesh Sahitya Akademi Award and the Sahridaya Sahiti Puraskaram. He passed away in January 2000.

S Krishnamoorthy, a cost accountant by profession, was a short story writer of repute in Telugu and was widely published in monthly magazines like *Yuva* and *Jyoti*. He won Jyeshta Literary Award for his collection of short stories, *Chaya Chtralu*. He translated many short stories from Telugu to English along with his nephew, N S Murty. Together they brought out a select collection of nineteen short stories titled *The Palette*. He died in July 2001.

N S Murty is currently working as superintendent in a government organization. He has one collection each of English and Telugu poems to his credit. He has also translated a Telugu novel and many Telugu poems into English.

URDU (India)

Joginder Paul has to his credit three novels, two novellas and many collections of short stories and "short" short stories – a genre enriched markedly by his contribution. Acknowledged as one of the leading Urdu writers of the subcontinent, his fiction has been translated into various Indian and foreign languages. He has been felicitated with a number of awards, the more recent being the Urdu Adab Award, the Modi Ghalib Award for Urdu Prose, the Shiromani Urdu Sahityakar Award, the All India Bahadur Shah Zafar Award, the Iqbal Samman, and an international award from Doha for his contribution to Urdu literature.

Bhushan Arora (His biographical details are given in the Punjabi section.)

URDU (Pakistan)

Saleem Agha Qazil Bash has three short story collections, three light essays collections, two prose poems collections and some research works in Urdu to his credit. His short stories have been widely published in different anthologies in India and Pakistan. He is the Vice President of Sargodha Academy, and a member of Sargodha Writer's Union. An agriculturist by profession, he also has a doctoral degree in literature.

Subhash Chandra Malik retired as additional director general of police, Himachal Pradesh, in 1996. He is now settled in Dharamshala, Himachal Pradesh.